Doug & Carlie's Love Conspiracy

By Lisa Smartt

www.lisasmartt.com

ISBN 978-0-615-79367-2

Front and back cover photo by Andrei Zveaghintev,
Shutterstock.com

To Mom and Dad,
for loving wounded souls

Table of Contents

Chapter 1 CARLIE: Matchmaker, Matchmaker 7
Chapter 2 CARLIE: Where Should We Look First? 13
Chapter 3 CARLIE: Getting Clara on Board 21
Chapter 4 CARLIE: Executing the Pigs and the Plan.......... 24
Chapter 5 CARLIE: Lighting the Matchmaking Fire 27
Chapter 6 CARLIE: Bachelor #1 34
Chapter 7 CARLIE: Christmas Conniving 44
Chapter 8 CARLIE: Southern Book Tour............................ 47
Chapter 9 CARLIE: Catching Up with Dave and Shannon . 50
Chapter 10 CARLIE: New Year, New Bachelor 54
Chapter 11 CARLIE: The Smoke-free Marlboro Man 59
Chapter 12 CARLIE: Preach On, Brother Jake 62
Chapter 13 CLARA LOUISE SPEAKS: Accidental U-Turn 77
Chapter 14 CLARA LOUISE: Dusty McConnell on My Mind 83
Chapter 15 CLARA LOUISE: Cars and Scars 87
Chapter 16 CARLIE: Redneck Writer Meets Hollywood ... 89
Chapter 17 CLARA LOUISE: The Joys of Routine, Sheer Boredom 91
Chapter 18 CARLIE Two Weeks Later: CALIFORNIA CARLIE 97
Chapter 19 CARLIE: Ashley Auditions 107
Chapter 20 CLARA LOUISE: Preachers and Car Thieves 109
Chapter 21 CARLIE: Alabama Ashley and the Georgia Peach 115
Chapter 22 CLARA LOUISE: Determined Dusty............. 126
Chapter 23 CLARA LOUISE: Marching Onward............. 128
Chapter 24 CARLIE: First Date and A Felon.................... 136
Chapter 25 CLARA LOUISE: Faith and Mary Kay 140
Chapter 26 CARLIE: Whomp Biscuits and Straight Teeth 143

Chapter 27 CLARA LOUISE: Blowing the Dust Away ... 148
Chapter 28 CARLIE: Trials and Bad Pork Chops 151
Chapter 29 CLARA LOUISE: Conquering Mountains of Stone 156
Chapter 30 CARLIE: Aunt Charlotte's Rural Detective Agency 160
Chapter 31 CLARA LOUISE: Pushing Forward or Pulling Back 172
Chapter 32 CARLIE: Burnt Tuna and Bad Drugs 175
Chapter 33 CLARA LOUISE: Confession is Good for the Soul 184
Chapter 34 CARLIE: Cheering for the Home Team 186
Chapter 35 CLARA LOUISE: Freedom, Sweet Freedom . 188
Chapter 36 CARLIE: Throwing Baby Bird Out of the Nest 193
Chapter 37 CLARA LOUISE: Perfect Family Dinner 195
Chapter 38 CARLIE: Love On the Run 205
Chapter 39 CLARA LOUISE: Don't Wimp Out at Wimpy's 211
Chapter 40 CARLIE Three Days Later: Here Comes the Judge 220
Chapter 41 CLARA LOUISE: A Family Gone Bad 232
Chapter 42 CARLIE: Funeral Pizza 239
Chapter 43 CLARA LOUISE: The Road to Recovery 242
Chapter 44 CARLIE: The Cocoa Bean Has Healing Properties 244
Chapter 45 CLARA LOUISE: Tater Tots and Tears 246
Chapter 46 CARLIE: Roman Holiday in Sharon, Tennessee 259
Chapter 47 CLARA LOUISE Five Weeks Later: Learning to Love 262
Chapter 48 CARLIE: Praise the Lord and Pass the Pickles 266
Chapter 49 CLARA LOUISE: Dark Corners and Cobwebs 272

Chapter 50 CARLIE Two weeks later: Movies and Moms276
Chapter 51 CARLIE The Finale..............................278
Acknowledgements...283

Chapter 1 CARLIE: Matchmaker, Matchmaker

I'm a married woman now. I know. It's shocking to me and everyone else I've ever known. I still remember what happened six months ago when I went to the post office in my hometown of Commerce, Georgia. Agnes Robertson said she was so proud to see my wedding picture in the local newspaper. Well, those weren't her words exactly. She said, "Carlie Ann, now don't you fret none 'cause everybody knows pictures add at least 30 pounds to a girl's physique." I didn't tell Agnes that the word "physique" hadn't been used since 1958 exercise shows on black and white TV.

"Oh Mrs. Robertson, I'm not worried about the picture 'cause I'm so deliriously happy being physically intimate with my good-looking husband every night. It doesn't give me much time for fretting."

I shouldn't have said it. That's my problem. You know those things people think in their minds but know not to say out loud? Yeah, I tend to go ahead and say them out loud. Sometimes it gets me in a lot of trouble too. Other times it makes me endearing.

Most people in Commerce, Georgia, thought I wasn't going to get married because I was 32 and experiencing a crisis in confidence. I tend to speak my mind without proper filtering. Plus, I'm 5'11" with a really big behind. Believe it or not, that's not every man's description of the ideal woman. But Doug Jameson is different. He's handsome and kind. He laughs at my jokes. And he loves me. Miraculous.

Getting married is not the most important thing in life. But it's not unimportant either. If you really want to be married, it hurts not to be. And I think it's really dumb when people act like it doesn't hurt or that marriage doesn't matter. That's why I'm a matchmaker now. Because I care a lot about marriage and mostly I care about women like me who think they'll never meet someone wonderful. I also help women re-define "wonderful." And gosh, there are a lot of women out there who need that kind of help.

I don't mean I'm a matchmaker for my job. I'm a writer by trade. I don't make money matchmaking. I'm kind of like Mrs. Grissom. She's a woman in Commerce who's an excellent baker even though she doesn't own a bakery. She bakes because she loves to hear my dad say, "Jolene, this chocolate pie will make you slap your grandma." Yeah, I understand Mrs. Grissom's baking now 'cause that's the way I feel about introducing single people to each other. I just can't wait until a newlywed comes up to me one day and says, "Carlie Ann, this beautiful woman you introduced me to is so wonderful. She makes me wanna slap my grandma." Yeah, that will be a banner day.

My name is Carlie and I got married to Doug six months ago. It's a long story how we met. Doug's Uncle Stanley wanted me to meet him even though he lived seven hours from Commerce in a tiny town called Sharon, Tennessee. But I didn't think it was such a great idea. I acted like it was because I thought there might be something wrong with Doug. But the truth is…well, the truth is…I thought there was something wrong with me. So that's why it scared me to meet Doug. I was in college (ten years late) and working at the dollar store when we met. But then I got a book published and I went on TV so I stopped working at the dollar store. But Doug's career has been gloriously consistent throughout our entire relationship. He's a bank loan officer. That whole journey is recorded in a book called, "Doug and Carlie."

Sometimes there is a certain grace extended to people like me who believe they are beyond help in the relationship department. I now live with my husband in a beautiful old farm house in Sharon, Tennessee. I'm 33 years old and Doug is 29. I love it when his Uncle Bart says, "Carlie, you done came up here to Tennessee and robbed the cradle." Then he always laughs real big and we're all scared he'll lose his dentures. His laugh speaks a lot of words into my heart. Those words are, "Carlie, we love you very much. We're glad you're in our family." Maybe that feeling right there is why I'm willing to devote a lot of spare time to matchmaking.

My first victim…uh, I mean, non-paying customer is my old roommate, Clara Louise Johnson, from Commerce, Georgia. She doesn't know she's getting ready to be a customer. I thought it best not to share that information quite yet. Clara is 32 years old and a kindergarten teacher at Commerce Elementary. She's really pretty but I think she believes she's ugly. This is a very common feeling among women. If you don't know that, you don't know much about women. Look out, Clara. A big, determined, happily-married woman in Sharon, Tennessee, is on the lookout for your future husband. Oh, and all you wonderful single men in Sharon need to be on your guard. I'm watching, boys. I'm watching.

The real question was whether Doug was going to join me in my sideline business of matchmaking. I decided to carefully broach the subject at supper one night.

"So, Doug, what's news at the bank today?"

"Sad news. Maxine fell and broke her hip at the ballpark last night. Her grandson, Bubba Junior, hit a triple and Maxine started jumping up and down with tremendous enthusiasm. Chester was there and he thinks she forgot about the grandstand bein' kinda dry-rotted. And Maxine, well, she isn't exactly a featherweight. She's still at Volunteer Hospital. They think she'll be gone from work till after Christmas."

"That's sad. I hate that for Maxine."

"How was the conference call about the book?"

"It went well. Everything is ready for release. It's just that now I have to start writing the next book. And that means work. And you know what they say about work? Work is always best accomplished tomorrow."

He bowed his head slightly and smiled because he isn't rude or judgmental or harsh. Doug is a faithful worker. He isn't sporadic or overly-creative. He can be counted on. He likes me even if it is hard for me to get stuff done. He knows I'll write the next book. He knows someday the barbecued chicken won't be as tough as it was tonight. He knows I care about Maxine and Chester and his Uncle Bart and Aunt Charlotte. He is the definition of gracious.

"Doug, I have a question."

"Shoot."

"Well, I'm worried. I'm worried about Clara. I was wondering if we could invite her for the weekend sometime?"

"Sure. But what's the worry? Has she been sick or something?"

Okay. Now here's a difference between most men and women. Doug assumed something was physically wrong with Clara. He never even thought about the fact that Clara was living in our dingy old apartment and that she might be dying of loneliness and that the Kindergarteners might be a daily reminder of the fact that she didn't have children or a man or even any prospects. Whew! Doug was handsome but he needed enlightenment.

"Well, she called yesterday. She got a new cat and now I'm really worried."

"She got a cat? And that's what you're worried about?"

"Oh, absolutely. I think it's the beginning of the end. See, when a shy lonely woman gets a cat, the universe begins to work against her in so many troubling ways. First, it's the cat hair on the furniture and then it's the wanting to get a 'cat friend' for the current cat. Doug, within a year, Clara could have 20 cats and be operating a failed recycling business out of her backyard. I'm serious. These things happen. We'd better intervene."

Doug smiled really big and started laughing. I knew what his laughter meant just like I knew what Uncle Bart's meant. Doug's laugh was saying, "Oh Carlie, you're so overly-dramatic and funny and obsessive…and I love you."

"Y'see, Clara wants to be loved. She needs to be loved. But she doesn't know how to start the process."

"And you think you're the person who can help her?"

"Oh, I know I can. I mean, we can."

"So I'm in on this too, huh? What role could I possibly play in keeping Clara from becoming a cat lady with a failed recycling business in the backyard?"

"I'm so glad you asked! You're from here and would know the available men and how we could work out the introductions."

“But don’t people usually end up hating the ones who try to fix them up?”

“Hate? No one could ever hate you, Doug. I’m asking you to step out and take a risk with me the way Uncle Stanley took a risk when he introduced us. He helped us find true love, remember? I think we owe it to Clara to do the same.”

I had him and he knew it. Oh, I don’t mean I was controlling him. Doug wouldn’t be controlled nor would I even try. No, I had him with the love part. And Clara Louise Johnson, a shy Kindergarten teacher from Commerce, Georgia, who was frightfully embarrassed to talk about pork chops with the pleasant-looking butcher at Pic Pac, was getting ready to be our first official beneficiary. Roll up those shirt sleeves, Doug. This won’t be easy.

Chapter 2 CARLIE: Where Should We Look First?

I decided to do some of the preliminary matchmaking work without Doug. Christmas was only two weeks away and he was busy down at the bank. Plus, I know enough about men to know that he only had a limited amount of emotional matchmaking energy. So the morning after our conversation about Clara I decided to wisely talk to him about other subjects. But don't worry. I had a plan cooking on the back burner. A great plan.

I poured a second cup of coffee and rubbed his back a little while he ate his ham biscuit. "Tell Maxine I want to bring a meal when she gets home from the hospital."

"Will do. I'm sure she'll appreciate that. What are your plans for the day, Carlie? Working on the book?"

If you're a disheveled, easily distracted person, it's always scary when someone asks what your plan is for the day. We don't know our plans. Distracted people make plans "in transit." We get ideas for great projects while we're supposed to be doing other great projects. I wasn't sure how to address Doug's question. So I played it safe. "Well, yeah. At some point I'm definitely going to do some writing. But this morning I thought I'd drop in on Aunt Charlotte and Uncle Bart for a while. Both parakeets have been sick and I need to check on them." Did I also tell you that distracted people sometimes say really stupid things that give them away completely? That's a constant problem for me. Several times a day.

"The parakeets? You're going to visit the parakeets?"

"Busted. Okay, not really. I mean, I am going to visit Uncle Bart and Aunt Charlotte but you're right. I'm not checking on the parakeets. I think Aunt Charlotte can help me, help us, with our little project."

"Wait a second, Carlie. You're not telling me you're letting Aunt Charlotte help you find a man for Clara? Are you serious? You think MY Aunt Charlotte, who has a raccoon in the house and washes out Dixie bathroom cups, knows where the right guy is for Clara Johnson?"

"Yes. I mean, maybe. Stranger things have happened, Doug. Here's the deal. She knows every person in town. She knows people in the county. She's a resource. I'm not saying she's the only resource. I'm saying it's a place to start."

"Have you even talked to Clara about this? Does she even know you're on this matchmaking project?"

"Well, no. I need to have a real game plan first. She needs to know I've done my homework and I'm serious. I need to have my first introduction all ready and waiting."

He stood up and put on his coat. "I hope you're not getting over your head here, Carlie. These things can get messy fast."

He was right and I knew it. Y'see, there are two kinds of people in life. There are cautious people, like Doug, and there are people like me. If you're a cautious person, you should marry someone a little more adventurous. Oh, and if you're a person like me, you should definitely marry a cautious person. If you don't, well, all kinds of bad things could happen. Those bad things include, but are not limited to: talking with Agnes Robertson about the joys of marital intimacy, saying you care about the health of parakeets, or matchmaking without permission.

"Doug, you need to trust me on this one."

He smiled and leaned in for a good-bye kiss. "I do trust you. Have a good day." He winked and added, "Tell Aunt Charlotte I hope those parakeets get better soon."

I smiled and said, "Oh, I think life for those parakeets is looking up."

I loved going to Aunt Charlotte's house. It was one part "crazy" mixed with another part "fun" and then there was, well, there was this foul-smelling element that no one was able to identify. But it had to do with cats and coons and strange casseroles. Oh, and you never had to call before you went to Aunt Charlotte's house. You know how some people would be mortified if someone dropped by and there was laundry all over the floor. Yeah, Aunt Charlotte wouldn't be mortified if there was laundry on the floor, dishes in the sink, and a coon doin' his business in the potted hydrangea. Dropping in on her and Uncle Bart is like opening a box of Cracker Jacks and digging for the prize.

One day we dropped by and she was making homemade sausage on the front porch. You don't want to know the meat source and neither did we. Another day she was cutting pictures out of an old women's magazine for framing. Then there was the time she and Uncle Bart were in the backyard castrating a calf for Chester and Ida. We chose not to ask questions. When Aunt Charlotte hears a car drive up, she always comes out onto the creaky wooden porch for a loud and welcome greeting.

"Carlie Ann Jameson, get your big purdy self in this house right now! Glad you came by. I've got biscuits and gravy, if you're hungry. I was jes gettin' ready to give the leftovers to the coons"

"This is the coons' lucky day, Aunt Charlotte. I've already eaten. But I do need to talk you. Do you have a few minutes?"

"Of course I do, Honey. Come sit down."

I knew to avoid the powder blue recliner. It was broken and crooked and I didn't want to be the source of its final breath. I chose the old lime green vinyl couch which I knew would still be around when humans travel by jet pack.

"Aunt Charlotte, I need your help. You remember my old roommate, Clara Johnson? Kinda plain but pretty? The redhead? You met her at the wedding."

"Yes, I remember. She looked like she lost her best friend that day. Also looked like she needed to eat a little more too, poor thing."

"Well, I think God wants me to help Clara. Maybe he even wants you to help her."

"Now, if you mean you want me to feed her, yes ma'am, I'm more than ready to feed the poor girl. A little biscuit and gravy, maybe a few deviled eggs and she'd be fillin' out that bridesmaid's dress a lot better, Carlie." Aunt Charlotte wiped her chubby hands on an old brown dish towel and retrieved a chunk of something from the freezer and tossed it into a bowl of water in the sink. (I didn't bother telling Aunt Charlotte that my high school Home Economics teacher, Mrs. Lawson, told us to never thaw meat in the sink for fear of food poisoning. Besides, that rule may not even apply to possum.)

"I appreciate your desire to feed Clara, Aunt Charlotte. I do. But I was thinking more in terms of finding a man for her."

Aunt Charlotte turned from the sink with a jerk. She looked as though the CIA had just asked her to carry out a dangerous and important spying mission. She pulled up a yellow kitchen chair and looked me square in the eyes, “A man? Well, now that may take some doin’, seein’ as how she’s a timid little thing. But I’m all in. What kind of fella you reckon would turn her head?”

“Well, she values education a lot. So he’d probably need to be a college graduate. Not a party kind of guy. You know, solid.”

“Yes, well, let me think about the single fellas ‘round here. Timbo is a fine mail carrier but he drinks too much. There’s a single Methodist preacher out in Sidonia but he done took up with that curly-headed librarian in Union City. Wait, let me think. The new insurance agent on Main Street? No. He’s engaged to some citified girl in Memphis. The basketball coach at the middle school is single but he has a terrible temper. Wait! You know Mabel down at Sammy’s, dontcha?”

“I think so. Does she have the big black beehive hairdo?”

“No, Baby. That’s Delores. Mabel has a great big rear end and short hair that’s been bleached half to death. About 65 years old, those fake white fingernails, and a real sweet smile.”

Aunt Charlotte had the gift of descriptive words. She should have been a writer. “Yes, I know who you’re talking about.”

“Well, Mabel’s grandson was always a real smart young’un. Went away to a bunch of schoolin’, but he’s back in town now. Livin’ in Martin, gonna be a teacher at UT Martin. Just got the job and is supposed to start in January. His picture was in Tuesday's paper. A math professor, I believe. Yes, that's it. Whatcha think, Carlie? Reckon we should give it a shot?"

"Sounds good to me. What do you know about his character, Aunt Charlotte?"

"I don't know Charles very well but now his parents are fine folks. His dad works as a lineman and his mama has done books for the phone company for years. God-fearin' people, both of 'em. Southern Baptist, I believe. Or maybe they's Assembly of God. Can't remember. But I can find out more, Carlie. Doug went to school with Charles so he might know more."

"This is sounding very hopeful, Aunt Charlotte. I'll talk to Doug about it. What does he look like? I mean, is he a pretty decent-lookin' guy?"

"I mean, he ain't no Marlboro man, Carlie. He's not a great big fella. I wouldn't hire him to chop wood or nothin' like that. But if you like the cleaned-up kinda fella without dirt under his fingernails, I mean, yeah, he ain't a bad-lookin' young'un. The name is Charles Parker."

"Aunt Charlotte, you've been a lot of help. I'll talk to Doug and maybe we can get this all set up before our Christmas party."

"Glad I could help, Darlin'. And you tell that husband of yours that his aunt needs to get some lovin' on 'em and he don't want me to have to come down to that bank and embarrass him right there in front of God and ever'body."

"I'll tell him, Aunt Charlotte. I will. And thanks again."

I hugged Aunt Charlotte quickly and almost ran to the car. The excitement level in my brain must have been overflowing because I'm not prone to run. Rather than bothering Doug at work, I decided to lay out the plan in a well-written e-mail that he could read at his convenience after lunch.

Dear Doug, 1:00 pm
12-13-11

I love you. And that love has motivated me to help people like Clara. I talked to Aunt Charlotte this morning and we have a plan. What do you think about Charles Parker? She said you went to school with him. He's moving back to Martin to be a math professor. Let's invite him to our Christmas party, yes? And we can invite Clara. Then they can get married and have kids and live happily ever after. When their oldest child becomes a famous Nobel Peace Prize winner for physics or medical research or something like that, Charles and Clara will say, "Oh Doug, we could have never experienced the joy of this moment if you hadn't stepped out on a limb and invited us both to your lovely Christmas party out on the farm in Sharon?"

I know. Life is sweet, isn't it? Just promise me you'll think about it. I look forward to your return home this evening. I have something special cooking for you and it's not on the stove.
Carlie

2:15 pm

Carlie,

Charles is a good guy. I'm willing to give it a shot if Charles and Clara are both willing. I'm sure you're not using your incredible sex appeal to get me interested in the matchmaking project. But if you are, it's working.

Keep things warm at home.
Doug

Chapter 3 CARLIE: Getting Clara on Board

"Hello."

"Clara, I'm so glad you picked up. Doug and I want you to come to Sharon and see us! We're having a Christmas party next week and you gotta make plans to come and spend the weekend with us! How about it?"

"I don't know, Carlie. Are you sure you won't be too busy? I saw that you're going on book tour right after Christmas. Don't you need your downtime?"

"I need some Clara Louise Johnson time. So c'mon, Clara, say you'll come! I promise to buy new flannel sheets for the guest room. I promise to make homemade hot chocolate every night you're here. I promise not to cook things that I tend to burn. Oh Clara, you'll be out of school by then. Say you'll come!"

"Gosh, you're annoyingly persuasive, Carlie. Okay. I'll come. Are you sure Doug doesn't mind?"

"I'm absolutely sure. But Clara, there is one tiny little thing I need to tell you about before you come."

"Let me guess. You don't want me to bring Hobo with me. Don't worry. My parents can keep him 'cause he's on feline antibiotics right now and probably shouldn't travel anyway."

"Well, you're right. I mean, I definitely wasn't inviting a cat who takes antibiotics to our Christmas party. But that's not what I was gonna say. Now hear me out and don't get all crazy or defensive or anything, okay?"

"Oh no. Now I'm worried."

"No need to worry, Clara. It's just that, well, we're inviting a young man to the party thinking that maybe you guys will hit it off. No pressure. Nothing weird or anything. Really. It will be fine. I promise. He's a good guy."

Silence from the other end prompted my escalating voice. "Clara? Clara? Clara, stop breathing into that paper bag. This is ridiculous. You're a beautiful woman. Stop hyperventilating and talk to me."

"I can't do it, Carlie. You don't understand. I'm not like you. I can't make conversation with someone I don't know. I'll be too nervous. It won't work."

"It WILL work. Now listen to me, Clara Louise Johnson. Don't make me drive to Commerce, Georgia, to drag your tiny little butt up here to this Christmas party. Let me tell you how it is GOING TO BE. You are going to drive to Sharon, Tennessee, on December 16th. You are going to drink hot chocolate with me and we are going to talk late into the night. The next day you are going to help me make pigs in blankets and tiny cupcakes for the party. Then that night you're going to put on the best outfit you have that accentuates your tiny little rear end and your gorgeous red hair. We are gonna do your hair real fancy and you're gonna wear some make-up, sister. I'm serious. As Grandpa Joe used to say, "If the barn looks better painted, paint the barn." You are a beautiful woman, Clara, and you're gonna start acting like one. Charlene is a family friend and the local Mary Kay pest, I mean, salesperson. She's great and will be glad to help us with hair and make-up. Then you're gonna eat pigs in blankets and drink eggnog and meet Charles Parker. You are going to be nice and engaging and wonderful because you ARE nice and engaging and wonderful. End of story. Any questions?"

"Who is Charles Parker?"

"Well, that's a pretty fair question, I guess. He's a decent-lookin' math professor at UT Martin. He's single and Doug is willing to vouch for his character. Aunt Charlotte knows his grandma and his parents and swears that they're all God fearin' people. So, I think a decent-lookin' God fearin' math professor is worth an eight-hour drive, don't you?"

Silence.

"Clara? Clara, put down your inhaler. I want you to know I'm not really giving you a choice on this. I love you. I love you like a sister. And it's time for some sisterly intervention. You need to come see us. SO, I'll be shopping for those extra-soft flannel sheets and we'll see you next Friday night, okay?"

"Okay."

"Can't wait to see you! Love you, bye!"

"You too. Bye, Carlie."

Whew! Some people sure are hard to motivate. But a win is a win regardless of how messy. Time was now ticking down. I had only a few days to get Charles Parker on board with the plan. Oh, and I also had to learn how to make pigs in blankets. I had a feeling those pigs would be a cinch compared to the matchmaking.

Chapter 4 CARLIE: Executing the Pigs and the Plan

After supper, Doug agreed to call Charles' mother to see if he'd be in town and willing to come to the party. Of course, I asked Doug to put the phone on speaker while he made the call so I could make careful note of everything she said. All great matchmakers know that effective matchmaking is in the details, the finer nuances of conversation. I needed to listen for certain voice inflections that would help me move forward with the plan. No, it wasn't just nosiness. Well, maybe.

"Mrs. Parker?"

"Yes."

"Mrs. Parker, this is Doug Jameson."

"Doug Jameson, how in the world are you, son? I haven't seen you since your mama's funeral. Saw in the paper where you got married to that Georgia girl. Congratulations, Doug. How's married life?"

"Oh, it suits me real well, Mrs. Parker. Real well. Hey, I heard that Charles is back in town or will be soon. Got the job at UT Martin, is that right?"

"That's right, Hon. Oh, you can imagine Jim and I are right proud of Charles. Gettin' the Ph.D. and then movin' back to Weakley County. Yeah, real proud. He's got an apartment in Martin but he's not movin' in until January. He's here right now. Would you like to talk to him?"

"Yeah, that'd be great."

"Doug Jameson? Hey man, how's it goin'?"

"Pretty good, Charles. Big kudos on the teaching job. Not an easy thing to get on at a university right out of the Ph.D. program. And UT Martin? That's great. I mean, we're glad to have you back here on the home front."

"Thanks. You know I'd have never made it if you hadn't helped me in Mrs. Burcham's Senior English class. You were always her favorite. Hey, I heard you got married. Is that right?"

"I did. She's a great girl. In fact, I'd love for you to meet her. We're having a Christmas party Saturday night. Why don't you come out to the farm for a little Christmas cheer?"

"That'd be good. I need to get out and start socializing again. The Ph.D. didn't give me much time for that."

"Okay. You remember where Mom and Dad's place is, right?"

"I do."

"Then plan to be here by 7:00."

By this time I was standing up and doing all sorts of graphic hand motions to communicate the importance of telling Charles about Clara. I could tell Doug was hesitant. But he plowed through his hesitation and came out the other side. What a man!

"Oh, and Charles, I feel like I need to shoot straight with ya, man. Carlie has this friend who is coming up from Georgia. She's a real nice gal and I think you'd like her. She's a kindergarten teacher, real pretty. You're not seein' anybody right now, are ya?"

"No."

"Well, no pressure or anything. I just wanted to give you the heads up. I mean, I don't want you to skip taking a shower Saturday night or using deodorant or anything like that. We all know how you 'academic types' can be. No offense." Doug laughed but it was a nervous laugh and Charles Parker and I both knew it.

"None taken, Doug. Well, hey, I'm always up for meeting a pretty woman."

"Good. We'll see ya Saturday night. And welcome back, Charles. Really. Congratulations on the job."

"Thanks, man. See ya Saturday."

Doug stepped out of his comfort zone when he made that call to Charles Parker. And I appreciated it. Now we just had to pray that Clara Johnson would be willing to step out of hers.

Aunt Charlotte called and asked if I wanted to use some of her homemade sausage for the pigs in blankets. Doug did his own version of charades. He put his pointer finger to his throat and went back and forth very quickly. "Oh, thanks, Aunt Charlotte. Thanks a lot. But we've got it taken care of."

Chapter 5 CARLIE: Lighting the Matchmaking Fire

Clara arrived exactly when she said she would. 9:00 pm Friday night. She and the Kindergarteners had been released early from school and I'm sure her bags were already neatly packed in her immaculately clean car. I knew all of that because I knew Clara. Everything she did was neat and clean and organized and well-planned. But life was getting ready to get messy. What a relief!

I ran out onto the big wrap-around porch and hugged her like she was a long-lost relative coming home from war. "Clara Johnson, we are so tickled to see you! Get yourself in this house and take a load off." I was starting to sound like Aunt Charlotte. This was either disturbing or endearing. I didn't have time to decide which one. Clara wore plain gray dress pants that were creased down the front just like those gray dress pants my grandma wore to church when it snowed or sleeted. A big ugly tan striped sweater swallowed her beautiful body. Her straight hair was perpetually pulled back in a pony tail and her face was washed clean of all color. For the first time in my life, I wondered if she did this on purpose. But why?

"How was your trip, Clara? No problems along the way?"

"No. Everything was fine."

Doug spoke words of welcome and kindness and I realized Clara was still very nervous around him. Doug was a man. This was new territory for her.

He realized this and excused himself to the bedroom, saying he knew we wanted to catch up on all our girl talk. He was very sensitive like that…or he wanted to watch the football game. Either way it was a win. Even though Clara and I had lived together for four years, we had never had much girl talk. I tried to be open. When we were roommates, I would complain about wanting a man, about wanting to be loved. I would dream aloud about my desire to meet Prince Charming. But not Clara. She was a closed book. Looking back, it was almost like she was trying NOT to meet Prince Charming. She never wore make-up and her clothes were always too big for her petite figure. She never spoke of wanting a relationship. She was like those old-fashioned diaries girls used to buy at the dime store. Each diary had a little lock on the side and a little metal key. But no one had ever found the key to Clara Johnson's lock. I was determined to start the search.

"So, Clara, are you getting excited about meeting Charles tomorrow night? He sounded pretty jazzed about it on the phone. Really. Said he didn't have much time for relationships when he was working on the Ph.D. and it would be fun to meet a nice woman." (Looking back, I'm not sure he used the word "fun." I may have embellished his enthusiasm a tad bit).

"I don't know, Carlie. I'm not sure this is a good idea. I'm feeling a little sick at my stomach."

"Oh, I know. I remember. I was SO scared when I first met Doug. What would I say? What would I do? I know it's not easy to meet someone like this. But life is about risks, right?"

"It's not just that, Carlie. I…I'm not ready for risk. I don't need a man. I don't have anything to give a man. I don't. Trust me. I don't."

"Clara, you do! What are you talking about? You're pretty and smart and well-educated. You're not out partying night and day. A good man, a solid man would love to meet someone like you. He would."

"No. He wouldn't." Clara started crying. It was the first time I had ever seen her cry. I had cried in front of her many times when we shared an apartment. I cried over my algebra grade. I cried when Jim Flanders rejected me. I cried with frustration because I couldn't seem to muster any romantic feelings for Dan Carlisle. But Clara? No. Clara never cried about anything. Not one time. Looking back, something wasn't right.

"Clara, Honey, what's wrong? Why are you crying? Is this about Charles? I mean, are you really that nervous about meeting him?"

"No. It's not about Charles. It's about all men. And me. It's about me." She put her face in her hands and continued crying. "I'm all used up, Carlie. Really. You have no idea. No, Charles Parker doesn't want me…and neither would Doug…or anybody else. You don't know what I've done. You don't know where I've been."

"Clara, come on. It can't be that bad. I mean, I've known you since you were a senior in high school. You're a good girl. An exceptional girl, in fact."

"Didn't you wonder why I never had a boyfriend? Didn't you wonder why no one ever wanted me?"

"Look, you're shy. I get that. Shy people are often misunderstood. We don't know whether anyone wanted you or not. You were shy and people stood back a little, that's all."

"No, Carlie. No, that's not it. I have a past. You don't know what you're talking about. I've already been with a man…with men. Lots of men. I even had a baby." She held her hands over her eyes like she was in horrible pain. "A beautiful baby boy."

At that pivotal moment Doug nonchalantly opened the bedroom door and headed to the kitchen for a glass of sweet tea. I was hugging Clara and she was sobbing like there had been a death in the family. I didn't bother speaking words because by this time Clara Johnson was crying so loudly, she couldn't have heard my words. Doug glanced over at me but wisely remained silent. I knew how to interpret his facial expression. He was saying, "Oh my gosh, Carlie! What on earth have you done? What have we done? Do I need to call Charles and tell him that the nice girl from Georgia is having a mental breakdown?" I smiled at Doug. I was sure he understood my expression to mean, "Don't worry, Doug. God's got this. He does. No worries."

"Clara, Clara, listen to me, Honey. Just listen for a minute. It's gonna be fine. It is. Breathe deeply. Yeah, like that. Just keep taking deep breaths. Okay. Now start at the beginning. Start over. I'm listening."

"Didn't you think it was odd that we moved to Commerce my senior year?"

"No. Why would I think that was odd? People move all the time. I figured your dad or mom got a different job. No, I didn't think it was strange."

"My dad HAD to get a different job. We were all too embarrassed to stay in Birmingham. Birmingham was all my parents knew. They both grew up there. I'd lived there all my life. But then I messed it all up. I messed it up for everybody."

"How did you mess it up?"

"I got involved with Jason Miller. It was the worst thing I could have done. The worst thing I've ever done." She looked down at the hardwood floor and I grabbed another Kleenex. "He was 25 when he moved in with his aunt. She lived next door to us and we trusted her. He was looking for work. She made us think he was just between jobs and needed a place to stay. But he was bad news." Her voice got lower and her face turned red. "He used me, Carlie. I was only 15 when he started using me. Of course, because I was 15, I thought he loved me. I knew what we were doing was wrong but he kept telling me that it was right because he needed me, loved me, wanted to marry me. But that's not even the worst. Oh no. It gets worse. Jason wanted to feel important. He wanted to feel like a big shot with his friends. So, he…" Her timid crying turned back to wailing. I worried that Doug would feel the need to call 911. But he knew I would help her, that I would take care of her. He wisely stayed in the bedroom.

"He what, Clara? What did he do?"

"He passed me around."

"What?"

"He told me that I was wanted, that it wouldn't hurt to be with his friends. So he'd invite men over and they would take advantage of me." Her soft voice turned angry. "I know. You're thinking, 'Why on earth would you let them do that? Why wouldn't you have more respect for yourself than that?' Well, that's the point, Carlie! I didn't have respect for myself.

And Jason knew it. He knew I would do whatever he wanted. And I did. For more than two years. By Thanksgiving of my junior year I was pregnant. I didn't know who the father was. Didn't even know some of their names. I was barely old enough to drive a car and I was going to have a baby. Daddy knew about Jason. But I never told him about the others. Daddy told Jason he would have him put in prison. But he didn't. He knew I wasn't raped. I was a willing participant. The shame alone kept him from pursuing any legal action. I had the baby in July and placed him for adoption. Daddy had already made a plan for us to move. So I started my senior year at Commerce High School. Not one person there knew that I had given birth to a baby only a month before. And that was the plan, for no one to know. Ever."

"Oh Clara, how in the world have you kept this bottled up all these years? Why didn't you feel you could tell me? I could have helped you, would have helped you. We lived together for the last four years and you never said a thing?"

"I couldn't. When we moved to Commerce, I made a decision. I was never going to be with a man again. Ever. And I haven't. I haven't touched a man in years. I lived at home and commuted to college. I looked for a way to take care of myself."

"Then why did you come? Why did you agree to meet Charles?"

"Because you are one stubborn and persuasive woman, Carlie."

I laughed and wrapped my chubby arms around her frail body. "Yeah, I'm kinda proud of that actually."

I pulled away and she spoke with unusual confidence. "And for the first time, I'm willing to face the fact that I'm lonely. Seeing you and Doug together on your wedding day made me realize that deep inside I still wanted to be loved. Not by Jason Miller or a man like him. No. I wanted something real." She wiped tears from her eyes and lowered her head again. "But obviously the man will have to be very understanding. And I just don't know if there's a man out there who is like that. I'm limping, Carlie. No one can see it. But I am."

"Clara Louise Johnson, you've come to the right place, sister friend! Yes ma'am. We're goin' on a dad gum full-out mission to find the right man for you. We just gotta find the fella who's plugged into the kind of love that's required. And oh, we'll find him too. Don't doubt me, Clara. When it comes to matters of the heart, I'm highly motivated."

Chapter 6 CARLIE: Bachelor #1

Party time was fast approaching. I forgot to dust or vacuum but Doug said no one would notice because the food would be so good and the conversation would be so exciting that they wouldn't even think about whether they could write their names on the coffee table. Doug must really be in love 'cause he's an obsessively clean person by nature. He may be the most organized person I've ever met. He has all his socks lined up like little sock soldiers in the sock drawer. It's scary. And you should see the way he eats toast. He doesn't like crumbs so he cuts each piece in nine exact pieces. I'm gonna quit explaining this before you stop liking him.

Those pigs in their blankets were delicious. I had to sample a few. The mini strawberry cupcakes were good too. Can't serve food that hasn't been properly sampled. Aunt Charlotte and Uncle Bart were bringing two gallons of boiled custard. Doug suggested we throw caution to the wind and not over think that decision. Charlene was bringing Ro-tel dip and two bags of tortilla chips. Charles wanted to bring something so we suggested Diet Coke and ginger ale.

Chester and Ida were bringing a layered red and green Jell-O concoction that Ida had seen in a woman's magazine at the checkout counter at Dollar General. She called and explained in graphic detail the risks involved in the Jell-O project. If it wasn't quite right, she wanted me to know that it's 'cause she didn't have a snowman mold and she had to scratch the recipe down real fast while she was waiting for Jed Henderson to check out two dozen eggs, a singing Christmas card, and two bottles of cheap hair tonic. I assured her that an ample dose of culinary mercy was available, if needed.

When she heard about the fix-up with Charles Parker, Charlene was happy to come over early to do Clara's hair and make-up. I think most normal people, especially women, have a soft spot in their hearts for matchmaking. Charlene was no exception. It didn't hurt that I told her I wanted to buy all the make-up she put on Clara. Clara needed a fresh start. A make-over inside and out. Charlene would work on the "out" and I would ask God to help me work on the "in." That's called teamwork.

I carefully explained to Charlene that she needed to go elegant but not too over-the-top glamorous, seeing as how Charles was a mathematician and all. And boy, did she hit the nail on the head. By 6:30 Clara Johnson was lookin' like a model out of the L.L. Bean Christmas catalog only with a little more lavender eye shadow. On Thursday I had gone to the stylish dress shop in town and asked my trendy friend, Christy, to pick out several new outfits for petite little Clara. I knew her size because when we lived together, I would sometimes find her clothes in the dryer. I knew she wore them too big so I went down a few sizes. When I held up the blue jeans, I realized I couldn't have gotten into them even when I was in first grade. God bless her. Maybe Aunt Charlotte was right. She needed to eat more deviled eggs. No time for that now.

When I showed Clara the clothes, she was overtaken with emotion. I'm not much of a fashionista myself so I let Charlene pick the right outfit for the party. She chose simple new dark jeans that were tailored real nice. Her red jacket was kind of shiny but not sparkly. Nothing that would make a mathematician run for cover or anything like that. Her hair was loosely curled to perfection and looked prettier than I had ever seen it. Charlene definitely has the magic touch. Clara Johnson no longer looked like a woman trying to be invisible. She didn't look like a child in sweat pants and no make-up. No. She looked like a beautiful full-grown woman. Everything on the outside was exactly as it should be. I asked

Charlene for some privacy and she gladly walked into the kitchen.

Clara and I stood in front of the full-length mirror. "Clara, you look beautiful. Strikingly beautiful. But it's not enough. It's not. You have to understand who you are inside. Your identity. You are loved, friend, and you are able to love."

It was 6:55. I hugged her and prayed God would show her the truth…and in less than five minutes too.

Charles Parker drove up right on time. I like punctuality in my matchmaking victims. When I get a little more experienced, I'll be sure to list that as a rule in my promotional material. Charles drove a 10-year-old white Jeep Cherokee which looked to be in pretty good condition. I liked that. A 30-year-old Gremlin covered in Bondo would have been no good. But a brand-new sports car that cost more than our house would have been even worse in my book. Charles Parker, in case you're wondering, I approve of your transportation choices. It made me think about what was said about baby bear's porridge all those years ago, "It was just right."

Of course, Doug and I went out on the porch to greet him. Aunt Charlotte was right. He was no Marlboro man. But Charles was a perfectly acceptable candidate for "Decent-Lookin' Math Professor of the Year." He was about 5'10", short dark hair, John Boy Walton glasses, and a neatly-trimmed goatee. He was dressed perfectly. Ironed khaki pants and a solid brown shirt tucked in. New lookin' trendy hiking boots. Not the big clunky mud-covered kind. You know, the kind that look like regular shoes. I don't know if he dressed himself or if his mama pulled a last-minute, "Charles Parker, you best not wear faded jeans and an old t-shirt to a Christmas party." I know. You probably think that a 29-year-old professional person like Charles Parker would know what to wear to a Christmas party. But if you do think that, it's because you don't know much about people who really love math.

Doug spoke first. "Hey Charles, welcome and welcome back to West Tennessee too!"

"Thanks, Doug! And I guess this pretty lady is your new bride, yes?"

Charles was now forever in my good graces. Don't worry. It's strictly platonic.

Doug flashed a big smile and proudly wrapped his arm around me, "It sure is! Charles, this is Carlie. Carlie, Charles."

I extended my hand and welcomed him with the first thing that came to my mind. "Charles, it's great to meet you. And don't worry. I don't hold your love for math against you. Or at least, I'm trying not to."

He laughed with warmth and sincerity, "Thanks, Carlie. Yeah, I didn't expect a famous writer to hold much affection for math. No harm done."

"Well, despite my disdain for your beloved math, I'm still happy to have you as a guest. Come on in, Charles. We've got lots of good food and I want you to meet a dear friend of mine."

A few hours earlier, when Charlene was working on Clara's make-over, Clara had been surprisingly calm. She talked of her favorite colors and an expensive perfume she bought at Macy's. It was like the make-up and clothes were helping to transform her. But now that calm was long gone. She looked pale and distraught. Come on, Clara. Don't do this. Don't go away right now. Stay with me. Stay with us. And for goodness sake, Clara, don't mess up your chances with a decent-lookin' math professor who has both a sense of humor and a well-trimmed goatee.

"Charles, this is a dear friend of mine from Commerce, Georgia, Clara Johnson. Clara, this is an old friend of Doug's, Charles Parker."

"Nice to meet you, Clara. Doug tells me you're a kindergarten teacher, yes?"

She looked down at the floor. "Yes."

Okay. I need to make a public service announcement right here and now. If you want to make a potential suitor think you're not interested at all, just answer his questions with one word answers. Oh Clara, I'm literally going to start crying and then I'm going to eat that whole pan of blanket-laden pigs if you don't pick up the enthusiasm. I might even hit you with the pan when I'm done.

Charles spoke with such kindness. "Well, I respect you for that, Clara. Really. It would scare me to death to face a whole room of little people. I don't have what it takes." Ten points for Charles Parker for trying to move things forward. Keep climbing that mountain, brother. Keep climbing.

Clara glanced down at the counter and nervously wiped up a punch spill with a paper towel. She moved away from Charles and toward the trash can to dispose of the towel. She shrugged her shoulders. "I guess I just like little kids."

He followed behind her and said, "That's a noble quality, Clara. So, tell me about Commerce. I mean, I'm sure it's not as much of a thriving metropolis as Sharon is, right?" Charles laughed and even touched her on the arm. He was doing everything he could to motivate eye contact. But I feared the Titanic had already hit the giant iceberg. Now we were just waiting for the body count.

Clara looked out the kitchen window as though she wanted to be somewhere else. Anywhere else. "Yeah, Commerce is pretty small. Not this small, but yeah, not very big."

I had never been so happy to hear Uncle Bart and Aunt Charlotte come in the door. Uncle Bart's booming voice provided a much-needed distraction, "Well, hey ho and Merry Christmas, ever'body!" Uncle Bart was wearing brand new overalls from Rural King and a plaid shirt that had been new in the early 70's. He was also carrying two big milk jugs filled with questionable light yellow custard.

Aunt Charlotte was in a full sweat and fanning herself with a church bulletin she'd found in the truck. "Sorry we're late but we took a quart of custard to Bill Donaldson seein' as how he's been laid up with the shingles."

I knew Aunt Charlotte would be wearing her beloved Rudolph sweater. The Rudolph sweater was famous all throughout Sharon because the little reindeer nose blinked off and on thanks to a tiny little battery pack secured in the right shoulder pad. Uncle Bart had kept that nose blinking long after the original battery pack had played out. I don't know the details but I know it involved a Triple A battery and wiring from an old CB radio. Every year he said, "Now Charlotte, don't get this here thing wet or you'll be squallin' for shore." The Rudolph sweater had been the stuff of family legend for more than fifteen years. It was also about two sizes too small and I'll just leave it at that.

Aunt Charlotte called it quits on the fanning and carefully cleaned her glasses with a Frosty the Snowman tea towel. When her glasses were securely back in place, she looked up and said with enthusiasm, "Charles Parker, well look at you! Now don't you look jes' like your Uncle Harold. My word. Bart, don't he look jes' like Harold Parker? Good golly, son, we hear a lot of fine things about you, yes, we do."

"Well, thank you, Mrs. Charlotte. It's good to see you and Mr. Bart again."

"Now Honey, tell me again where you've been. Somewhere out west, yes?"

"Yes ma'am. Colorado"

"Well, law mercy, I never been to Colorado but I tell ya right now I got no use for high mountains. One slip of the foot and you're dead as a dog."

Charles was such a good sport. He laughed and said, "Yes ma'am. Those mountains are pretty awesome. But in a twist of good fortune, I'm back in the farm country of West Tennessee now."

"Yes, sir. You should be thankful God done brought you back to HIS country."

I was relieved that Aunt Charlotte was entertaining Charles. But where in the world was Clara? I wanted to believe she was desperately searching for a lifeboat. But, no. She was hiding in the bathroom evidently. She finally entered the kitchen looking paler than before. Even Aunt Charlotte couldn't bring her to life. And here's some wisdom you can take to the bank. If an older woman—wearing a battery-charged Rudolph sweater—can't bring you to life at a Christmas party, you've got one foot in the grave already.

Here's the whole evening in a nutshell. We all chose to trust God when we courageously drank Aunt Charlotte's custard. Uncle Bart told us what he heard at the feed store, how the local school board election had been rigged by a lawyer in Nashville. We all bragged on Brother Dan's German potato salad and then listened intently when he explained how the recipe came over on a big boat with his German relatives at the turn of the century. Charles entertained us with funny stories from his time in Colorado. And Clara? Clara spent the whole evening silently convincing Charles Parker that she wasn't much of a catch, and he shouldn't even bother baiting the hook.

At 10:30 everyone left and the three of us sat in the living room drinking cocoa. Doug made small talk for a while but was planning his exit strategy. "Well, girls, ya'll feel free to stay up as late as you want, but I'm ready to call it a night." He reached down to kiss me. "G'night, Honey."

"G'night, Doug. And thanks for drinking the custard. It really was a leap of faith."

He laughed and winked at me. I was completely enamored with Doug Jameson. As Aunt Charlotte would say, "God done blessed me real good."

Seeing Clara curled up in a blanket on the couch brought me back to the mission at hand. I decided it was time for the direct approach. "Okay, friend. Start talking."

"About what?"

"About Aunt Charlotte's boiled custard. Gosh, Clara, what do you think? About tonight. About Charles Parker. About you. Where were you?"

"I was right here. You told me to come and I came. If Charles Parker doesn't like me, so be it."

"But that's the thing, Clara! How could he know if he likes you? How could anybody know? You never let him in. At all. You were shutting him out completely. You never even gave him a chance. Why? I thought he was a great guy. He's cute and nice and he seemed really friendly."

"Well, that's the thing, Carlie. You think Charles Parker is gonna have to settle for a girl like me? No. He's not."

"Settle? Who even said anything about settling? I'm just talking about a conversation, Clara! You never even made conversation." My frustration level was growing. "Gosh, you made him think something was wrong with him! And incidentally, there doesn't seem to be much wrong with him in my book. So no, that wasn't very smart!"

Clara's voice cracked with emotion and she rose from the couch. "See? I told you this wouldn't work! I tried to tell you that I wasn't like you, that I couldn't be friendly and outgoing. Guess what, Carlie? Not everyone can walk into a room and just start making conversation. I'm sorry that I'm not funny or entertaining enough for you or your friends. Oh, and I'm sorry I'll never write books or be on TV talk shows either. Look, I'm a kindergarten teacher. I live alone. I have a cat. That's who I am. You and Charles Parker can be disappointed in me all day but it won't change anything. It won't change me."

She was crying now and I was feeling terrible. Yes, the Titanic crashed into an iceberg tonight and Charles and Clara were both casualties. But we all know who was captaining the ship.

I stood and embraced her. "Clara, Clara, I'm sorry. Really. It's all my fault. It's my fault for inviting him. It's my fault for trying to make you someone you're not. Gosh, it's even my fault if you get food poisoning from questionable boiled custard or mystery Jell-O." We both laughed. "Can you find it in your heart to forgive me? Please?"

"I forgive you, Carlie. I do. Let's just put it behind us, okay?"

"Absolutely."

A lot of people would have given up matchmaking right then and there. Yep! A lot of people would have seen the handwriting on the wall. Clara Johnson doesn't want Carlie Jameson's matchmaking services. Thankfully, I found the writing completely illegible.

Chapter 7 CARLIE: Christmas Conniving

The morning after the Christmas party was much more enjoyable than expected. It's like all the pressure was off. Off of me, the ship's captain. And off of Clara too. I made giant cranberry muffins and the whole house smelled like coffee and leftover pigs in blankets. At the breakfast table Clara managed to have a long and detailed conversation with Doug about marketing and international business practices. I made note of the fact that she could actually have a pleasant and meaningful conversation with a man. But it needed to be unscripted. Casual. Spur of the moment.

Clara loved our country church which wasn't surprising to Doug or to me. Everyone was especially friendly and Brother Dan's preaching was always excellent. I scoped the crowd as I had been for several weeks. No available men. None. Well, none under the age of 70. No worries. It's never over till the fat lady sings "Bohemian Rhapsody" at the top of her lungs.

The afternoon found us saying our tearful good-byes. I had known Clara for 13 years but for the first time, I felt genuinely close to her. I would miss her and I knew she would miss me too. She had opened up her heart to me. She had told me things that no one else knew. Now I would need to safeguard those revelations and try to help her move forward. But she was a fragile soul and I had to be careful.

"Clara, come again soon. Tell me you will."

"I will. Thanks, Carlie. Really. It may not have turned out the way you planned, but I appreciate your trying. I do."

Clara Johnson drove out of our driveway on December 18th in an immaculately clean tan Ford Focus. She thought I was done with matchmaking. But I don't give up that easily. I spent the next few days Christmas shopping and writing and trying to become a better cook. But always in the back of my mind I was looking for Clara Johnson's Doug. Early one morning I realized I hadn't really addressed the painful things she had shared with me during her weekend visit. So I grabbed a cup of coffee, sat in the comfy chair in my office, and wrote a letter.

Dear Clara,

Thanks for coming last weekend. We loved having you here. There are a few things I want to tell you that I didn't get a chance to tell you. So here goes:

I am very angry at Jason Miller for hurting you. I hold him fully responsible. Clara, even though you say you were a willing participant, you weren't. He was a 25-year-old man and you were a 15-year-old child. That's not called sex. It's called a felony.

The forces of darkness would like to convince you that what happened all those years ago means that no man will ever want you…or even worse, that the wrong man will want you. I'm sure those forces are working night and day to convince you that you're worthless, Clara. But it's not true. And we all know it takes a lot of effort to propagate an effective lie. So stop listening to all that whispering in your ear about your poor self-worth. You're worth a lot to your family, to me, and to God. So when the lies come, try to remember that and speak the truth to yourself.

We never even talked about the fact that you gave birth to a baby. A real, live, breathing, beautiful baby boy. I never asked if you met his parents or how you worked the plan. I never asked if you held him or if he had red hair. I'm sure he was beautiful. I guess that means he's about 15 years old right now, yes? Clara, I know the adoption decision couldn't have been easy. I want you to know how very much I respect you for it. A wonderful, handsome, smart young man is out there right now with all the opportunities in the world because you loved him. You loved him in spite of his immoral father. You loved him because he was a person, your baby boy. I'm sure he's having a great life. That life began with a young girl's courage.

Doug and I will be going on the book tour a few days after Christmas. I just wanted you to know we're ready for a return visit anytime in January. Oh, and Doug talked to Charles a few days after the party. Charles said you were a beautiful young woman but he figured something was holding you back from being in a relationship. He didn't know what it was. Doug didn't tell him anything. Doug just said that you thought he was a good guy but maybe you weren't right for each other or maybe the timing was off. Charles agreed. No harm done, Clara. So, it wasn't a match.

I'm sure you think I'm done with the matchmaking. Sorry. I'm not. I'll keep you posted. And by the way, the more you tell yourself the truth, the more likely my matchmaking will someday result in a match. This is a mystery of life. But it's true. I promise.

Love and hugs,
Carlie

Chapter 8 CARLIE: Southern Book Tour

Doug had four days off for Christmas. Every morning, he built a fire in the fireplace. I cooked country ham for breakfast. Even though the ham pieces were tougher than a crocodile cowboy boot, we were thankful. I learned a valuable lesson those first six months of marriage. Selfish little annoyances can be lessened through frequent sexual activity. And no, I haven't written to Dr. Phil to ask if he agrees with me. But I think he should agree and probably does. When Doug and I would have conflict or I would have a hormonal meltdown, physical intimacy seemed to remedy some of that conflict. I need to write a book about this except someone has probably already written a book about it. It would be called, "Don't Worry about His Dirty Socks on the Floor: How to Forget About Laundry and Get Busy in the Bedroom." If I tacked on something like "30 days to a great marriage" it would be a best-seller. Americans love stuff that can be fixed in 30 days. I guess we have relationship ADD. This book should be given to every newlywed couple during their pre-marital counseling.

Doug's relatives came over for a potluck dinner on the afternoon of Christmas Day. No boiled custard and no Jell-O so we deemed it a great success. My parents, along with my two brothers and their wives, came for a visit the day after Christmas. It was like a big slumber party and I felt blessed to be the host. Well, I wasn't the only host. My handsome husband, Doug, was also the host. Still seemed unbelievable sometimes, those words…my husband. It's like I'd spent my whole life believing that tall chubby girls don't get married. But they do. Hallelujah. They do.

Doug took a few extra days off to join me on a whirlwind book tour through the South. Nashville, Birmingham, Atlanta, Savannah, Pensacola, and Orlando. I was promoting my most recent book, "A Married Woman's Guide to Ordinary." See, when I was 32 and single, I got a book published which was called, "A Single Woman's Guide to Ordinary." I guess tons of people liked it and bought it. And because tons of people bought it, I got to go to cool places and meet famous people and do a bunch of stuff I had never done.

Becoming a published author also ended my ten-year career at the Dollar General Store in Commerce, Georgia. Some people might think I'm embarrassed by those years. But I'm not. I learned a lot about people and about pork n beans. Anyway, so then I married Doug and the publisher knew that I would have to stop writing funny books about being single because...well, I wasn't single anymore. So they figured everyone who liked my book about being single would like to read about my meeting Doug and getting engaged. That's the first half of the book. The second half is about getting married and the funny stuff I learned in the process.

You may think a book tour would be exciting and glamorous. But Doug and I aren't much into excitement and glamour. We like meeting the people at the book signings and Doug and I like traveling together. But what we really love is a nice quiet evening at our farm house in Sharon accompanied by my mediocre cooking. We could buy another house, a bigger house, quite easily. But we won't. Why would we buy a different house when we already like the house we have? Plus, our farm house has been in Doug's family a long time. So it's one of those deals where we wish the walls could talk. At least I think we do. I don't know. Talking walls would be weird and scary so maybe that's not a good idea.

When we were in Atlanta, my publisher called with big news. Huge news. I mean, this was probably the biggest news since Doug asked me to marry him at the Crowne Plaza while we were eating biscuits and gravy. A big movie studio wants to make a movie based on my first book. It'll even be called, "A Single Woman's Guide to Ordinary." I hope it doesn't turn out to be a spoof or something like "Bill and Ted's Excellent Adventure." The publishers hired a script writer who developed a main character who's chubby and single and funny and a lot like me. She'll even work at the dollar store and everything. So it should be pretty good, if you like dollar store humor. And I do.

The movie studio representative said they like making movies based on best-selling books because it's like printing money. No, the movie studio didn't say that. At least not out loud. They said a lot of mumbo jumbo about my book being a fresh and honest paradigm shift for the modern single woman. But I wasn't born yesterday. It was all about the dough. Nevertheless, as the author, I get some editorial privileges and for that I'm grateful. We'll be heading to Hollywood in early March. Great weather. But lousy gravy.

Chapter 9 CARLIE: Catching Up with Dave and Shannon

The best part about the book tour was stopping in Chattanooga to visit Doug's cousin, Shannon, and her husband, Dave. I met Dave and Shannon on the same day I met Doug in person for the first time (all recorded in that "Doug and Carlie" book).

I mean, Doug and I had been writing and talking on the phone but the first day I met him at the Cracker Barrel in Chattanooga was the same day we went to their house for dinner. They made me feel loved and appreciated at a time when I was very insecure. They made me feel a part of their family even before I was a part of the family. And you don't ever stop loving people like that.

I could feel intimidated by Dave and Shannon because they're real smart and beautiful and everything but I choose not to. He's the pastor of a growing church. Shannon looks like Jennifer Lopez. Except I think Shannon is probably way cooler than Jennifer Lopez because I doubt Jennifer Lopez changes her own sheets, makes her own lasagna, or makes tall chubby girls feel beautiful. Well, I don't know. Maybe Jennifer Lopez does do all that. I shouldn't be so quick to judge. Anyway, Dave and Shannon are our closest true friends. Ringing the doorbell to their house made both of us giddy.

Dave opened the door barefoot and wearing a Hawaiian shirt from college. "Doug! Carlie! Come on in. Come in!"

Doug laughed, "We're not keeping you from a luau, are we, man?"

"You're just jealous because I'm so much cooler than you."

"Yeah, I've always been jealous of men wearing floral print."

They hugged really big. I loved seeing them together. Dave was the brother Doug never had, the brother he so desperately needed. Shannon walked from the kitchen and hugged both of us but something seemed amiss. She was always so cheery and enthusiastic. But not today.

"Shannon, is everything alright? I mean, Dave said it was fine for us to come for supper tonight. But if you're not feeling well, hey, that's no problem. Really."

"No, I'm fine. Besides, I've already made taco soup. It's all good."

Dave looked down at the carpet. "We've just had some disappointment lately. That's all."

Doug sat in a floral wingback chair and leaned forward. "What kind of disappointment? Anything Carlie and I can do to help?"

Shannon sat in the leather recliner, put her head in her hands, and started weeping.

I kneeled beside the recliner and grabbed her hand. "Shannon, what's wrong? You guys can tell us. Did something happen? Something with your job or the church?"

Dave spoke up. "No, it's not the church. Everything's fine there. It's us. Our family situation hasn't turned out to be what we'd hoped. We've been trying to have a baby for a few years now and…well, it's just not happening, that's all. I mean the 'trying' part is happening just fine…but the baby…yeah, the baby part doesn't seem to be working out the way we planned."

Doug and I were uncomfortable and sad and unsure of what to say next. I just stared at the coffee table. I noticed that Shannon had all the magazines lined up in the most bizarre and perfect order. She was definitely Doug's cousin.

Shannon grabbed a Kleenex from the end table and spoke quietly, "We're trying not to get depressed about it. But really, after two years, it's hard not to get down. This time the doctor thought he had us all fixed up. But today we found out it didn't work. Again."

"I'm sorry, Shannon. Really. I had no idea. I mean, Doug and I knew you guys had kind of talked about it, but we didn't know you were really trying to have a baby. That must be hard. Really hard."

Shannon wiped her eyes and patted my hands. "It is hard, but we'll get through it. Well, hey, let's change the subject. No use bringing you guys down too. So, how did the tour go? Are the books selling pretty well? I mean, well enough to make the publisher happy?"

"Yeah, everybody's happy right now. Good crowds. And some good buzz from the press."

Doug smiled really big and said, "Carlie should tell you about her latest project. She's working on it night and day. I think she's more enthusiastic about it than about any book she's ever written. Go ahead, Honey, fill Dave and Shannon in."

"Well, if you must know, I've decided to become a matchmaker."

Dave started laughing. "A matchmaker? Carlie, are you just wanting people to hate you?"

"Gosh, that's what Doug said! Look, matchmaking is an art form and I'm determined to learn the art of it. Besides, if I feel blessed by my marriage, why wouldn't I want to bless other people with the same?"

"Hey, you'll get no criticism from me. I counsel people every day who should have been screened through a process before taking the leap. So knock yourself out, Carlie. Really."

"Thank you. You remember Clara, don't you? My roommate from the wedding?"

Shannon said, "Sure! She's the redhead. A little shy maybe, but she's a beautiful girl."

"Well, Clara, she's my first non-paying customer."

"So, have you found a match yet?"

"Uh, not exactly. Close maybe, but no. It may take a while. I mean, the Sistine Chapel wasn't painted in a day, right?"

I moved toward Doug and he wrapped his arms around me, "That's right, Honey! You just keep on painting and I'm sure someone decent is going to come to the surface any day now."

I was fine with their laughter. They weren't making fun of me. They loved me dearly. Dave and Shannon had shared the painful news of not having a baby. And we didn't know what to do or say. So we all found a reason to laugh. I didn't even bother telling them about the movie deal. It didn't seem to matter so much anymore.

Chapter 10 CARLIE: New Year, New Bachelor

Aunt Charlotte was not the best source of advice about recipes or household cleaning tips or proper pet maintenance. But people? Oh, now Aunt Charlotte knew people. So I expressed my matchmaking frustration to her over coffee one cold January morning. We were sitting in her living room which is the living room of mismatched furniture. Two old broken-down recliners in dusty blue and dusty rose. Dusty being the operative word. A lime green couch Uncle Bart had found in a discard pile on the edge of town. Orange and green throw pillows handmade by Mrs. Simpson, an older woman at our church, and proudly displayed by Aunt Charlotte, saying, "You just don't see that kind of handiwork anymore." A scratched-up coffee table made of particle board and old yellow lamps shaped like squirrels from Uncle George's estate sale. No, Aunt Charlotte would never have her own show on HGTV. But decorating help was not what I desperately needed.

"We mustn't give up on our matchmaking, Aunt Charlotte. We can't."

"I hear ya, Darlin', but that Clara, she's gotta perk up a little. I mean that little ol' Charles Parker gave it his all and she done nothin' but throw 'em overboard and he drowned, Carlie! He drowned right there in your livin' room with all of us just sittin' there watchin'. It was a pitiful sight too."

"Yeah, but she's working on that. She is. I think she's gonna try harder next time. Maybe Charles Parker was a little too friendly, too I don't know, too perfect. I just know we shouldn't give up. She does want to meet someone, but she's scared."

"Okay. Now I was a figurin' last night all the fellas 'round here that I consider decent. I'll be honest, Hon. The list ain't that long. But then I thought of Dewayne. He cuts meat down at the market and we all like him real well, but he's kind of odd."

"Odd in what way?"

"Hard to put my finger on it. Uh, I reckon he's a little bit of a mama's boy."

"You mean he lives with his mama?"

"Yeah. And she ain't helped him none either. She babies him. He's older than Doug and she still brings him his lunch every day. Plus, he smokes. Would that be a problem for Clara?"

"She's highly allergic so I'm afraid it would be. Who else you got, Aunt Charlotte?"

"Now there's always Pete Thompson. He owns the gas station out on Hwy. 22 but he's 'bout 45 years old. His wife left him last year. Ran off with some highfalutin car salesman she met in Jackson. Yeah, he said he ain't never gonna buy a Dodge fer the rest of his life. Ever time he sees a Dodge, he says it's like the food poisonin' we all got at the community center last 4th of July. Polly Johnson's tater salad nearly caused us to meet our maker so I knew zactly what he meant, poor thing."

"I don't know, Aunt Charlotte. I think Pete needs some healing time, wouldn't you say?"

"Yeah, I reckon. Well, I didn't wanna have to do this, but we're gonna need to move over a county. I'm callin' someone who can help us. Just give me a minute."

Aunt Charlotte took off her bright red apron that read, "Kiss me. I'm from the South." She picked up the faded yellow telephone receiver as though it were 1979 and dialed a number she had memorized. The phone base was secured to the dark brown paneled wall and had a mile-long cord which gave Aunt Charlotte the opportunity to plop down in the broken powder blue recliner. What a woman of faith! The whole scene reminded me of an episode of the Brady Bunch except Alice would have never made squash/macaroni casserole and there were no coons in the Brady household. Of course, speaker phone was not even an option so I knew I would only hear one side.

"Debbie? Debbie, this here's Charlotte. I need your help, Baby. I do."

"Well, there's this lonely, right pretty, little skinny woman who needs a good man. She's a teacher and a God fearin' woman so he don't need to be some kind of wild fella. He needs to love God, go to church, and be a hard worker."

"Yes, uh-huh. He can't be a smoker or a heavy drinker. She ain't that kinda woman, Debbie. She's a cute little thing, about 30 years old, needs to eat a little more, kinda shy. But not a bad young'un"

"Yes. Okay."

"Yes. Hmmm. Yeah, I do remember."

"Now you're talkin', Debbie. Uh huh, that sounds good. Tell me more."

A few minutes passed as though it were an hour. Aunt Charlotte was clearly getting good news because her short chubby body rose from the broken chair with Olympic enthusiasm.

"Yes, ma'am! I reckon we could all be Baptist for a day. Grandpa Joe might roll over in his grave but it wouldn't kill none of us. Yeah, that sounds real good. Okay. We'll plan on bein' there on the 27th. And it's just regular potluck? I'll bring deviled eggs and baked beans with the ground beef and onions all cooked up in 'em. Oh, and this little redheaded kindergarten teacher will be with me too. Yeah, go ahead and give him fair warning. Thanks, Debbie. See you soon, Baby!"

Aunt Charlotte hung up the phone and then cheered like she won the lottery! "God done smiled on us, Carlie Jameson! He done smiled on us good!!"

"I can't wait to hear the details. Lay it on me."

"Well, Bart's niece lives over in Troy. That's in Obion County. She's a fine lady too, married about eight years, four kids. And Debbie knows people over in Obion County and I knew she could help us. Turns out one of her old high school friends is preachin' at a Baptist Church way out in the country. He sells insurance in Union City during the week and preaches on weekends. Anyway, he's 29 and was datin' this little gal from Illinois but she turned out to be trouble. He found out she flew to California to see some fella she met on the computer. God, help us, Carlie! What's wrong with these poor young people? Anyway, that was almost a year ago and he's still single. Debbie says he's a real good man but most ever'body in the church is married or old enough to be his grandma. They're having a potluck lunch in a few weeks and we're gonna be there, Carlie. You, me, Doug, Bart, and o'course, Clara. So get on the phone with 'er and tell 'er to eat as much as she can in the next two weeks. She needs to be filled out real good 'cause she's gonna be meetin' Jake Smith.

And Carlie, 'tween you and me and the fence post, Debbie says Jake really does look like the Marlboro man. A big rugged country boy who don't smoke and carries a Bible? Oh Baby, God done smiled on us real good."

Chapter 11 CARLIE: The Smoke-free Marlboro Man

I called Clara at 4:20 because she loves to watch Jeopardy at 4:30. I'm sensitive like that.

"Hello."

"Clara? Hey, how was your day, friend?"

"Well, two of the Kinders came down with the stomach virus right after lunch. I'll never eat a Chuckwagon sandwich again. But other than that, it's good. How are you?"

"Oh, we're good. Clara, I've never been one to mince words. So I'll shoot straight with you. It's time for your late January visit to the farm. And yes, there is some matchmaking involved. But there's no use to fight me on it. I'm ornery. And it's best to just surrender."

"Ha Ha. So, who is the poor victim this time? Let me guess. Uncle Bart has a brother."

"Well, aren't you funny? I've totally underestimated your sense of humor. Yes, Uncle Bart does have a brother but he lives in Alabama and is married to a manicurist who sings country music on weekends. They've been married for over 40 years AND she wears rhinestones so you don't have a chance, friend."

"Well, darn. Then I'm not even going to bother coming."

"Aren't you in a good mood today? Okay. Here's the deal. Uncle Bart's niece knows someone in a neighboring county who would be perfect for you. Really. He's an insurance agent and a preacher on weekends."

“You’re kidding?”

“No, I’m not kidding. Why would I be kidding?”

“You think I could be a preacher’s wife? Me? A shy woman who can’t meet people and has a sordid past? You think that’s what he’s praying for? You think he’s saying, ‘God, please bring me a woman who is so shy that people think she’s unfriendly and then go ahead and throw in a horrible past that involves childbirth.’? You’re over your head this time.”

“No. You’re the crazy one. You’re living in the past, Clara. You’re listening to the stupid voices. And you have to quit listening. Really. So stop listening to the crazy talk and make plans to come up. We’re going to his church on the 27th and they’re having a potluck afterward. No pressure at all. We are literally just going to visit Uncle Bart’s niece for the day. Come on.”

“Would it matter if I put up a fight with you?”

“Absolutely not. I’m a big woman and I’ll always win. So don’t waste the energy.”

“I’ll see you in a few weeks then.”

“And we’ll be looking forward to it.”

When Doug got home from work, I explained the plan.

“Doug, how do you feel about being Baptist for a day?”

“Excuse me?”

“Well, Aunt Charlotte and I have planned a little family field trip to a Baptist Church outside Troy in two weeks.”

"Oh, let me guess. This involves Jake Smith and a certain shy woman from Georgia, right?"

"Well, aren't you the smart one? You're already ahead of me. How do you know Jake Smith?"

"I've known his daddy for a long time. He's a big soybean farmer and has done a lot of business with the bank. Jake's a pretty good fella. He's a little young though, isn't he?"

"Well, if that ain't the pot callin' the kettle black." Note to self: I'm spending way too much time with Aunt Charlotte.

Doug grabbed me from behind and started feverishly kissing my neck. He laughed and said, "I couldn't help it, Carlie. This big blonde bombshell robbed my cradle. I was powerless."

"Well, let's hope a skinny little redhead can rob Jake Smith's cradle. I hold out a lotta hope this time, Doug. A lotta hope."

Chapter 12 CARLIE: Preach On, Brother Jake

The weekend of Clara's visit was extraordinarily cold. Of course, I love cold weather. I think most chubby women love cold weather 'cause we look much better in black pants and sweaters than we do in sundresses. That's just a cruel fact of life and I'm one of the few people willing to say it out loud.

Saturday night I helped Clara lay out all the clothes she brought. I knew what I was looking for but hadn't seen it quite yet.

"We're walkin' a fine line here, Clara. We want modesty while also accentuating the positive. Just remember, he's a Baptist preacher, not a blind man."

"I guess. I mean, I'm not sure any of these clothes will really work, Carlie."

"Of course they will. Let's see. Okay. What about these brown pants and that green sweater? That green is your color!"

"Yeah, and I've got a big multi-colored scarf that goes with that too. Let me find that in the pile. I know those are really in style right now."

"No. Absolutely not. No scarf."

"Why not?"

"Well, because a big chunky scarf is, uh, well, a distraction. A big chunky scarf draws the eye to the scarf. Y'know what I mean?"

"Not exactly."

"Look, just trust me on this. Women love scarves. But men? No. Men never give women big chunky scarves. Stop and ask yourself why that is." Clara looked at me like she just found out that 2 + 2 = 5. I tried to put her mind at ease. "I promise I'm right on this, Clara. Just wear the green sweater and leave the chunky scarf for a day with the Kinders. I promise all the middle-aged female teachers in the teachers' lounge will ooooh and aaaah over that chunky scarf like it's Christmas mornin'. But when it comes to Jake Smith, well, that scarf needs to stay in the suitcase. Trust me. Have I ever steered you wrong? On second thought, don't answer that."

Whew! Matchmaking is so much harder than people think. It's not just finding a preacher who looks like the Marlboro man. Oh no. Then there's all the late-night emotional support. The fashion advice. The counseling regarding lipstick color. And of course, I planned to cook a high-protein breakfast too. Clara needed plenty of raw strength for the day ahead. I mean, I may be a slacker on cleaning out closets. I might even be running a tad bit behind on writing my next book. But sloppy matchmaking? Not a chance.

Because it was a potluck event, I got up early Sunday morning and made my granny's crock pot chicken and dressing to take. Then I cooked up a big pan of bacon and some eggs.

"Carlie, somethin's sure smellin' good this morning!" Doug walked into the kitchen wearing navy blue sweat pants and an old gray t-shirt that said UTM in bright orange letters. Sometimes I was still taken aback by his good looks. A chiseled face that was warm with kindness. Strong arms. Man hands. I wrapped my arms around his waist and he gently kissed me while he twisted my hair. Then we both remembered Clara was in the next room. So we straightened up and pretended we weren't newlyweds. Not easy. At all.

Because we ARE newlyweds and being newlyweds is better than beating Meryl Streep out of an Oscar. (Okay. I don't really know what it's like to beat Meryl Streep out of an Oscar but it's not better than being married to Doug Jameson. I know that for sure.)

Doug reached for a piece of bacon and said with enthusiasm, "Honey, I'm afraid all your good cookin' is gonna expand my waistline." But we all knew the truth. Six months of my cooking would cause most men to lose ten pounds. Doug was giving it his best effort so he probably only lost five. And as for his waistline, I thought it was perfect. Just right.

Clara walked out of the guest bedroom looking like the perfect wife for a fully-sighted Southern Baptist preacher. Modest. Tasteful. But with a little zing thrown in because a smart happily-married woman convinced her to lose the chunky scarf.

"Wow! Who let the high-fashion model in the door?"

"Thanks, Carlie. Are you sure this works? I mean, it doesn't look like I'm trying too hard?"

"Clara, it's perfect. Worry not. Today's gonna be a great day. I mean, we're eatin' bacon and cookin' chicken! What could possibly go wrong?"

A word to the wise. Saying, "What could possibly go wrong?" is never a good idea.

Even though it was cold as a frog, the sun was shining and the drive to Troy was peaceful and pleasant. Clara turned pale and started fading like a morning glory at dusk. I tried to resuscitate her. "Look! You can do this, Clara! You can. You're a beautiful woman. You're smart. Any man would be

BLESSED to get even a little bit of your attention. You're bringin' the goods, girl! Stand up straight. Speak clearly. Let's do this, Clara Louise Johnson. It's time for a knock out!"

I felt like a manager for a featherweight boxer. I was in Clara's corner cheering her on and telling her she could do it. But I couldn't help but notice the Russian boxer in the opposing corner who was bigger, stronger, and had been boxing since preschool. I found myself praying a simple prayer. Lord, please defend the weakling.

The church looked just like I knew it would look. It looked like Doug's and my church. It looked like my grandparents' church. It looked like every small country church in my rural southern memory. Faded white with a tall steeple. Concrete front steps attached to a small concrete porch. Doug parked the truck in the grass behind the church as the tiny parking lot was starting to fill in. We saw Uncle Bart and Aunt Charlotte visiting with a good lookin' man near the front porch. If that man turns out to be Jake Smith, well, I'll just say that Debbie Walker is a truth teller for sure.

I didn't expect Jake to look like a mannequin in a Macy's window. No. A country preacher would look silly dressed like a fashion designer. But I also think it's not very smart for a man to look like he slept in his clothes either. Jake was probably 6'2" and looked like he had done plenty of farm work. He wore nice khaki pants with a blue unwrinkled oxford shirt and a navy blue striped tie that was too short. But I forgave the short tie travesty in honor of it bein' a Sunday and all. Overall, Jake looked like a decent dresser. It was kinda like when Charles Parker drove into our driveway in that really clean 10-year-old Jeep Cherokee. That Jeep Cherokee told me that Charles wasn't a materialist. But it also told me he wasn't a slacker. Jake was puttin' out the same vibe.

Aunt Charlotte came running up to Clara. "Baby, don't you look like a Christmas tree all purdied up! Yes, ma'am. You sure do. Come on over here, Clara. There's some folks we want you to meet."

I wasn't sure that an insecure woman wanted to be compared to a Christmas tree but someone with a butt as little as Clara's really shouldn't be worried about the comparison. Aunt Charlotte was in charge of introductions which was frightening. So at that moment we all had to place our trust in the providence of God.

Jake had been pulled aside by another family. But Aunt Charlotte got started without him. She cleared her throat and put her arm around a short round-faced blonde woman with dark brown eyes. The young woman was carrying a small baby and a pink diaper bag that looked like it had been through two world wars. "Clara, this is Debbie Walker, Bart's niece. Debbie, this is Clara Johnson from Commerce, Georgia. Clara's a real good kindergarten teacher too. And this here's my nephew, Doug. Ain't he handsome? Yeah, we always said he looked like his daddy's people. None of our people was handsome. Some of 'em was downright homely. Why Uncle George could'a killed a Grizzly bear with just one look. Poor thing. Anyways, and this here's his big purdy wife, Carlie. She's famous, y'know? Yeah. Been on the Today Show and ever'thing. She's a famous writer and a talker at places. I shore never thought I'd be kin to a famous person but I am. Yes, ma'am, I shore am."

I prayed that Aunt Charlotte would quit while she was behind. That's when Jake approached us and put his hand out to Doug. "Doug, it's been a long time, man."

“It has. We’re glad to be here, Jake.”

“Yeah, I’m glad you guys could visit with us today. And this is your new wife, yes?”

Doug proudly replied, “It is. This is Carlie. And this is our friend from Georgia, Clara Johnson.”

Jake extended his hand to me, “Welcome, Carlie.”

He reached out to shake Clara’s hand, “And you too, Clara.”

Clara actually looked Jake straight in the eyes and said, “I’m glad to be here.” I gave myself a pretend pat on the back. Keep it up, Girl. Keep dancin’ around the boxing ring until you throw your hands up in victory.

We all filed into the tiny church one by one. A big bald man was gettin’ after his teenage son about smackin’ bubble gum on the back row. An older lady in a wheel chair rolled up to Jake requesting we sing at least one verse of “Trust and Obey.” That’s when I knew Jake was a really good country preacher ‘cause he said without hesitation, “Mrs. Emerson, we’ll sing all the verses. How ‘bout that?” She beamed from ear to ear.

Jake wasn’t just the preacher. Evidently they expected him to lead music, make announcements and be the ring leader of the whole shebang. His first words to the congregation were, “We’re blessed this morning to have some visitors from Weakley County and beyond. Bart and Charlotte Nelson and Doug and Carlie Jameson live in Sharon. Welcome. And Clara Johnson comes to us from Commerce, Georgia. We’re glad to have all of you here with us today.”

There's something everybody needs to know about country churches. Country churches are about connections. So I knew, I absolutely knew, what was going to come next. Jake was going to explain to his small congregation just how he knew us and how we knew him. Or at least he was gonna die trying.

"Mr. Bart here is Debbie's uncle and he's married to Mrs. Charlotte and Mrs. Charlotte's sister was Doug's mama. And Doug is someone I've known most of my life. His mama and daddy were farmers there in Sharon and he works at the bank and has done some business with my daddy and helpin' with the bean fields and all. Carlie is Doug's new wife and Clara was Carlie's roommate back when Carlie lived in Georgia. Clara still lives in Commerce, Georgia, and is here visiting the Jamesons for the weekend."

Whew! That's one intelligent country boy wearing khaki pants. The fact that he could keep all that straight without ever stuttering made me realize that ol' Jake Smith was more than just a looker. The man's got skills.

I knew the first song was going to be "Trust and Obey." Mrs. Emerson looked like her days on earth were numbered so it was wise for Jake to prioritize what could be her last request before Glory.

He wasn't much of a song leader though. I mean, he just stood there, held open the book, and sang. He looked out at the congregation pleasantly but he didn't do all that other "song leader stuff" that people do sometimes. I always thought it would be fun to be a real song leader and get to do that right-handed musical sign language and everything. Jake Smith might be good at keeping people's names straight but clearly he didn't know musical sign language. That's okay, Jake. I don't take off points for musical talent or lack thereof.

After a few people shared prayer requests, Jake prayed and began his sermon. I was glad he wasn't a yeller. I don't like preachers who feel the need to yell. Plus, I think we all knew that Clara Johnson had a timid countenance and a yelling preacher would not help to alleviate that timidity.

Jake brought a simple message from the book of Romans. God's grace. Christ's payment. Our thankfulness. We sang all the words to "Turn Your Eyes Upon Jesus" and then an older man wearing brand new overalls closed in prayer. I deemed it a blessing from beginning to end.

Jake walked to the back of the sanctuary to greet the 30 or so parishioners as they filed outside. Now it was time for my matchmaking to go into overdrive. I'm glad Clara ate bacon this morning. As a big game hunter would say, "It's time to go in for the kill."

Doug walked up to Jake first and told him how much he appreciated the sermon. I nodded my head in agreement. Aunt Charlotte asked for directions to the bathroom and Uncle Bart unfolded a bag of Red Man chewing tobacco and headed to the church yard.

But Clara? Clara had gotten sideswiped on the way to the back of the church. Mrs. Emerson had taken it upon herself to explain to Clara that all her daddy's people had come from northern Georgia. She began to go into detail about who lived where and who married who and who went west to find their fortunes. It was time for an intervention. I graciously waited for Mrs. Emerson to take a breath.

"Mrs. Emerson, my name is Carlie. We sure did enjoy being with all of you today. Sure did."

"Well, we was glad to have you, ever last one of you. Why, you nearly doubled the congregation."

I laughed and patted her shoulder. "Yeah, I guess we did. We're lookin' forward to eating with you. But Clara and I need to go out to the car to get our food. We'll see you downstairs."

I grabbed Clara by the arm and gently led her to the back. I was glad that the night before I had taken it upon myself to explain stuff to Clara about men, other than just the scarf thing. I like to think of it as a matchmaking tutorial. Men love respect. It's a good idea to compliment them on things they do rather than the way they look. I mean, I could tell Doug that he has a cute butt and that's fine. He does have a cute butt and I'm sure he's happy to know that every now and then. But what he loves, what he craves, is for me to tell him how much I appreciate his ideas, his strong leadership skills, his ability to keep our new little family afloat. The way to a man's heart is with respectful words. Well, that and a well-crafted sweater minus the chunky scarf.

Jake was now in the church yard discussing soybean farming with Uncle Bart, between spits. This gave me a chance to whisper one final admonition to Clara, "Initiate some conversation, Girlfriend."

Clara walked up meekly and stood next to Uncle Bart and Aunt Charlotte. I prayed that just this once the Lord would shut Aunt Charlotte's mouth, just like He did for Daniel in the lion's den. The Lord saw fit to answer.

There was a moment of silence and then Clara spoke softly. "Jake, that was a powerful message on forgiveness. Really. I want you to know that I took notes. Thank you. It was really an honor to be here today."

I could not have been prouder of Clara Johnson if I had given birth to her on a Sunday. She hit a homerun. Knocked it out of the park. She hit that ball so hard it was unraveling and traveling to a neighboring town.

Jake smiled. "Thank you, Clara. I'm glad you were here too. You guys are staying for lunch, aren't you?"

"Yes, Carlie made chicken and dressing and I know Mrs. Charlotte brought something too. So, yes, we're staying."

"Good. I'd love to hear more about your life in Georgia."

Score one for the home team. I wondered what color bridesmaid dress I would wear in the wedding. I hoped it wouldn't be yellow as that had never been a good color for my skin which is a shade lighter than school glue. No. I look best in blue or some decent shade of pink as long as it's not that gut-wrenching Pepto-Bismol color. Jeannie Parker (a girl I went to high school with) made her bridesmaids wear that loathsome Pepto-Bismol color and several of them still hold a grudge against her to this day. I'm not supporting that kind of bitterness but I also don't support Jeannie's flawed decision making. Asking your closest friends to wear the color of a well-known stomach remedy in front of the whole town seems unusually cruel.

As we headed to the basement stairs, Doug was engaging Jake in some heated discussion about crop pesticides. I gave him the look that says, "Stop talking to Jake and push Clara into the picture." We've only been married seven months so he didn't read my look correctly. He just went right on talking about bug killers and sprays and those little planes that dust the crops. Finally, I hurled myself into the conversation like an atom bomb. "Jake, Clara's grandparents lived on a farm outside Birmingham. Yeah, I think they grew turnips or beets or…I forget." I put my arm around Clara and shoved her up between Doug and Jake and then asked, "Which was it, Clara? Turnips or beets?"

"They were hog farmers."

"Oh, yeah, I always get turnips and bacon mixed up. Crazy me."

Jake and Clara laughed and then immediately started talking about farming and I was happy. It didn't matter that I had made a blunder. My blunder got them talking. I was crazy alright. Crazy like a fox.

The church basement was small and smelled like every country church basement I had ever experienced; a musty combination of old crayons, Lysol, and cheap dusting powder. When you add the smell of chess pie, field peas, fried chicken, and baked beans…well, there's only one word for it. Comforting.

Sadly, the members of the church were uninformed about the matchmaking purpose of the potluck dinner. They all sat around Jake and left no room for the visiting kindergarten teacher. I wanted to stand on a metal chair and make a simple announcement. Excuse me. Uh, this meal is intended to eventually bring these two adorable young people into holy matrimony. I really do want to wear that blue bridesmaid dress with the dropped shoulder so you guys need to all back off and give 'em some room. But I'm sure that kind of announcement would not be considered "appropriate" plus I wasn't sure the metal chair would hold me. So I just politely asked Mrs. Emerson if my friend, Clara, could squeeze in between her and Jake. Mrs. Emerson seemed delighted and so did Jake. Mission accomplished. I need to put that little move on my matchmaking resume.

By 2:00 everyone seemed ready to go home and take a nap. The little kids were crying and the grown-ups were gathering trash. Jake was saying his good-byes but, sadly, he hadn't yet given Clara that knowing glance. You know, the glance that says, "If all these people weren't here, I'd move those Sunday School tables up against the wall, spritz myself with Drakkar Noir, put on some Lionel Ritchie, and we would dance the night, I mean afternoon, away." No. No such glances. Maybe it was the Lysol that was killing the mood. But I was getting a weird vibe that made me wonder if Jake was really interested at all.

Jake and Doug talked pleasantly about local football rivalries while they folded up the tables. Mrs. Emerson interrupted their work to say good-bye and to kiss Jake on the cheek which I chose to find charming because she was old enough to be his grandma. The experience did kind of remind me though of that elderly Baldwin sister on the The Waltons. You know, the one who was always dreaming that Ashley somethin' or other was going to come back and claim her for his bride. I mean, I did catch a little twinkle in Mrs. Emerson's eye. But I chose not to over-analyze it. Watching Jake bend over and gently remove her from her wheelchair and carry her up the stairs while a teenage boy carried her wheelchair, well, it was inspiring. I thought Clara would have married him right there on the spot, had he not been the only one in the room qualified to do the ceremony.

But my matchmaking inexperience was on display because I didn't have a way to close the deal. Everyone knows you have to have a clear exit strategy. Finally, in desperation, I spoke. "Jake, if you'd like to get Clara's number or e-mail address, I'm sure she'd be glad to give it to you."

Silence. Deafening silence. May I share a word of counsel with all potential matchmakers? The words, "Finally, in desperation, I spoke." are words you should always avoid. If the situation becomes desperate, whatever you do, don't speak.

I had put Clara in an embarrassing position. Again. The worst part? This time the real Clara had shown up. She talked about hog farming on the way to the church basement. She made eye contact and asked Jake about insurance and family. She drove eight hours to come with all of us to a tiny Baptist Church…when everyone in town knew we were Methodists. She didn't wear the chunky scarf because I told her not to… and she trusted me.

Jake finally spoke timidly, "Sure. That'd be great. Do you have a card or something?"

Clara turned red and scribbled her phone number and e-mail address on the back of a Taco Bell coupon Aunt Charlotte found in her purse. Jake put the coupon in his pocket and I had a sneaking suspicion that it was going to "accidentally" go through the wash. I also had a terrible feeling that Jake was going to feel a sense of relief when he pulled those khaki pants from the dryer and realized the opportunity to call Clara Johnson had been magically eliminated.

When we reached the top of the stairs, Uncle Bart pulled the bag of Red Man from his pocket. The rest of us shuffled our feet nervously until all the good-byes had been spoken. I dreaded getting into the truck.

Doug remained silent as he pulled out of the church parking lot. So did Clara. I'm sure they were waiting for my verbal assessment of the situation…that or they were both silently plotting a way to kill me.

I broke the silence. "That went well. Clara, you really were very engaging. It was a lovely afternoon."

Clara spoke softly, "I guess."

"Look, if he calls, great! If he doesn't, well, it's not like he's the only nice-lookin' insurance-sellin' Baptist preacher in the world. Good golly, no. There's a whole sea full of fish like him. Absolutely."

She smiled and patted me on the arm.

The quiet ride home was painful. I remembered something Doug had said about people eventually hating the matchmakers. He was right. Clara should hate me. But she won't. She's kind and loving and she'll forgive me. That almost made it worse.

When we arrived at the farm house, Clara tried to muster a smile but said she needed to leave in order to get back at a decent hour. We understood. She drove away and Doug and I got into the biggest argument of our newly married life. I don't even remember what it was about. I just remember feeling sad and miserable. I lashed out in horrible anger. I even broke a plate on the kitchen floor. Ridiculous. I guess I wanted Doug to be miserable too. I apologized for such childish behavior and suggested he watch the game in the living room while I took a nap. I laid on the bed and cried like I had lost my best friend. I was mad at Jake Smith. Mad at Aunt Charlotte and Debbie Walker for thinking he was such a catch. Mad at myself for being such a rotten matchmaker.

I was almost asleep when the phone rang.

"Hello."

"Carlie, it's Clara. I'm stuck on the side of the road. I don't know what happened. The car made this rattling sound. I pulled onto the shoulder and opened the hood. The oil is fine. I just had the belts checked. But now it won't even start."

"Don't worry, Clara. We'll come get you. Where are you? Are there any signs around?"

"I just passed the Bradford city limits."

"We'll be there in 20 minutes."

Chapter 13 CLARA LOUISE SPEAKS: Accidental U-Turn

I can't cry. I won't cry. If I start crying, I'll never stop. Jake's rejection was one thing. But now my car is broken and it's probably going to cost a fortune. And I'm stuck in Tennessee for at least another day. I'll have to get a substitute. Oh, and I'm not letting Carlie Jameson fix me up ever again. Ever.

Oh no. Now some crazy man is coming up to the car.

Tap. Tap. "Ma'am, can I help you with the car?"

"No. No thank you. I'm fine. My friend is on his way."

Oh my gosh. He's gonna kill me. He's gonna break the glass and kill me right here in Bradford, Tennessee, home of the Doodle Soup Festival.

He determined to speak through the glass. "Ma'am, I'm a mechanic by trade. And really, I could just give it a look. I'm not a criminal. I promise."

Oh my gosh. Everyone knows the first thing a criminal would do is deny bein' one.

I felt nervous and afraid. "Uh, no. That's fine. Really. You can just go on."

He leaned in closer to the window. "Did the car just stop? Or did it make a lot of noise first?"

"I'm not sure. It rattled a little and then I pulled over. Now it won't start at all."

"It's probably the alternator. I can go get my tow truck and take it in, if you want."

"No. I'll just wait for my friend."

He stood up straight and said, "I'll just wait here with you then until he comes."

"No, you don't have to. Really. He's not that far away."

"So he lives around here?"

"Sharon. He lives in Sharon. Doug Jameson."

"Yeah, I know Doug. I know his aunt and uncle real well. Used to live next door to them."

For the first time, I studied his face. He was dark but I couldn't tell whether it was sun or whether he just had a dark complexion. There was a black patch over his left eye and he had a scar on his chin. His hair was dark and thick and long enough to be seen under a Titans ball cap. I couldn't tell whether he was 30 or closer to 40.

"Really. You don't have to wait. Doug will be here any minute now."

"I don't mind. I'd never leave a lady with car trouble on the side of the road. I wasn't raised like that."

"Well, okay then."

He stood there silently in the cold. Stood right there by my car window. He didn't get back in his truck. He didn't try to look under the hood because I had asked him not to. He just stood there occasionally rubbing his hands together and looking at the highway.

I felt ridiculous with the car all locked up like I was afraid of him. But I couldn't bring myself to unlock the door. I was afraid. But not for the reason he might think. Not because he had an eye patch or a scar or because his face looked weathered. No. I was afraid of him because he was a man.

He looked into the window and said, "Sure been havin' some cold weather lately. Yeah, sure have."

"Yes, it's been pretty cold."

He then looked straight ahead and didn't even lean toward the window when he spoke. "Do you live in Sharon? Is that how you know Doug?"

"No. I live in Georgia. His new wife was my old roommate and I was here visiting them."

"Yeah, that's right. Saw in the paper where he married that famous girl from TV. Some kind of writer, I believe. Yeah, that was big news round these parts. Big news."

"Yeah. It's really somethin' cause when we roomed together, she worked at the dollar store. I mean, sometimes I even lent her money for the electric bill. And now she's famous. But really, it hasn't changed her that much. I mean, she's still nice and kinda fun and crazy. Everybody likes her."

"So, you were just here for a visit, huh?"

"Well, not really. I mean, not just a visit." Good night. What am I thinking? Am I honestly getting ready to open up to a stranger wearing an eye patch who's hovering over me and my disabled car? Don't do it, Clara. Don't do it.

He rubbed his hands together, adjusted his cap, and said, "Can't imagine much that would bring somebody out to these parts." He chuckled and looked down at the ground.

It was shocking how we managed to have a conversation through the glass of the car window. I don't know why but I opened up and told the truth. It was so unlike me. "Carlie, Doug's wife, well, she's determined to be my matchmaker. She's determined to find the right guy for me. But she's struck out twice now. So I don't know. Maybe she'll throw in the towel this time."

He laughed and when he did I saw that his teeth were perfectly straight and white. He took off his ball cap and straightened his hair before putting it back on. The navy blue coveralls had a few grease patches and his tan Carhartt coat was worn around the sleeves. But despite the scar and the grease and the eye patch, there was something about him that was handsome.

"Well, you don't need my advice in the relationship department. I'm not the one you should listen to."

"Maybe you have more wisdom than you know." Why in the world am I talking to him? I don't even know this guy.

"Yeah. I know about relationships alright. But I found out too late, I'm afraid. I messed it up real bad and then it was too late to fix it. But that's none of your concern, ma'am. You've got car trouble and that's what you need to worry about."

About that time I could see Doug's truck in the rearview mirror. A part of me felt sad.

Doug got out and extended his hand, "Dusty McConnell. It's been a long time, man. Are you helping our lady in distress here?"

"I could. But she won't let me, Doug. Reckon she's seen too many of those cop shows."

Doug smiled, "Yeah, I guess it's better to be safe than sorry. Well, if you could get your tow truck and take it in for us, we'd sure be appreciative. I know you can't work on it today. But she's trying to get home to Georgia so if you could work on it tomorrow, that'd be great."

"Yeah. No problem. I'll be back in about ten minutes. If you want, you can just go ahead and give me her keys and you can take her back to your house. I'll let you know somethin' by tomorrow mid-mornin' and should have her on the road by afternoon."

"That'd be good, man. Thanks."

I opened the car door with embarrassment and handed him my keys, "Thank you, Mr. McConnell. I'm sorry I acted like I didn't trust you. But you understand why a woman can't be too careful, don't ya?"

"Absolutely. A pretty woman like you could get taken advantage of real easy. You're smart to play it safe. That's what I think." His face was friendly and I realized he was probably 30, not 40. He reached out to shake my hand. "Don't worry. I'll get your car fixed up and have you back on the road by tomorrow afternoon. And that'll give you time to rest up before the next round of matchmaking." He laughed, took off his cap and did that thing with his hair again, and headed to an old red truck which was parked right in front of the car.

"Thank you, Mr. McConnell. And my name is Clara. Clara Johnson!"

He turned around, tipped his hat and said, "Nice to meet you, Clara. And you can call me Dusty."

When Doug and I got in the truck, Carlie was full of questions.

"Who was that? Were you freezing to death? Were you scared, Clara?"

"No. I wasn't scared. He seemed nice really."

"Well, looks like you'll be getting a substitute for tomorrow, friend. Just don't get Mrs. Peterson 'cause remember how she brought those Tootsie Pops that got stuck in the carpet? Oh, and she let the kids make glitter snowmen with hot glue guns."

"Thanks, Carlie. I remember."

Chapter 14 CLARA LOUISE: Dusty McConnell on My Mind

Doug left for the bank early the next morning which left Carlie and me to talk, make muffins, and hash out plans for the day.

"Clara, you might better check your e-mail this mornin'. Jake could have gotten some late night inspiration and decided to write of his undying affection."

"Doubtful."

"Look, crazier things have happened. We don't know he's not interested. We don't. I think he just felt on the spot and needed a little time to process it all. I mean, he did take your number and e-mail address."

"It's on a Taco Bell coupon and you pretty much forced it on him. He'll be eating a free burrito by noon today and never give it a second thought."

"Yeah. I was kinda surprised Aunt Charlotte was willing to give up a free burrito for the cause of love. Bless that dear woman's heart."

"Look, Carlie, he's not interested. You could see it in his eyes. It was obvious to everyone. Besides, we need to be thinkin' about my car, not Jake Smith. Dusty said he'd have it done by this afternoon. So maybe he'll call sometime this mornin' with an estimate. He seems to know what he's talkin' about when it comes to cars."

"Dusty, huh? You guys are on a first name basis?"

"Oh my gosh. Don't you EVER stop? Even for a minute?" We were both laughing when we heard Aunt Charlotte at the back door.

"Mornin' Girls! I come bearin' gifts! Homemade sausage for everyone. Clara, I even brought a pound for you, Darlin'." She reached out to hug Clara like she thought she was ill and hadn't seen her in months. "I heard the bad news, Baby. How you was all stuck on the side of the road down there in Bradford. Willie Carlisle saw ya and woulda stopped but Dusty had already pulled over."

"Thanks, Mrs. Charlotte. Yeah. Dusty stopped right away. Kept me company till Doug got there. He seems real nice."

"Oh Baby, tell me you're not takin' a shine to Dusty McConnell."

"No, ma'am. I mean, I don't even know him."

"Good. 'Cause that Dusty, he's had a hard time. Life dealt him some painful blows." She paused at the sink to wash her hands. "And well, he dealt some back too."

"What do you mean?"

"Bart and I always felt sorry for Dusty. He was a smart young'un but he couldn't read good and was treated like a dog by his daddy. Meaner than a snake, that man. When he was in high school, his daddy up and left and we never heard tell of him again. Nobody has. He could be in prison. He could be dead for all we know. Dusty's mama was a sweet woman but she took up with some bad fellas and none of them kids had a decent raisin'. Bart and I tried to love 'em as best we could, but well, by the teen years, they was long gone and in trouble."

"What kind of trouble?" I'm not sure why I felt the need for Dusty McConnell's criminal history but I did.

"He stole a few cars. Got in with some real bad guys. Did a few years in prison over 'round Nashville. But about five years ago he was released and he got all straightened out too, got married, had a baby. Ever body was real proud of Dusty McConnell. Chester said, 'The Lord did a miracle in his life.' And it was true. He was a changed man."

"But?"

"But that was before his wife and baby died last year."

"Died? His wife and baby died? How in the world?"

"It's a miserable story, Baby. Miserable. Dusty had some debt to take care of so he took this extra job down in Jackson, workin' in the evenings. He was wore out and decided to sleep on a friend's couch one night. Word was that he'd had a few drinks after his shift. Didn't find out til the next mornin'."

"Find out what?"

"It was February and we'd had some terrible tornadoes, which was a little early. That night there was a warning but Melissa must not have known. She went to bed early. They found the trailer all mangled up in a field early the next morning. She and the baby was dead. Because of his criminal history, the law was pretty rough on him too. Bob Miller was the sheriff at the time and he thought there was something fishy about it all. But Bart and me, we always knew he loved Melissa and that baby girl. It was just a tragedy. A terrible horrible tragedy. His family was gone. The trailer was torn to pieces.

Thank God Carl and Betty Jenkins asked Dusty to move in with 'em or he'd a been dead. Really. I think he'd have drunk himself to the grave…that…or killed himself. He lived with them a few months and then last summer he bought a little house outside Greenfield."

Carlie and I stood in disbelief. I had rarely seen Carlie speechless. But neither of us knew what to say next.

Finally Carlie said, "My word, Aunt Charlotte. I think that's the saddest story I've heard in a long time. What a wounded soul. Poor Dusty McConnell."

Now I knew what Aunt Charlotte meant. I needed to steer clear of Dusty McConnell. It didn't matter that he had white teeth or a ruggedly handsome face. It didn't matter that he stood in the cold until Doug got there because he didn't believe in leaving a woman alone. It didn't matter that I felt happy when he tipped his hat. Dusty McConnell was a felon. A felon whose wife and baby were dead. Aunt Charlotte was right. I needed to drive straight back to Commerce, Georgia, and wait for an e-mail from Jake Smith even though Jake Smith was never going to write. End of story.

Chapter 15 CLARA LOUISE: Cars and Scars

Aunt Charlotte shook her head and grabbed a muffin after telling the details of Dusty's sad story. Carlie still looked shell shocked when the phone rang. She managed a cheerful "Hello." Soon she was moving her arms to get my attention.

"Clara, this is Dusty. Says he needs to put an alternator in. It's gonna cost about $250. Doug trusts him. Said he can get you on the road by 2:00. You okay with that?"

"I don't really have a choice, do I? So yeah, that's fine."

"Dusty, she said it's fine. Yeah. We'll be here. Just call here or let me give you her cell number. Doug gave it to you? Good. That's fine."

I was glad to be going back to Commerce. The Kindergarteners needed me. Mom and Dad needed to be free of my cat. I needed to get back in the routine. It didn't even matter that Jake Smith wasn't going to call or write. It was all a silly idea anyway.

2:00 pm

Carlie dropped me off at Dusty's shop with a big hug and a promise to keep in touch. The shop looked just like I had visualized. I didn't expect it to look like a hotel lobby at Hilton Head. It looked like a place where fixing cars took priority over decorating or cleaning. Two dirty green naugahyde couches. A dusty bubblegum machine that hadn't seen gum since the 90's. Old fishing and hunting magazines on a broken coffee table. Stale cold coffee in an old Bunn machine.

But Dusty? Dusty looked different than he had yesterday afternoon. He wasn't wearing the cap. He was clean-shaven and wearing tan coveralls. His expression was different too. Maybe because he wasn't in the cold trying to talk through a car window. He looked more at ease.

"We got ya fixed right up, Clara. If you have any trouble, you call me at this number, okay?" He handed me a business card and I touched his hand, which stopped us both for a moment. He continued, "I mean, anywhere between here and Commerce, you call, okay? I want to guarantee my work and I sure don't want a woman on the side of the road in a car that I said was workin'."

"Thank you. Really. But unless it stops right away, I'll just call my dad. He'll take care of it." Dusty's expression fell. He wanted me to need him. But I didn't. I might be lonely but I'm not stupid. This would be the last time I would see Dusty McConnell. And that would make Aunt Charlotte and me both very happy. Deliriously happy.

Chapter 16 CARLIE: Redneck Writer Meets Hollywood

Clara is on her way back to Commerce now. Matchmaking effort #2 seems to have been a massive failure. But at least I tried. Besides, I never told anyone I was a GOOD matchmaker. Just a motivated one. And I'm still motivated. I still hold out hope that there's a man out there who will love Clara. I just haven't found him yet. But that's okay. There's still time. Plenty of time.

Matchmaking can't be my only project in life anyway. I'm a newlywed. Sometimes I forget that I'm also a writer and I'm supposed to be writing stuff, and calling my publisher, and caring about my career. I get easily distracted by making chicken and dressing and tracking down Baptist preachers to fix Clara up with. But this afternoon I have to get serious. I have to put on my business hat and do some real business.

The folks in Hollywood have set a date to talk about the movie. Two weeks from today. They call it "collaboration." That means the author and the movie makers work together to bring about a good result. But I wasn't born yesterday. I have a feeling the meeting will consist of the Hollywood folks telling me that they know about movies and I should trust them. And I will tell them that I know about funny southern single girls and they should trust me. It may take us a while to properly "collaborate."

Doug and I got a great idea last night. We decided to invite Dave and Shannon to go with us on our redneck Hollywood adventure. They needed to get away and this would be the perfect trip. That's why I like having a lot of money. I liked working at the Dollar General Store just fine but when I did, I never could have paid for a trip to Hollywood for a couple who are having a hard time having a baby.

Doug called them last night to share the news. At first they acted like they weren't gonna go with us, that they were too busy. But Doug convinced Dave that he needed to take his woman on a stress-free California adventure. And it would be stress-free for Dave and Shannon. They wouldn't be the ones in meetings surrounded by trays of food that no one ever eats trying to convince a bunch of thin California movie people that Angelina Jolie couldn't play the main character and that women in small towns never order non-fat sugar-free soy lattes extra hot, no whip. Whew! This trip made me tired just thinking about it.

Chapter 17 CLARA LOUISE: The Joys of Routine, Sheer Boredom

The car made it back to Commerce with no problems. It's been three days now. Jake never called or sent an e-mail. The burrito coupon is long gone, I'm sure. The Kindergarteners have been acting like, well, Kindergarteners. All is at it should be, I guess.

Coming home to homemade soup in the crock pot made getting up 20 minutes earlier well worth it. As I turned the key and opened the door, the aroma poured out of the apartment and it made me feel like a grown-up. Like I was making plans with my life, plans with my future. And it all started by making plans for my dinner.

When the cell phone rang, I knew it was Carlie. Or my mom. Well, sometimes colleagues called me at home but rarely. I didn't recognize the number.

"Hello."

"Clara, this is Dusty McConnell. Uh, I wanted to check on your car, make sure you're not having any trouble or anything."

"Oh, thanks. No. No trouble. Seems to be running really well."

"Good. That's real good. Okay. Well, I figured you'd have called if there was any trouble."

"No. Running like a top."

"Well, then I guess I'll let you get back to what you were doin'. I mean, I'm sure you're real busy and all."

"Okay. Well, thanks, Dusty. Thanks for taking the time to call."

"Uh, okay. Have a nice night, Clara. Good night."

"Bye."

That was weird. I can't imagine that a mechanic from eight hours away would call a customer just to make sure the mechanic had done good work. I mean, I figure he knew he put it in right. Every mechanic would know how to put in an alternator, right? Right.

That phone call was clearly unnecessary. It was kind of nice, I guess. But I'm not going to think about it. At all. I already have to take Hobo to the vet tomorrow afternoon for gastro-intestinal distress. That's plenty of messiness and drama for me.

The soup was good. But watching the evening news while sitting at the table listening to my cat cough up a hair ball wasn't very exciting. I was still lonely. I'd been asking God to bring me someone for more than a year. Nothing. The butcher at Pic Pac flirted sometimes but he never pursued me. Some of the teachers said I should ask him out. But that's not my style. Besides, that seems backwards. It's not that I'm all "Pride and Prejudice" or anything but I'm not "Sex and the City" either. At all. Why is it all so complicated?

Sitcoms are stupid now. Crass and unintelligent. I tried to do some lesson plans on my laptop, but found myself fading in and out of sleep. In desperation, I checked e-mail one last time before calling it quits and going to bed. I couldn't help but wonder if Carlie had called Jake and lit a fire under his behind. His name was in bold, sent at 8:32 pm. It had been more than three days and the subject of his e-mail? Nice to Meet You.

Clara,

It was nice to meet you Sunday. I hope your trip back to Commerce was uneventful. If you're ever in the area, let me know, and I can show you the sights. Not that there's that many actual tourist sights. But West Tennessee does hold more treasures than some people realize. I hope the Kindergarteners are well. Everyone at church was talking about how great it was to have visitors. They're right. It is great to have new folks to shake it up a bit. Well, I guess it's still not that shaken. By God's grace, I'm trying.

Jake

I can't write back tonight. Too forward. Plus, I need to call Carlie and ask what I'm supposed to write. Maybe she'll even write something for me. That would be the best. I dialed her number and tried to remain calm.

"Hello."

"Carlie, I got an e-mail from Jake tonight. Just now."

"Well, hallelujah! Now see, I told you it was crazy to give up so fast. So, what did he say? Give me the scoop. The whole scoop and nothin' but the scoop. Why aren't you talkin', Clara? Is something wrong? Did he write something insensitive? You're not having a hard time forgiving him for the short tie, are you? 'Cause really, Clara, you should let that short tie go. Lord knows I'm tryin' to forget that poor striped little thing every day. I mean, yes, it was pretty awful but he's a tall long-waisted man, Clara, and without a woman to pick out his clothes too. It's not a federal offense to wear a tie that's a tad too short. I mean, it probably should be a federal offense but it's not. Well. Well, why aren't you talking?"

"Are you finished?"

"Yes, I'm just waiting on you, friend. Waiting. Waiting. Waiting."

"Look. The e-mail is no big deal. Really. I'm going to forward it to you and you can analyze it, over analyze it, and then let me know what you think. You can call me in a few minutes. Bye."

Five minutes later.

"Hello."

"Clara, I think he may be madly in love with you. Seriously. These seem like the words of a man who is smitten, in love, making plans for the future."

"You cannot be serious."

"Dead serious. I mean, what 'treasures' is he talkin' about in West Tennessee? There's no treasure 'round here. No gold or diamonds. He's referencing his heart, Clara. His heart. The man is saying that the treasure of his heart is ready and willing to be given to a pretty redhead Georgia girl with a tiny little rear. Yes ma'am. It's as plain as the nose on your face."

"Well, you're crazier than I thought. Just don't tell anyone about it, okay?"

"Ooops!"

"Carlie, you couldn't have told anyone. It's been like five minutes. How could you even have time to tell anyone?"

"Well, Aunt Charlotte is over here and we're makin' pickles."

"Pickles? It's winter. You're not makin' pickles in the winter, Carlie."

"Well, we sure are. Y'see, Aunt Charlotte buried this whole mess of cucumbers in the ground at the end of summer and put some kind of 'secret' preservative around them to see if they could be preserved. It was an experiment of sorts. She and Uncle Bart dug 'em up this mornin'. Yes, ma'am. Crisp as the day they were buried. We're makin' pickles right here in my kitchen. And when I told Aunt Charlotte about the e-mail, well, of course, we ran to the computer and looked at it together. She said she'd even buy a new dress for the wedding, which is huge because she doesn't shop, Clara. Really. But don't worry. I'll go with her. Aunt Charlotte can't be trusted shopping for clothes by herself because she goes too bold on the color and too small on the size. Sorry, Aunt Charlotte!! But it's true. You know it's true!!"

"I'm hanging up. Look, don't start losing sleep over this, Carlie. Don't you dare look at wedding invitations online or pick out dresses or go all crazy on me. It was a simple e-mail greeting. That's all. I'm going to write a simple e-mail greeting back to him. Get back to your pickles. I'll talk to you soon."

"Love you, Clara. Praying for you and Jake tonight…and for your tall redheaded future children."

"Bye."

I don't know what Aunt Charlotte put on those cucumbers to keep them from rotting. But I fear those pickles are fermented. That e-mail meant nothing. He probably just felt like a burrito and thought he should e-mail me one time before my address got sent to the corporate office of Taco Bell. Jake Smith is not in love with me. At least, not yet.

Chapter 18 CARLIE Two Weeks Later: CALIFORNIA CARLIE

Airport security is hard for me for the same reason life is hard for me. Organization or the lack thereof. There were always business men who seemed at ease taking off their shoes, putting their computer in a tray and removing their watch all at the same time. Like it was one fluid motion. Beautiful. But not me. Nothing is one fluid motion for me. I always dropped things or spilled make-up or forgot that bottles of hairspray were considered contraband. Every time I went through security, something was confiscated. Hairspray or mousse or a bottle of Orange Fanta. Blessedly, Doug was often there to help me and make me feel at ease.

"Honey, don't worry. We can buy hairspray when we get there. Everyone forgets about an orange soda now and then. Really. No one thinks less of you."

Dave and Shannon enjoyed a good laugh. Dave said, "Carlie, I think you're the only famous person in the world who grieves the loss of an orange soda like it was a family heirloom and who acts like they've never been through airport security. I died laughing when the woman behind you said, 'This must be her first time to fly.' I wanted to say, 'Are you kidding? This woman is famous. She's been on the Today Show and met Matt Lauer.' But of course, she'd have never believed me."

"Of course not. No famous person would spill make-up all over the security personnel. Oh, and that whole 'use your seat cushion as a flotation device' propaganda? Not gonna happen. I can barely get my rear end out of the seat. I'll be the only one floating in the ocean in an upright position with the arm rests still squeezing against my behind."

We all enjoyed a laugh at my expense. I didn't mind. The truth of the matter is that I'm not famous. Famous people can't go to Disney World because people chase them down. Famous people have private jets because the general public can't handle their presence without making squealing noises. No one ever makes squealing noises around me. I have been on TV and my book has sold a lot of copies. But rarely do people recognize me and if they do recognize me, they don't seem to care enough to squeal or chase me. They just make nice comments and move on with their lives. I doubt they even text their cousin in Mississippi with the news. And truthfully, I'm glad I don't get chased through airports. I'm not a very fast runner.

Doug smiled and put his arm around me. "I love you, Carlie."

"I love you too."

We arrived at LAX with no trouble. The studio sent a car to pick us up. I should have been happy but something about California made me nervous. The women were too beautiful and tan. The weather was too warm and perfect. Plus, I didn't feel comfortable making decisions about the movie and I didn't feel comfortable NOT making decisions about the movie either. That's why Doug came. Doug was always the voice of reason in any given situation. He would help the negotiations go well because he was thoughtful and never seemed caught up in the glitz and glamour of any of it.

At dinner, Dave and Shannon were almost giddy as they made plans for the next day. They were getting up super early to stand in line for The Price is Right. I envied them terribly. My grandma and I used to watch The Price is Right every day in the summer. I was probably the only kid in the fourth grade who knew that 60 oz. of Tide cost more than a Wonder Mop.

I was the only one who knew that a trip around the world cost more than a brand new Ford Escort, even if it was red.

I wanted to be going to The Price is Right instead of to the studio tomorrow morning. But I was on a mission, a mission to keep Angelina Jolie out of a movie about a funny, chubby, southern girl. And I had to charge that hill.

Doug tried to sound enthusiastic. “It’ll be fine, Carlie. Really. We go to the meeting, speak our minds, shake hands, and that will be that. They respect you. They’ll listen. And if they don’t listen, well, we can always pull out. No one says there has to be a movie. If they don’t share our vision, we can just let it go. We haven’t signed a contract yet.”

“The publishers will be livid. No, the movie deal has to work out. I can’t disappoint Joan. She’s worked too hard.”

“Well, alrighty then. No disappointment. We’ll negotiate and make it work. And then we’ll be done. We can go home to Sharon and let the movie people make a movie and let the Sharon people make the sausage.”

All four of us laughed. What would I do without Doug? He was the only man I knew who would still wear JC Penney pants even though his wife had a best-selling book. The only man who would re-sole shoes rather than buying new ones. The only person who could intelligently negotiate with movie people and go to work at a small town bank two days later. And be happy about it too. Wildly happy.

The next morning I was feeling nauseous and scared. I still have a LOT of insecurities. Just ‘cause you wrote a book a lot of people want to read doesn’t mean you’re not insecure about your looks or your business sense or your clothing choices or your ability to go through airport security without public humiliation.

The studio was busy and loud and very "California chic." I'm not chic. At all. I mean, I'm not even really sure what "chic" is, but whatever it is I know I'm not it. Wait. I'll look it up. Okay. According to the IPhone dictionary chic is: attractive, fashionable, stylish. See? I shouldn't have even wasted time looking it up.

Doug and I were clearly overdressed. I forgot that some Hollywood young professionals take great pride in wearing really expensive clothes that make them look like they shop at the thrift store. If you want to know why some people buy really expensive clothes that make them look like they shop at the thrift store, well, you'll have to ask them. I have no idea. Doug and I buy brand new clothes at JC Penney. That's how we roll. (I know. People who buy brand new clothes at JC Penney never say, "That's how we roll." Someone get me out of this town…and quickly.)

Chance, the young man who greeted us, wore faded jeans, a gray t-shirt that said, "Ghandi=Brilliance" and an old tan professor's jacket. You know, those jackets your uncle wore that fit really big and had dark brown patches on the elbow.

"Ms. Jameson, welcome to California! I'm Chance Baldwin, no kin to Alec Baldwin."

I extended my hand, "Nice to meet you, Chance! This is my husband, Doug Jameson."

Doug smiled and said, "Great to be here."

"Chance, it's kind of too bad you're no relation to Alec as he might be able to hook you up with those free flights he's always touting on TV."

He barely cracked a grin. Boy, I sure miss Aunt Charlotte and her homemade sausage right about now.

The meeting room was filled with young and old who shopped at the same place Chance shopped. I tried to be quiet and listen to their ideas without being harsh or judgmental. And I liked most of what they said. Well, until the woman in charge said, "As to the lead role, well, we can't go 'chubby' as you'd say. It doesn't work on screen. We don't have to go super thin but we can't do something crazy and cast someone repulsive either."

Doug scowled. I remained quiet.

She looked at her assistant, "We can go size eight or so, but that's it. I mean, a woman size ten would cover the screen and it would make a mess everywhere. Really. A travesty."

Doug remained calm and spoke intelligently, "Well, speaking from a guy's perspective, I don't think a woman with a little more to grab is repulsive. At all. And I don't speak for women, but I would think they might want to see women on screen who more closely represent them. Plus, this movie is targeted to women, right? It's not supposed to be a James Bond movie. It's supposed to be about real humorous women and their lives and their issues."

A thin young woman with curly blonde hair wearing chunky dark glasses clad in thrift store fashion started clapping wildly, "Hear, hear!"

The lady in charge said, "Calm down, Emily. Doug here seems like a perfectly nice fellow, but he's not a movie maker or a movie critic. He doesn't understand the business."

Doug retorted, "You're right, Ms. Watson. I don't understand the business. But I do understand people. I understand this story. I understand the story because I understand the person behind it." He glanced at me kindly. "She's a gifted woman. And she's not a size eight or a size ten even. And this book, this best selling book, is her book. Her story and the stories of women like her. So if I were a movie maker, and you're right, I'm not one, but if I were, I'd listen to her and find out what she thinks about the lead role. But maybe that's just me."

Silence. Dead silence.

Finally Ms. Watson looked up from her bright blue reading glasses. "Well? What does the star of the negotiations have to say?"

I put my hand on Doug's leg. "Well, first of all, I think I married well. And I'm thankful. I'm thankful whether we make a movie or not. My reality is far better than any make-believe story we can concoct in this room. Secondly, Doug is right. I'm not asking for an obese actress. But no, a size eight is not going to do this role justice. It won't work with the story. And if we can't agree to someone who looks…well, a little closer to the way I look, I'll need to find a studio that can agree to that. So I guess that's my position."

Ms. Watson wrote some things on a big piece of paper. "Give us 24 hours and we'll get back to you, Ms. Jameson. How's that?"

"No problem. Thank you, Ms. Watson. Thank you all for being here today."

Doug and I sat in the quiet little diner down the street from the studio. It reminded me of home because the sign said, "Sit wherever you'd like." They sold hamburgers and meatloaf plates. No sushi or fancy food.

We chose a comfortable booth with a few tears in the plaid fabric. "Thank you for saying what you said in there, Doug. I think some of those women wanted to ask you to marry them right on the spot."

"I'm already taken." He winked. "But I meant what I said. They're crazy. I mean, I don't even know if they know what pretty looks like anymore."

About that time a lovely waitress with thick dark hair spoke pleasantly from behind the cash register, "I'll be right with ya!" She was wearing solid black stretch pants and an old-fashioned light blue double-knit uniform shirt.

She hurried to the table. "Welcome to Lou's Diner! My name is Ashley and I'll be takin' care of ya'll. What can I get you to drink?"

My first response came blurting out, "Ashley, where are you from? You're not from California, I take it."

"No ma'am. I'm from Florence, Alabama. That's up in the northern part of Alabama."

"Oh yes. We know. We know it well. I'm from Northern Georgia. What brings you so far from home, Ashley?"

"It's a long story but I'll shorten it as best I can. A few years ago I got cast in some commercials. You may have seen me.

Probably the most popular was 'Delicious Doggie Delights.' Yeah. I was the dog trainer with the hiccups."

Doug piped up, "Yes, I do remember that. You wore an Oakland A's cap, right?"

"I did! And for a while, I thought I was gonna really have a career in acting. But like most of the actors out here, I spend more time waitin' tables than acting. And as for my name up in lights, well, I am in charge of turning on the neon open sign every morning. So it's not so bad really. I'm thankful. I am." She spoke with a chuckle and real enthusiasm.

I wanted to be encouraging. "It sounds like you've got a great attitude, Ashley. Maybe it's not quite time to trade in your dreams. You never know when you'll get your big break."

She paused and smiled. "Thanks. I guess I needed someone to walk in here today and say that. So, thank you so much. What would you guys like to drink today?"

Doug spoke up, "We'll both take water with lemon."

"Okay. I'll be right back with those."

As she walked away, I smiled like a cat who'd found the bird cage open. "Doug, I have an idea."

"Carlie, I know what you're thinkin'. But we can't. We can't even get her hopes up. I mean, we just got the studio to even CONSIDER hiring someone a little more normal looking. But you think we could literally walk in there tomorrow afternoon and say, 'Oh, and guess what? We found our own lead actress. Yeah, right down the street at the diner.'"

“Crazier things have happened. Doug, hear me out. Let’s at least give her a little audition, yes?”

Ashley gently set the water glasses before us. “Here you go. Now, what can I get you two today?” She leaned in and whispered softly, “The meatloaf is as dry as the Sahara and my grandma’d be plum embarrassed by the chicken ‘n dumplins but you didn’t hear it from me. The hamburgers are always real good.”

I liked Ashley from the diner. I liked her really well. I think God had answered our prayers about the negotiations and the lead role and well, about a lot of things.

Doug said, “Honey, you okay with a burger?”

“I certainly am.”

“Okay. We’ll take two burgers, but just one order of fries. We’ll share.”

“I’ll get that right out. Thank you. It’s nice to hear people talk like the folks back home.” She paused and looked out the window at the busy street and added, “Yeah, sure is.”

Ashley walked away and I took careful notice of her appearance. About 5’8”, probably a size twelve or fourteen. She was beautiful but not haughty. Intelligent but not proud. Good hygiene but not glitzy. Perfect.

“Doug, I’m sorry. I think this may be a sign.”

“A sign? A sign of what?”

“Well, this may be the answer to our prayers AND to Ashley’s. Let’s at least hear her read a few lines. I mean, we should ask her to meet us somewhere after her shift. We wouldn't be getting her hopes up. We'd just be kind of auditioning her."

"Auditioning her? Do we know anything about auditioning anyone? I'm a bank loan officer. You're a writer."

"No. But a really good-looking man, I mean, a FANTASTIC-looking, intelligent man just said, in a BIG meeting with the movie people, that the woman behind this book would be the person who would best know how to cast it."

Doug smiled and looked down at the table. "Touché."

Chapter 19 CARLIE: Ashley Auditions

Ashley agreed to meet us in the hotel lobby at 3:00. We told her we couldn't make any kind of promises but we might have an audition lined up. Maybe.

She walked in wearing a big smile. Black dress pants with plain black flats. Her peasant top was bright pink with a wispy striped scarf that looked homemade.

I handed her a copy of the preliminary script and asked if she would mind doing some reading.

She looked startled. "This, this is for a movie. I mean, BAM Studio only makes movies. Big movies. Real movies. Are you for real?"

"Look, Ashley, Doug and I are not in the movie business. We're not. We live in a small town in Tennessee. We're regular folks like you. But, 'A Single Woman's Guide to Ordinary?' I wrote it. I'm the author, I mean, of the book. And now, well, now it's been translated into a movie script and we're trying to hash out some negotiations about it all. They want a thin woman to play the lead role. But Ashley, that just can't be. I mean, the main character is supposed to be based around my real life persona. And who better to judge who that person should be played by than me, right?"

"Oh my gosh. I mean, you just can't even be saying what you're saying. I've stayed out here five years longer than expected. I can't tell you the number of times I've almost gone home. I have. I have prayed 1000 prayers. And now, now this?"

Doug added a voice of reason, "Ashley, listen. We can't make you an offer. We can't. We don't have that kind of power.

What we're saying is that if we hear you read the lines and we like what we hear, we can give your information to the studio for consideration. They'd have to agree on all that. We're not casting people. We don't pretend to be."

I had a feeling Ashley would read the lines perfectly. And I was right. Tears literally came to my eyes when she read the first portion.

"I can't decide whether havin' a man is even worth washin' my hair. All that blow dryin' and curlin' and nonsense just to turn the head of some man wearin' a ball cap 'cause he wasn't willin' to wash his own hair. I don't know. It seems like a ridiculous system. On the other hand, a Friday night Hallmark movie never expects me to wash my hair. I can curl up on the couch and snuggle into a pillow and watch a good Hallmark movie with no personal scorn. I can even eat Funyuns if I want to and not worry about whether they give me fake onion breath." She threw her hands in the air. *"Glory Hallelujah, I may have to wash my hair in order to get a man,"* Ashley winked with delight, *"but givin' up Funyuns is where I draw the line."*

That was it. It was as though a voice came thundering out of heaven. The lead role of "A Single Woman's Guide to Ordinary" would go to Ashley. Ashley from Alabama. I didn't even know her last name. You're right, Aunt Charlotte. "The Lord done smiled on us real good."

Chapter 20 CLARA LOUISE: Preachers and Car Thieves

I let 24 hours pass before returning Jake's e-mail. I didn't want to seem too eager. The new music teacher said I should have written back right away. But she doesn't know anything about men. She dates a city planner from St. Louis who sends her mean text messages that make her cry.

9:00 PM

Dear Jake,

Thanks for your e-mail message. We all liked visiting your church. The people were very nice and made us feel right at home. I would like to visit West Tennessee again soon. So maybe I will take you up on your offer to show me the sights. Northern Georgia also has some wonderful things to see. So if you're ever in the neighborhood, I would be glad to show you Georgia's treasures as well.

Thanks,
Clara

I knew Carlie wouldn't like my reply. I could hear her booming voice now. "It's a little dry, Clara. Let him know you're interested. Be a little more cyber-friendly." But that was the problem. I wasn't interested. I should be but I wasn't. I couldn't talk to anyone about it. Not Carlie. Not Aunt Charlotte. Definitely not my mother. I wasn't interested in the right man. I was interested in the wrong one. Oh God, please help me. I'm going the wrong direction. Or am I? Make my path straight.

I got out Dusty McConnell's business card again. There was a little smudge of black on the top right corner. Perfect for a mechanic's card. It's almost like it was done on purpose. Dusty McConnell had some smudges on him too. I thought about what Aunt Charlotte said about him, how he'd been dealt some painful blows but how he'd dealt some back too. I should be afraid but I wasn't.

I saw the e-mail address at the bottom. What could it hurt? I mean, I live 8 hours away. He's clearly not dangerous. Everyone in town trusts him. Even Aunt Charlotte didn't say anything about not trusting him.

Dusty,

I wanted to thank you for taking such good care of my car when I was in Tennessee. When I showed my dad the bill, he said you gave me a significant discount. Thank you. I guess there are still people who have compassion on a stranded school teacher, even if she won't open the door to have a conversation.

Thank you for staying with me until Doug got there too. That was kind. The car is doing well and the Kindergarteners are fine. I hope you are doing well. I hope business is good too. The way I see it you and I are in the right jobs. There will always be kids who need to learn to read and there will always be cars that need fixing. We are both blessed.

Appreciation from Georgia,
Clara

God, please help Dusty McConnell to answer my e-mail. Give me a sign.

Two days passed. Neither of the Tennessee men responded. Their silence confirmed my greatest fear. I wasn't worth a man's love or attention. Not even worth an e-mail message. I was a loser, a castaway. The rejection was trying to speak truth to me, telling me that I needed to be alone. But I refused to listen. One man was too dangerous and the other was just not interested.

When the phone rang, I prayed it would be Carlie. She would know what to do. But it wasn't. Blessedly, it wasn't.

"Hello."

"Uh, hello, this is Dusty McConnell up here in Bradford, Tennesee."

"Oh uh, hi, Dusty."

"Yeah, I got that nice message from you and everything and I'm not much of one to write at all. I had problems with writing in school and I never got much help with it. Anyway, I don't write a lot. It's not that I'm stupid. No, they said I'm not stupid. Just have a hard time with writing and spelling, I guess."

"You're probably dyslexic, right?"

"I did have one teacher that thought that's what it was. You know, a lot of Hollywood actors have that. Tom Cruise and some others. But I'm doin' fine. I mean, I own my own business. I can read good enough to do what I need to do. It's more the writing. I didn't want to send something that would make you think I'm stupid."

"I would never think you're stupid. I have no idea how to put an alternator in a car. Do you think I'm stupid because I can't do that?"

"No."

"Then why would I think you're stupid for not being able to spell?"

He laughed as though my words relieved a fear. "I guess that's one way of lookin' at it."

"Everyone has strengths and weaknesses. Take me for example. I like working with little kids but sometimes I'm scared around adults."

"Why?"

"I don't know. I guess I trust little kids because, well, because they can't hurt me. They wouldn't even want to hurt me."

"Yeah. I get that. I do."

"So, what's been going on at your shop today?"

"Poor ol' Mrs. Reeves brought in her van again. She has 8 kids and 'er oldest two boys are always in trouble. She told 'em they couldn't drive the van for two weeks. So they got the bright idea of hotwiring it late last night for a joy ride. But they're both a brick shy of a full load, if you know what I mean. They wouldn't know how to plug in a George Foreman grill much less hotwire a van. They fried her electrical system pretty bad. God bless the poor woman. Van trouble is the least of her worries. Other than that, some oil changes and a few flat tires. I guess that's about it in the big city of Bradford."

"Wow! 8 kids? She's a busy woman even if her oldest two weren't trying to become car thieves."

"Yeah. She's had it rough lately. She has. But, she definitely doesn't have to worry about 'em becomin' car thieves. Neither of 'em are smart enough for that…thankfully."

"I guess you would know. Uh, I mean, you know about cars and uh, engines and stuff so you know what it would take to do that 'cause you're a car mechanic and mechanics know those kinds of things, right?"

"Look, I'm sure Mrs. Charlotte has told you about me. It's okay if she did. I'm not trying to hide anything. Mrs. Charlotte, she does like to be a little dramatic, I guess. But I'm sure she told you the truth. I went to prison for bein' a car thief. I did three years over near Nashville. I was in with a bad group of guys at the time. Prison was the best thing that could have happened to me. I got in some church groups, met some men who were trying to help me. It was life changing. Really. And yes, I came back to Bradford and two years later I married the greatest girl in the county. Her parents were hesitant at first until I proved to 'em that I was a changed man. You know, you can't blame 'em for not wanting me as a son-in-law. But then, I messed it up and…"

Dusty's voice cracked and I wished I had never brought up the stupid car thief subject.

"Yeah, I know about the tornado and your family. And I'm sorry. So very sorry."

"Well, anyways, I guess I just wanted to thank you for the e-mail. It was real nice. I don't get many thank you notes. A few returned checks now and then, but not very many letters." He laughed nervously, but his laughter was comforting. "I probably need to let you go so you can work on your school stuff or somethin'."

“Well, thanks for calling, Dusty. Really. I’m glad you called.”

“No problem. Bye, Clara.”

I felt joy and sadness. Joy because I liked talking with him. Sadness because no one knew about my feelings. I thought about what Carlie told me once. Things that are hidden are usually not helpful. She was right. Plus, I didn’t feel a need to hide anymore. I knew she was still in California but I texted her a few simple words, “When you get a minute, I need to talk to you about Dusty McConnell.”

Chapter 21 CARLIE: Alabama Ashley and the Georgia Peach

We still couldn't believe it. Dave won a pool table on The Price is Right. If I had been there to yell out the correct price for Chicken Rice-A-Roni, he would have won the boat too. But sadly, me and my uncanny Rice-A-Roni pricing knowledge can't be two places at once. Still, a pool table is not too shabby.

"How did the big collaboration go?" Dave asked the question between bites of waffle in the hotel breakfast area.

My answer was enthusiastic. "We found our lead actress!"

Shannon said, "Oh, I didn't know they let you choose your own person."

"They don't. But we did."

Doug looked concerned. "Well, we haven't yet. I mean, we did listen to her read a few lines. And she is an actress. But the studio will have to agree."

I tried to explain the situation. "They will love her. She's perfect. Perfect. And she's going with us to the meeting this afternoon. They called a meeting at 2:00 and she's going to walk in with us. And when she walks in the door, they'll love her immediately. It's impossible not to know she's right for the part. Impossible."

Dave was a brave man and he asked a brave question. "What if they don't love her? I mean, what if they say no? What are you going to do then?"

"I have no idea. We'll cross that bridge when we come to it. Well, we'll cross the bridge or push all the movie people in the water. Either way, it'll be a win."

2:00 pm

Ashley looked perfect for the big meeting. Her friend, a hairdresser, had given her an up do with loose curls around her face. She wore black jeans and a bright blue sweater which was directly from the pages of the book. She stayed up late reading the book so she would be ready.

Chance greeted us in the lobby and scowled when we told him that our friend, Ashley, needed to come with us to the meeting. His scowl didn't look very good with his yellow smiley face t-shirt. I wanted to say, "Chance, don't worry. Be happy." But I patted him on the back and chose silence instead. I like to think my silence indicated a lot of personal and emotional growth on my part. Oh, and if you're wondering if Doug and I decided to wear shabby chic clothes on day two of the negotiations, we didn't. I figured we should be who we are and not try to fit in. I remember what Pappa always said, "Ya better dance with the one that brung ya."

When we walked in the door, all the players from the day before were in the same chairs. Different day. Different thrift store fashion. They all stared at Ashley so I decided to get the ball rolling. "Thank you all for agreeing to another meeting. Really. I know you're having to make some decisions about casting and that's a big deal. I don't pretend to understand movie casting. But I do know about life. I mean, about my life, about the life the book portrays. This is Ashley Harrison and she's an actress. She's done some big commercials. She's from Alabama. And well, Doug and I think you should give her a chance."

Ms. Watson spoke first, "A chance for what?"

"A chance to play the lead role. You know, the character based on my life. I think she's perfect. She's got the look, the accent. I heard her read some lines yesterday and she has talent."

Ms. Watson removed her glasses and broke out in laughter. Her underlings followed suit with their own fake laughter which was nauseating. Well, everyone except Emily. She wrote something down on her tablet.

"Carlie, I'm afraid there's been a misunderstanding. We never asked you to go out and find the lead role. We have teams of people to do that. Besides, we haven't even tried A or B list folks yet. If we can negotiate a deal, we should try to get someone with a name. No one knows your friend here. So, the answer is 'No.'"

"But you'll give her a chance, right? I mean, you'll let her audition?"

"I'm afraid not."

I reached out to shake Ms. Watson's hand, "Thank you for considering us. Thank you for spending your time at these meetings. But I'm afraid we're not on the same page so I'll need to take our script somewhere else. It was nice to meet you though. Really nice."

"Mrs. Jameson, don't be silly. You want our studio to make this film. The publishers want us to make this film. We can give it the credibility it deserves. Don't let this one thing dampen your enthusiasm for the project."

"Oh no, Ms. Watson. My enthusiasm is not dampened in the slightest. No. I'm more enthusiastic now than ever. And yes, I know you make good movies. You do. And I want you to make this one. It's just that, well, you're not willing to take chances. And I need to work with a studio that IS willing to take chances. That's the whole theme of the book, y'see. And you haven't even heard Ashley read any lines. You haven't experienced her flavor for the character. So, that's pretty close-minded in my book."

Ms. Watson removed her glasses and leaned back in her swivel chair and said, "Well, let's hear her then."

"Thank you. You won't regret it. Ashley, why don't you read page 12."

Ashley stood and nervously pulled the script from her bag. I prayed that the Lord would do a miracle. A miracle for Ashley Harrison. A miracle for the movie. A miracle so Ms. Watson would see that sometimes taking chances pays off.

Ashley pretended to be fixing her hair while looking into a mirror. *"J.C. Collier's sister said he wants to ask me to the Rotary Club Pancake Breakfast and what would I say if he did ask me. Of course, I'd say 'Yes' even though it makes me horribly nervous. First of all, I get chatty when I eat too many carbs. Secondly, the flourescent lighting at the elementary school cafeteria will age me at least 10 years. And this is yet another reason I'm sad not to be married. I don't think there'll be ONE married woman at that pancake breakfast worried about the cafeteria lighting. A married woman is right to assume that if her husband can watch 'er give birth under flourescent hospital lights, he oughta be able to watch 'er eat pancakes on a Saturday mornin' under harsh cafeteria lighting. That's called intimacy. Real marital intimacy. And seein' as how the Rotary Club is rightfully afraid of exposing elementary school kids to mood lighting, I'll have to bite the bullet and brave the storm this time."*

Some around the table looked nervously at Ms. Watson while others looked down at the table. Emily was brave though. "Wonderful! Wonderful!" I didn't know if Emily's daddy was a famous person or if Emily was just a trendsetter. But I was appreciative either way.

Ms. Watson said in a matter of fact way, "Nice job, Ashley. We may ask you to come in and read a few more times before we make a decision." She asked sarcastically, "Are you okay with that, Carlie?"

"Yes, ma'am. I understand that you can't jump the gun on something as important as this. I'll stay in contact with you and with Ashley. But she IS wonderful, isn't she? She's got presence."

"She does. Now, Chance will take you on that set tour he promised. If you need anything at all, contact Chance or Emily. They'll get it worked out. I'll be in touch with a contract. Don't worry."

Doug chimed in, "Thank you all for everything. Carlie and I'll be going back to Tennessee tomorrow but here's Ashley's contact information." He slid a promotional packet toward Ms. Watson. Ashley and I had worked on it yesterday afternoon and it was good. It wasn't perfect. But we didn't need perfect. The book wasn't perfect. The movie wouldn't be perfect. Life isn't perfect.

The next morning Ashley met us at the hotel lobby before we left for the airport. We introduced her to Dave and Shannon. She asked Shannon if they had any kids and I winced. But it wasn't like that was the first time someone asked. It was a normal question, a question they were used to.

"Not yet. But we wish we did. We're hoping for one soon."

"That's great. Kids are a blessing. It took my parents eight years to have me so don't give up. Sometimes it's the best kids that take the longest." She smiled pleasantly and touched Shannon on the hand.

I hugged Ashley and insisted that she could call me day or night regarding the movie or just life in general. She promised she would. I was ready to be done with the movie business for a while. I was letting it go. Trusting that they would do right by the script. Unless something went drastically awry, I would sign the contract and move on with my life. Besides, I had gotten off course on one of my missions in life. Finding a man for Clara Johnson. She had sent me a disturbing text about wanting to discuss Dusty McConnell. But of course, Dusty was just a distraction. I would take care of it as soon as we got home. No problem. No worries

On the plane, I leaned over on Doug's shoulder and said, "Thank you."

"For what?"

"For inviting me to meet you at the Cracker Barrel that day."

He grinned and laughed. "I was so nervous."

"You didn't seem nervous."

"I'm a guy. I'm good at covering things up, remember? And thanks for agreeing to meet me too."

"Are you kidding? A good-lookin' Christian man with green eyes and a great butt? Really. It was a no-brainer, Honey."

I texted Clara from the Nashville Airport. "Back in TN. I can talk to you at 8 2nite. Call the home phone. Luv U."

8:05 pm

"Hello."

"Carlie, it's Clara. How was the big California trip?"

"Great! You won't believe all the excitement. Dave won a pool table on The Price is Right. Doug and I toured the movie studio AND we found the lead actress for the movie, too….at a diner! Can you believe it? It was just like an old movie! It's like God literally dropped her from the sky."

"Oh, I didn't know the studio let you pick the actors."

"They don't. I mean, not really. But we found her and she's perfect so I guess that's that, right?"

"Gosh, Carlie, only you. Only you would meet a woman at a diner and know that she was the lead actor for the movie and then be able to convince a studio that she is too."

"They're not convinced yet. They're going to let her audition several more times. But I'm not worried. They know I think she's perfect and that works in her favor. Okay. But enough about us. Tell me about you, Clara. What's this strange message I got about Dusty McConnell?"

"I like him, Carlie. I do. I can't explain it. I know that Aunt Charlotte's unsure about him. I know you want me to ride off into the sunset with Jake Smith. I get that. But I'm not interested in Jake. And I don't think he's really interested in me either."

"Clara, I hate to point this out. But you don't even know Dusty McConnell. I mean, he visited with you for ten minutes through your car window. He talked with you for a few minutes when you picked up your car. But you're not saying that in that twelve minutes you've fallen for him? That wouldn't be like you. At all. You've waited all this time to get out there and trust men again. And now you call and tell me that you're interested in a felon widower?"

"I haven't just talked to him those times you mentioned."

"What?"

"A few days after I got back home, he called on my cell phone. He was checking to make sure my car was running fine. It was a courtesy call. That's all. But it was nice. I was happy to hear from him. Then Jake sent an e-mail that night and the next night I wrote back to Jake. I did. But after I did, I don't know. It just felt like I was going through the motions."

"And?"

"Well, I did something very out-of-character, Carlie. I sent Dusty an e-mail message too. I'm not trying to hide it. I'll even send it to you if you want to read it. But mostly I just thanked him for taking good care of the car and told him that we were blessed to have the jobs we had and so on and so on."

"And?"

"Well, a few nights later, he called and we talked a little longer this time. He even told me about the prison time, and about how he'd messed everything up with his family. I listened. And I have to say, it didn't scare me, Carlie. It didn't. You always go around telling people to show mercy. Be quick to forgive. Don't hold a grudge. Well, here's your opportunity to live those words. I'm asking you to be merciful to Dusty McConnell. He's repentant of his crimes."

"Well, there's nothing left to say then. I'm not the one who'll throw stones. Not me. What about Jake? Have you heard from him again?"

"I sent him a message the very next night. Then four days later I got a quick paragraph from him and half of it was stuff that was happening at the insurance company with some kind of new government regulation. I haven't even written back yet. Truthfully, I'm not that motivated to write back."

"I see. Well, it looks like we've gone from having no men to having two men, Clara Louise Johnson. My word. What a strange, strange world we live in, friend. Well, so what's the next move with Dusty then? He called. Now what?"

"I sent him a message last night through e-mail. I express myself better through e-mail. He doesn't send e-mail because he has dyslexia and so he's not much of a writer. So, um, well, I figure he'll call sometime. I hope so anyway."

"Clara, I just have one question. And I need ya to just shoot straight with me on it."

"Yeah?"

"You're not interested in Dusty because you figure it'll be easier for him to understand your past, right? If so, it's not a good enough reason. Everybody's done things they've regretted. Yours are no worse or better than someone else's confessions."

"No. That's not it. I mean, yeah, I do think he'll be a little more understanding than the average guy. But that's not why I like him. It's not. I don't know. There's just a gentleness about him. Maybe all the pain and suffering, I don't know. Maybe it made him nicer. Not so haughty or proud."

"Jake didn't seem haughty or proud either."

"Carlie, it's not about Jake. He's nice. He's good-looking. Yes to all of it. He's even a good preacher and you don't see that every day either. I'm not saying I don't like Jake. I'm saying he seems mildly interested, if he's interested at all."

"Well, you know me. I'd never try to run your life or anything."

"Ha Ha. I love ya, Carlie. I do. Don't worry."

"Me? Worry? No way. See ya soon, friend. Bye."

Wow. If Aunt Charlotte could have heard the things I just heard, she'd say, "Ol' Clara Louise Johnson done got a fire lit under her rear." I sat down and explained the whole Clara/Jake/Dusty scenario to Doug. He listened intently. Smart married men listen intently to their wives. There's a very good reason for that that I won't go into right now. You'll just have to trust me. When I explained the final detail, he leaned back in his leather recliner and said, "Well, looks like we're out of the matchmaking business, Carlie. Sounds like she's got it all under control."

Doug is so darn cute when he's naïve. Out of the matchmaking business? Not even close. We were just getting started.

Chapter 22 CLARA LOUISE: Determined Dusty

It's after 9:00 pm. If Dusty were going to call, he'd have already called. Besides, he's probably tired and needs his rest. I agree. A working man needs plenty of rest, right? Right. My heart jumped for joy when the phone rang.

"Hello."

"Clara, this is Dusty."

"Hi Dusty. I was hoping you'd call. I'm happy to hear from ya."

"Well, I know it's late and all but I wanted to ask you a question. I was thinkin' maybe I'd come to Georgia next weekend and check on things, you know, your car, and uh, I'd even be glad to change the oil, if you want, while I'm there. I mean, if it needs changing. I don't know who usually changes it, but if you need me to, I could do it. I wouldn't mind."

"Well, yes, to your coming but I don't need an oil change. So I guess we'd have to find something else to do. Have you ever been to Stone Mountain?"

"I haven't."

"Well, you need to see it. I could show it to you. If you don't mind, you could stay with my folks while you're here. I mean, that wouldn't be weird or anything, would it?"

"Not if they don't mind. You think they'd mind?"

"I'll talk to them and work it out."

"I can't leave the shop 'till noon on Saturday. I'd wanna get cleaned up and all, so it'd probably be 9:00 Saturday before I got there. I could stay till late afternoon Sunday. That'd give us at least a little bit of time."

"Yeah, that'll work fine. I'll look forward to it. I'll talk to my mom and dad to make sure and let you know."

"Thank ya, Clara. Thank ya for givin' me a chance, okay?"

"Okay."

"Well, I better hit the hay. I've gotta get to the shop early in the mornin' to get some paperwork done. Paperwork is the one thing I don't love about this job."

"Well, no job is perfect, right?"

"Right."

"I'll send you the address by e-mail. Thanks for wanting to come see me, Dusty. Good night."

"Good night."

I loved hearing his voice. It didn't even bother me that I loved hearing his voice. I wasn't hiding any longer. I told Carlie. I would tell my parents tomorrow.

I like Dusty McConnell. And amazingly, Dusty McConnell likes me too.

Chapter 23 CLARA LOUISE: Marching Onward

I awoke to pure happiness. I needed to craft a plan concerning how I would tell my parents about their future house guest. What was the appropriate amount of information to distribute? Would Daddy be put off by the eye patch and the scar? I couldn't be sure. I'd never been close to him. When the phone rang, I jumped. No one calls me this early.

"Hello."

"Clara, I'm sorry to be calling so early and on a school morning, too."

"No problem. I have a few minutes. What's wrong, Carlie?"

"Are you sitting down?"

"No. What's happening?"

"Dusty McConnell was arrested early this morning. Just heard it on the radio. A policeman stopped him last night. His tail light was out and for some reason, he ended up searching the truck. He found cocaine in the glove box. Clara, I'm sorry. Really. I'm so very sorry. You have to know that I get no joy from this whatsoever. It hurts you and that means it hurts me too."

I couldn't contain my tears. "Is he in jail? I mean, he's there in jail?"

"I'm afraid he is, Clara. I mean, they'll get him a lawyer and I don't know what happens next. But yes, he's in jail right now."

I got a tissue from the kitchen counter. "Thanks for letting me know. I appreciate it. I need to get to school now. It's fine. I think we all know I'm not very good at choosing men. This is confirmation of that fact. So really, it's no big deal."

"Clara, this doesn't say anything about you. It's not about you. Everybody likes Dusty McConnell. There's no way you could have known. Call me as soon as you get home from school. I mean it. If I don't hear from you by 4:00, I'm gonna call your cell phone."

"No problem. Bye."

I walked into the bathroom calmly and then doubled over with grief. I wasn't crying. I was wailing. Crying represents sadness or happiness or even great joy. But wailing? Wailing represents the most horrid of human emotions. Grief. "God, why? Why can't I get this right? What is SO very wrong with me that I only garner the attention of bad men?" I kept wailing until I realized I would be late. I dried my tears, put on my shoes, and walked out the door wearing old clothes and no make-up. Carlie would have been very disappointed. I didn't care. Commerce Elementary School was going to see me au natural today. It no longer mattered. Nothing mattered but the loss, the loss of something I never even had.

4:00 pm

"Hello."

"Clara, I told you I was going to call if you didn't call me."

"Oh yeah. Sorry."

“Look, Doug went to the jail to see Dusty this afternoon. He swears up and down he’s been framed. He has no idea who put the drugs there or why.”

“Wow. I bet he’s the first convicted felon with that defense. Gosh, Carlie, you can’t say you believe him? Isn’t that what anyone would say who gets arrested for drug possession?”

“What’s changed your tune so quickly? Maybe he HAS been framed.”

“Maybe. It doesn’t matter to me.”

“Yes, it does. It does matter. At least tell the truth.”

“Okay. It matters. I got my hopes up. Those hopes are dashed now. We need to move on.”

“Look, Clara, I’ve gotta get on a conference call. Tell me you’ll call me tomorrow. Really. I want to help.”

“That’s fine. Bye for now.”

“Bye.”

The phone rang an hour later. No doubt Carlie was checking on me for fear I was sinking into a gruesome depression which would be stupid. I didn’t even know Dusty McConnell. Yet she would be right. I was grieving. The highest form of stupid.

“Hello.”

“Clara, this is Dusty. I only have a few minutes, and I’m so sorry but I need to cancel the plans for this weekend.”

"Yeah, I know. Carlie called me."

"It's not what you think. I promise I've been framed. I have no idea how it happened or who is behind it, but those drugs weren't mine. I've haven't done drugs in years, gosh, ten years probably. I haven't. But because I have a record, well, it makes them a little less likely to believe me. But I'm workin' on it. I am."

"That's fine. Look, Dusty, I have to go. I have a lot of things to work on and I need to get busy. I hope you get stuff worked out and get out of jail soon. I'm just glad I hadn't told my parents about the weekend plan yet. They probably wouldn't understand a guy not being able to visit me because he's in jail."

Silence.

"Good bye, Clara."

"Bye."

I wanted to believe that people had the capacity to change, to grow. That they could choose a life not controlled by their past. But maybe not. Dusty was a criminal and still is a criminal. I was used and abused, and now lonely. Life.

I went to work the next morning and tried to put it all out of my mind. I came home from work, made a grilled cheese sandwich, and determined to move on with my life…without a man. But the crying started around 7:30 and I couldn't make it stop. I wasn't crying about Dusty's or Jake's rejection. I was crying about things that happened many years ago. Things that defined me. The prospect of a man had brought up this whole truck load of nasty baggage and painful memories. No one was there to help me unload it nor would they even want to. I was alone, alone with a cat who coughs hairballs. The phone rang at 8:00.

"Hello."

"Clara? Clara, this is Jake Smith. Do you have some time to talk?"

"Oh hey, Jake. I'm in the middle of something right now. Can I call you back? I mean, in just a few minutes? Is that okay?"

"Sure. I'm home all night."

I went to the bathroom, dried my eyes, and asked God to help me see the truth. Jake was a good man. Dusty was a criminal. It didn't seem much more complicated than that. I'm a grown-up. I finished sniffling and dialed the phone.

"Hello."

"Jake, sorry about before. I needed to finish something up. But I'm done now. Really. Thanks for understanding."

"No problem. Actually, I just called to apologize. I re-read the last e-mail I sent and realized I probably talked shop a little too much. That was stupid. I guess I don't know much about what a woman wants to talk about. But I'm sure it's not insurance regulations."

I laughed. "Yeah, it's not that insurance regulations aren't fascinating, it's more that I don't know anything about it so it's not something I could intelligently discuss. On second thought, uh, no, they're not fascinating. Not fascinating at all."

His laugh was surprisingly genuine. “At least you’re honest. Okay. So I blew it. Give me another chance. I think I can reach into my bag of tricks and write about something better. How about bulletin boards? A kindergarten teacher would be fascinated with that, right?”

“Is that all kindergarten teachers are to you? Just bulletin board creators?”

He laughed. “I’ve messed up again. I’m an idiot. You should never write to me again. Pretend you never met me.”

“Relax. I’m joking. As to writing back, well, I got busy and distracted and I’m sorry. It wasn’t your e-mail. It was me. I got sidetracked. But I’ll definitely try to do better.”

“Do you plan to be back in West Tennessee anytime soon?”

“Yeah, I’m thinking this weekend maybe.” What was I saying? I wasn’t planning on being there this weekend.

“Great! Maybe we could go somewhere on Saturday. I’d like to take you to Reelfoot Lake and then maybe to this little diner in Union City. Are you up for an afternoon at the lake?”

“Sure. You can pick me up at Doug and Carlie’s.”

“I’ll see you at 1:00 then. Thanks, Clara. This’ll be fun.”

“It will. See you Saturday.”

I didn’t want to engage Carlie in a big and joyful celebration. So I wrote a simple e-mail.

Carlie,

I hope it's okay that I come visit this weekend. Jake is picking me up at your house at 1:00 on Saturday. He called tonight. And yes, I see the handwriting on the wall. You're a better matchmaker than I gave you credit for. A far better matchmaker than I am.

Let me know if this works for you guys. If so, I'll see you Friday night before 10:00.

Love,
Clara

6:30 am The Next Morning

"Hello."

"Oh Clara, I am SO excited! I'm jumping up and down! Aunt Charlotte will just be beside herself. Really. This is a banner day, friend! A BANNER day!!"

"Carlie, it's no big deal."

"No big deal? So I guess a Nobel Peace prize is no big deal. An Oscar or an Emmy is no big deal. Clara, this is a HUGE deal. You're going out with JAKE SMITH!! This is a dream come true, an answer to prayer. Really. I'm thinking of canceling any plans I have today so that Aunt Charlotte and I can run a victory lap…only it'll be hard for her to run 'cause she has foot spurs, and bad knees, and well, well, anyway, we'll be celebrating in Sharon tonight!"

"It's one afternoon. That's it. Nothing more. Yes, I'm excited. But no, I'm not flying to New York to have my hair done. Don't you have anything else to think about? Aren't you working on a movie deal?"

"It's all settled. Well, almost all settled. They just have to audition Ashley one more time, but Ms. Watson said they're leaning towards her. They really are!"

"Good. Look, I need to get ready. So I'll see you Friday night late, okay?"

"We'll be waiting, Clara! Oh, and before you go, promise me something, friend. This is very important. Promise you won't make me wear yellow or Pepto-Bismol pink in the wedding. Really. I couldn't bear it. It would be atrocious."

"You are beyond ridiculous. Have a good day, Carlie. Love you, Bye."

"Bye, Clara!"

Chapter 24 CARLIE: First Date and A Felon

I took a few phone calls from the publishing house, wrote 2000 words on my next book, and then raced to Aunt Charlotte's for a late lunch.

She was on the back porch when I arrived.

"I'm 'round here, Carlie! I'll be done in just a minute."

I turned the corner to see her releasing two little birds from a cage. "Bart found these little ones a while back, nearly killed by that dad blame cat of 'is. They was hurt and we got 'em goin' again. Now they need to go out and find their own way. They're strong now. They try to fly around the cage. But there ain't enough room in there. They're wild and they should be free. You sounded so happy on the phone! This must be good news."

"It is. Guess who's going out with Jake Smith this Saturday?"

"Well, I pray it ain't you, cause you know I don't take to that kind of nonsense, Carlie. I don't." She laughed.

"Clara is coming up late Friday night. Jake's pickin' her up at 1:00 Saturday. So, looks like we weren't such bad matchmakers after all. This might work out, Aunt Charlotte. And you and me, we'll be on the front row of the wedding too."

She wrapped the thin gray sweater around her chubby middle as she put the cage down by an old metal chair. "Well, I figure this egg ain't hatched quite yet so we best not count on the chicken."

"Oh, I know. I mean, it's just one date. But still. It's pretty good news in my book."

"It IS good news, Child! It is! And I think we should have a meatloaf sandwich in honor of it. I do. Oh, and some of them pickles too. Bart says them's the best pickles he ever ate in his life. We must be real good pickle makers, Carlie. Good pickle makers and good matchmakers. The whole package."

We walked inside and Aunt Charlotte took off her sweater and said with a sigh, "Sad news about Dusty McConnell, Baby. Sad news."

"Oh, it's heartbreaking, Aunt Charlotte. Do you know any more details?"

Aunt Charlotte started pulling beets and pickles out of the fridge. She retrieved a loaf of Wonder Bread from the top of an old freezer that hadn't worked in years. "Ricky's cousin is a lawyer over in Martin. Says Dusty has declared his absolute innocence. Swears up and down he's been framed. But Honey, ain't nobody been riding with him in that old truck. Both of his work hands checked out clean. So it all points back at him. I can't figure it out."

"I don't know, Aunt Charlotte. I thought Dusty was on the straight and narrow."

"Me too, Baby. Me too. And he may be. What's that thing they say…innocent till proven guilty."

"Yeah, you're right."

Saturday 12:50 pm

I knocked on the guest room door and provided a gentle admonition. "Okay, Clara! Get your tiny little rear out here and let's see you!"

Clara walked out wearing dark blue jeans and the cutest girly lavender sweater set. That trendy little Christy Jacobs downtown is ridiculously chatty about unimportant local news but she sure knows her stuff when it comes to picking out skinny girl clothes. Clara applied her make-up exactly like Charlene had showed her. Using a little sponge and everything. She knew to not even consider wearing a scarf. God bless her. She looked perfect. All she needed was to fall madly in love with Jake Smith today. Oh, and of course, Jake Smith needed to fall madly in love with her too. That process would begin in less than ten minutes.

"Clara, you look marvelous! Now look into my eyes. You, my friend, are a confident and beautiful woman! Walk out this door and knock him dead. He'll never even know what hit him. Really. It'll be like a line drive that just bowls him over or a like a bat that hits him over the head..."

She smiled with such confidence, "I get it, Carlie. I get it. Thanks. For everything. I'm going to run to the bathroom. Just let me know when he gets here."

Jake knocked on the door six minutes before one. Doug shook his hand and asked about his daddy. I loved watching Doug answer the door because it was a reminder that he lived here, with me. It was still unbelievable. A good-lookin' man was walking through the house in his sock feet because this was his home, the home he shared with me, his wife. I wanted Clara to experience the same joy.

I walked into the dining room. “Hey! Jake, nice to see you again. Can I get you some iced tea? Clara will be out in a minute.”

“No, I’m fine, Carlie. Thanks.”

Jake was wearing new blue jeans and a plaid long sleeve shirt. I didn’t love the odd burgundy color of the plaid but I chose to be thankful he wasn’t wearing a short tie. Glass half full, y’know?

I knocked on the door and told Clara he was here. When she walked out, I decided to watch Jake rather than her. He smiled broadly. Happily. Zing zing zing. This train was movin’ down the track at record speed. Everybody just needed to get out of the crossings. If I could keep Clara away from chunky scarves and Jake away from short ties, I felt confident the wedding would be within six months.

Chapter 25 CLARA LOUISE: Faith and Mary Kay

Jake Smith was kind and nice-looking and he had a pleasant way about him. I determined to give him every opportunity to knock me off my feet. And I did. I gave him opportunity. I listened to his stories. I even laughed at the appropriate times. I walked around the lake and asked him questions about eagles and boats and things he knew about. I tried to think about what it would be like to kiss him. Not that I would. I mean, not today. But I did wonder what it would be like if I did. It still seemed horribly scary and nauseating. By the end of the night, well, by the end of the night, I knew that Aunt Charlotte and Carlie were absolutely right. Jake Smith was perfect. Absolutely perfect. On the front porch, I shook his hand quickly, thanked him for the evening, and started to head into the house.

"Look Clara, what if I came and picked you up in the morning and you could come to our church again? I mean, are you open to that? I hate for you to not be with Doug and Carlie, but if you're willing, I'd sure love for you to come out to Troy. I'll even take you to lunch, if you're game."

"Sure. Thanks."

"It's no problem. Really. I'll be here by 9:00. That should give us plenty of time."

"I'll be ready."

When I walked in, the door made a familiar squeaking sound. Carlie was waiting at the kitchen table pretending to read a magazine. But I knew the truth. She was like a lioness waiting for the right antelope to walk by so she could spring to life from behind that Woman's Day.

When she saw Jake's truck pulling out of the driveway, the coffee kicked in and she pounced, "Spill it, sister. What did he order? What did you order? What did he say? Did he seem nervous? Were you nervous? Did he ask questions? Did you ask questions? Well, out with it. Out with it, Clara."

"Okay. No, he didn't seem nervous. I'm sure I did. He asked a lot of questions about my job and my family. I asked him about work and family too. And why do you care what we ordered?"

"Are you kidding? Good night, Clara. Do you never read blogs or magazines? You can tell a lot about a relationship based on what people order."

"You're not serious."

"Dead serious."

"For example, tell me he didn't order a baked potato."

"No. Why?"

"Ordering a baked potato indicates a total lack of interest. And if he put sour cream on the potato? Oh, sour cream is a death march, friend. A death march."

"We both ordered the burger and fries. I didn't eat my fries. He ate every one of his and mine too. So, what do you see in that, Madame Carlie?"

"I see a big farm boy with good metabolism."

I managed a smile. "Look, if you're asking if I'm happy, I am. He's a good guy and he's coming to pick me up for church in the morning."

"Well, Glory Hallelujah and AMEN! Ol' Clara Louise Johnson's got a boyfriend."

"You're jumping the gun. I have a friend who happens to be a boy. A man, actually."

Chapter 26 CARLIE: Whomp Biscuits and Straight Teeth

"Doug, wake up! It's 8 o'clock and you've got to be ready when Jake gets here!"

"Why? Honey, I'm not going with her."

"I know. But you need to be available in case he wants to ask you questions, get advice, or something."

"Carlie, we're guys. He's not gonna talk to me about Clara this morning. I'm not gonna tell him his hair looks good. And he's not gonna ask me where I got my shoes either. He's coming to pick her up for church. We don't leave till 10:00. Come back to bed, Honey."

"I can't. I'm too nervous. Plus, I want to make something good for Clara before she leaves. She needs to eat. I'm gonna start the bacon…and the eggs…and biscuits to provide ample carb loading."

Doug started laughing. "Has anyone ever told you you're beautiful when you talk about bacon?"

I reached down for a kiss, "You're the first."

Clara was less nervous than the night before. She looked relaxed. Relaxed and confident. Black dress pants and a multi-colored smock that made her look like a college student. Her hair was in an up do that normally I would have discouraged. But not today. Strands of wispy red hair framed her face. Romantic perfection.

"Carlie, you can't make a big deal about this. You can't."

"Who's making a big deal? I'm making bacon, Sister."

Jake pulled in the driveway at 9:02. I know. I have an odd fascination with time. And if you want to get on my bad side, just be late. Two minutes was fine. But ten would have had me pacing the floor eating excessive pork meat.

I opened the kitchen door. "Good morning, Jake. Come on in. Clara just finished her breakfast. Can I get you something? We've got bacon and whomp biscuits."

"Pardon me?"

"Whomp biscuits. You know, the kind that come in a tube and you whomp 'em on the counter."

He smiled and I noticed his teeth were really straight. Truthfully, Jake needed slightly crooked teeth so he didn't seem so over-the-top. But I can't convince his parents not to spring for the braces now. Sadly, the deed is already done.

"No, I'm good, Carlie. Thanks."

"Well, I'll run get Clara."

I knocked on the guest room door and then walked in and whispered, "Clara, I've got big news, good news."

"Yes?"

I whispered loudly, "He went tie shopping. I'm serious. He's wearing a white shirt and the tie goes all the way to his pants and it's all shiny and silver and modern-looking too."

"My word. You are a mess, Carlie Jameson."

Clara walked out of the guest room with incredible confidence. She and Jake looked beautiful together. A modern tie. A stylish smock. An up do and a shiny silver Camry. This day was nearing perfection.

"Okay, you two. Stand in front of the fireplace and let me get a picture. I know. It's embarrassing. And both of you want to throttle me right now. But that's okay. I have good self-esteem and I'll recover quite nicely."

They both laughed, stood by the fireplace, and smiled. But just before I got the camera focused, Jake put his arm around her shoulder. She turned bright red at the exact moment I pushed the button. Jake Smith had put his first "move" on Clara Johnson. And I was there to snap the picture. It shall now be preserved for their great grandkids. Thank you, God, for small photogenic favors.

Doug was making a light snoring sound when I entered the bedroom. "Oh Honey, good news! Jake and Clara are getting married!"

He rubbed his eyes and looked startled, "What? Getting married?"

"Well, not today. But yeah, eventually. I can just feel it inside. I can."

He rolled over and laughed. He was the sexiest man in the world when he laughed. "I love you, Carlie Jameson. With or without the early morning bacon, you're the best thing that ever happened to me."

We made homemade pizza after church and I paced the floor.

Doug was clearly bothered by my nervous pacing. "Honey, you need to relax. It'll still be another hour or more till she gets back. Come take a nap with me."

Doug has the best ideas. A girl just can't turn down that kind of offer. I woke several hours later to the sound of glasses in the sink. It would be just like Clara to wash dishes before the eight-hour drive home. And it was just like me to have left them in the sink in the first place. I ran into the kitchen. "Oh Clara, why didn't you wake me? I know you need to get on the road."

"It's fine. I just got back a few minutes ago. Besides, I wanted to wash these dishes before I left. I could never thank you enough, Carlie. I'm serious. It's been a good weekend."

"That makes me so happy. SO, how was church?"

"It was good. Everyone was happy to see me. Mrs. Peterson asked if I was sweet on Jake. I said I didn't know yet. We went to lunch with some folks from church and everyone was nice to me, really nice."

"You went to lunch with folks from church?" She must have seen my countenance fall.

"Yeah, what's so odd about that?"

"Well, I guess I just expected you and Jake to have some alone time, some time to get to know each other better."

"This family asked us to go and we just went along. It's no big deal."

Hmm. I didn't like that bit of info and I wasn't sure why. But I chose not to focus on it.

I had plenty of other things to think about.

Monday morning:

The movie people called and told me Ashley was being cast in the lead role but they were still looking for a more well-known actress to co-star with her. I called Ashley and she was ten feet off the ground. I felt blessed. God had thrown us together in a diner and now she would be starring in a movie. It's true, Aunt Charlotte. God watches over fools and insecure women.

Shannon called in a state of despair. They'd had another failed fertility procedure. I didn't get why God was answering our prayers with a "No." This seemed like a no-brainer. They're a fantastic couple. They need a fantastic baby. But if there's one thing I learned a long time ago, it's that I don't run the universe. And as hard as it is for me to accept, that's a good thing.

I know this. If someone asked me five years ago what I would be doing today, I wouldn't have had a clue. When I was working at the Dollar General in Commerce, Georgia, I would have never predicted that I'd marry a good-lookin' Tennessee banker and move to a farm, write a best-selling book, or talk to people in Hollywood about a movie. But the one thing I did know? Even five years ago, I knew that Clara Louise Johnson was an undiscovered treasure. By God's grace, maybe someone had finally turned over the rock.

Chapter 27 CLARA LOUISE: Blowing the Dust Away

While I was wandering aimlessly through the cereal aisle, the cell phone rang. I hoped it was Jake. But I had a feeling it was Carlie. When I saw the number, I started to push "Ignore" but I didn't.

"Hello."

"Clara, this is Dusty McConnell."

"Uh, Dusty?"

"Look, I'm out of jail on bond awaiting the trial and I need to visit with you. I can't leave the state so I can't come see you. Not yet. But Clara, I don't know. I just need you to know that I didn't do it. I didn't."

"Well, that's good, Dusty. I'm sure it'll all come out in the trial then and you'll be fine. I hope you have a good lawyer."

"I think I do. We still can't figure out who put the drugs in there. And now, well, now it's gonna affect my business. I've owned the shop for three years and I've got a good reputation. I'm afraid people are gonna be afraid to do business with me now."

"Maybe not. Look, I'm sure it'll be fine once the trial is over. Really."

"Thanks, Clara. I don't guess you're comin' to Tennessee anytime soon, are ya?"

"No. I was just at Doug and Carlie's yesterday. So, no. I won't be comin' for a while."

"Not another one of Carlie's matchmaking projects, was it?"

"Uh, not really."

"I'd be glad to come to Georgia. I wanted to come. I did. It's just that now, right now, I can't. But I hope this, this whole mix-up will be straightened out soon. And I hope this hasn't messed up the way you think of me. I've done a lot of bad things in my life. I don't deny it. But not this time. That wasn't my cocaine. It wasn't."

"I don't even know you, Dusty. We met on the side of the road. You don't need to be worried about my view of your character. You need to be worried about the jury's view. I'm sure it'll all turn out fine and I'll be happy for you. I will."

He sighed as though he were disappointed. But I didn't know if he was disappointed with me or disappointed with himself. He paused and then said, "Yeah, well, thanks, Clara. Sorry to have bothered you. Have a good evening. Bye."

"Bye."

I got home with the groceries and was happy to see an e-mail from Jake.

Clara,

It was a fun weekend. I'm glad you could come to Tennessee. I thought about coming to Georgia in two weeks. I could take Friday off, and be there when you get out of school. I'd leave Saturday afternoon to be back in time for Sunday. Well, are you game?

Jake

I wrote back immediately.

Jake,

Your Georgia tour guide awaits your arrival. I'll be here and ready for the adventure.

Clara

Chapter 28 CARLIE: Trials and Bad Pork Chops

I can't decide if tonight's dinner was a complete failure or just a minor setback 'cause, truthfully, some things in life aren't pass/fail. I think the dinner was a C+. Pork chops are just ridiculously hard to get right. I mean, if you overcook 'em they're hard and dry. But if you undercook 'em, everybody goes to the hospital. That's really a lot of pressure. I always feel it's best to err on the side of physical safety, right? But tonight's pork chops were so hard I thought they might inflict dental damage. So we finally gave up and made ramen noodles. Doug didn't seem traumatized in the least. He said my skills in the kitchen were not what kept him a happy husband. So we laughed and ate Ramen noodles and ice cream. It was a carb-loaded supper, just in case we needed to run five miles or something. Thankfully, we didn't.

We curled up on the couch and watched Andy Griffith. You know, that one where Barney gets taken in by the old lady selling the car. It was just at the good part when we heard a knock at the back door. I stayed on the couch but I could hear Doug's voice. "Dusty, hey man, good to see you. Come on in. Have a seat."

I stood up and rearranged the blanket. Dusty smiled as he walked toward me. He had removed his NAPA ball cap and when he did, he ran his fingers through his hair a bit to keep the brown curls out of his eyes. He was wearing jeans and a gray t-shirt. Clara was right. He was handsome. Not in a movie star way. And not even in a "bad boy" way either. No. He was handsome in a humble, understated kind of way. He wasn't as tall as Jake. He was a little thinner. But something about him was attractive. I was dying to know about the eye patch and the scar. But of course, I wouldn't ask. I guess that was one of the blows life had dealt him…or maybe the result of one of the blows he had dealt back.

"Hey Dusty, good to see you! Can I get you something? I'd offer you dinner, but my cookin' is still pretty bad. We've got yogurt. Oh, and we always have sweet tea. I'm a killer at makin' sweet tea."

"No, I'm fine, Carlie. Thanks. I hate to barge in like this. It's just that, well, I need to talk to both of ya. Do you have a minute?"

"Oh, sure. Yeah. Let me turn off the TV."

By this time, Doug had joined me on the couch. He said enthusiastically, "Glad to see you're out, Dusty. I hope it gets settled soon. I mean, I hope the trial is soon and you can put this behind you."

"Yeah. For sure. The lawyer just called and he's still doing some investigation. There's still some things we don't know, but yeah, I think they'll get it straightened out." He looked down at the rug and rubbed his hands together nervously. "Actually, I'm not even here to talk about my legal trouble. I have faith that'll get worked out. I mean, I know those drugs weren't mine. So I have to believe the court system will work for me."

Doug smiled and said, "Then I'm guessing you're here to talk about a woman, yes?"

Dusty looked down at the rug and didn't make eye contact. Then he turned his head and smiled as he looked out the window. He rubbed his lips together. "Yeah. I know. It's crazy. I get that. I don't know her. She doesn't know me. And I haven't been interested in a woman since, well, since Melissa. I haven't. It's been nearly a year now. I've been trying to build the business up, trying to re-build my life. I was living with Carl and Mrs. Betty at first. But nine months ago, I got my own place. Nothin' to brag about, but it's home. A two-bedroom place off of 119." He looked straight at us. " I've been goin' to church, makin' a plan for my life, savin' some money, you know, tryin' to get it together. Most decent girls around here, they remember me from before. They steer clear of me and I get that. I do. But Clara, she was different. I mean, she acted like she didn't care that I was a mechanic or even that I'd done some time. And now…now I've messed it all up. I mean, I haven't....but someone did."

I was glad Doug was sitting next to me. I have a tendency to get all weepy and emotional and ridiculous when a man shares something personal. I wanted to run over and just hug the stuffins out of Dusty McConnell. I wanted to make an omelet for him (even though my omelets are dry and crunchy and completely worthless). I wanted to tell him that I'm mad that his dad was mean, and I'm sad that he used to steal cars, and uh, well, that God loves him…very much.

Doug spoke with confidence, "Dusty, your reputation hasn't been ruined. There's been no trial. No real outcome yet."

Dusty bent the bill of his cap back and forth in his hands, then looked up. "C'mon, Doug. You live here. You know life in a small town. It's been on the radio, in the paper. My name already had some black marks beside it and now it has another black mark. A big one."

"When's your trial date?"

"Two months from now."

"So, you can still operate the business during this time? I mean, it won't hamper your work schedule?"

He smiled. "Not unless people stop coming to the shop."

"They won't, man. It might lighten up a little, but people are still going to come."

Dusty looked down at the rug again. "Business is not the only thing I'm worried about."

This was my cue to break into the conversation. "Dusty, if you mean Clara, well, that was never a sure thing, right? You hadn't really even gone out with her."

"No. But I was makin' plans to go to Georgia. And she was happy about it too. She acted like she really wanted me to come, like she was giving me a chance. And when I told her I couldn't write good, she acted like she didn't care. She said she couldn't put an alternator in a car so that made us even." He laughed and rubbed the side of his face like he was thinking.

I had a feeling Dusty McConnell could recall every single detail of that conversation with Clara. I was proud of her too. Even though I knew Dusty was not her soul mate, I was still glad she had taken the opportunity to make him feel good about his work. That effort had filled his soul. And God knows somebody should be filling Dusty McConnell's soul.

"Dusty, have you talked to Clara lately? I mean, in the last few days?"

"Yeah, I told her tonight I was out on bond. I told her I couldn't leave the state, asked if she was comin' up here soon." He stood and grabbed his coat. "But no, she said she wasn't. And well, I could tell she didn't even want to." He looked at both of us like a puppy who'd been kicked. "So I guess that's that, huh? Sorry I took up your time."

I spoke up. "Dusty, it's not you. It's probably my fault. Truth is, I introduced her to a guy in Obion County a few weeks ago and they saw each other this weekend. And I think things went pretty well. I'm sorry."

He ran his fingers through his hair, put his cap on, and headed toward the door, "Not your fault, Carlie. Really. Thanks." He turned back and looked at Doug. "Let me guess? This guy's not a felon or up on charges or a car mechanic either, right?"

At that moment I stopped caring about the sensible thing. I reached out to hug Dusty McConnell with every bit of enthusiasm I could muster. "I'm so sorry, Dusty. So very sorry." He smelled like pine trees. A pleasant and happy smell.

He hugged me back and it's almost like I could feel his pain being transferred into my own heart when he said, "Don't worry about it. It's okay. I'll be fine."

Doug put out his hand and grabbed Dusty's shoulder. "Dusty, you come by anytime you want. Anytime. Day or night. We're here for you. And we'll be prayin' for a swift resolution to your legal trouble too."

"Thanks, Doug. Oh, and if you have any car trouble, I'm open for business, y'know?"

"We won't forget."

Dusty McConnell drove out of our driveway in a 20-year-old red Chevy pick-up truck that looked like it had been through some rough years. But I had a feeling he wasn't interested in doing a trade-in. He knew just how to care for it, battle scars and all.

Chapter 29 CLARA LOUISE: Conquering Mountains of Stone

I recognized Jake's Camry as I walked out to the school parking lot.

He waved and shouted, "There's one of Georgia's treasures right there."

"Thanks! Welcome, Jake! Welcome to the Peach State!"

His hug was pleasant and almost familiar. We were planning to eat supper at a place in Atlanta I had seen on the Food Network. But first, we were off to my parents' house. He would put his stuff away, eat some of my mom's brownies, and shake my dad's hand. That was the plan. The entire operation should take less than ten minutes because my parents have almost no social skills. Mom was going crazy with cleaning and brownie making and breakfast plans. I guess she and Daddy had long given up on my ability to find a man. And now this. None of us were even sure what to call Jake. He wasn't my boyfriend. But he wasn't just a friend either. I decided we would all just call him, well, Jake.

Everything went fine. The brownies. The parental meeting. The burrito place that served everything with banana peppers. His clean car. My favorite sweater. His perfection. My ability to cover my imperfections.

Saturday morning Mom made some pancakes she had seen on the internet but the batter was too thin and it made a mess and stuck to the pan. The tiny kitchen was filled with smoke and tension as she struggled against the old cast iron skillet. She put her face in her apron and began to cry. Daddy yelled some obscenities, grabbed a paper, and sat in the recliner. Jake stood in the kitchen propped up against an old countertop covered in coffee stains, unsure of what to do next. I hugged Mom and explained that we needed to get going anyway and that we had had such a big supper that we weren't really hungry.

When I pulled the car door closed, I decided to lay it all out. "Jake, I'm sorry about that. Mom and Dad haven't had the best relationship. Ever. Mom's real emotional. Dad's volatile. It just makes for a bad situation. I'm sorry. Really."

"No, it's fine. I just wasn't sure what to do. I wanted to help your mom. But I wasn't sure what would help her."

"You did fine. The fact that we didn't add to the chaos was a help. Mom's probably crying on the bed now and Dad's in the living room ignoring her. It's been this way my whole life."

"So what did you do? I mean, when you were a kid, what did you do in a situation like that?"

"I read. I went to my room, closed the door, and went somewhere else through the pages of a book."

"Did it work?"

I smiled and looked out the window. "Not really. But it made the time pass. And that's what I wanted. I wanted time to pass quickly so I could grow up and get out."

Jake looked uncomfortable. He asked if I wanted some gum. I declined. In an effort to find a more pleasant subject, he said, "Well, I guess all that reading motivated you to want to teach folks to read."

"I'm not sure what motivated me. I knew I didn't want to live at home. I knew I didn't want to depend on Mom and Dad financially so I made a plan and carried it out. I've been happy as a teacher. So yeah, I feel blessed."

"I guess your dad, seein' as how he's a little rough around the edges, was pretty hard on your boyfriends probably."

I held onto the car door and said, "Uh, I don't know. I guess."

"Well, I know if I had a beautiful daughter, I'd be pretty strict with the guys comin' around."

"He could have done a better job in that department."

"What do you mean?"

"Oh, nothing. Let's change the subject. So you've never been to Stone Mountain, huh?"

"No."

We talked about Stone Mountain, about insurance regulations, and about his family. It sounded like the most imperfect thing about his family was that his sister didn't graduate college. It broke his parents' hearts and they did everything they could to change her mind. I wanted desperately to tell Jake Smith that I knew what family trauma was. Up close and personal. And trauma was not a sister who didn't graduate from college. He explained the family tree. One brother is an orthodontist in Memphis, got married five years ago, has a little boy and one on the way. Another brother, a CPA in Jackson, has a wife and baby girl. And of course, the wayward uneducated older sister was happily married to a local history teacher and the proud mother of three. Yeah. That's traumatizing alright.

We had a lovely morning. Pleasant. Happy. He needed to leave at 2:00 so he retrieved his things from my old bedroom and thanked my mama and hugged her. He shook my daddy's hand and said, "You have a fine daughter, Mr. Johnson. She's a great girl." Daddy sighed and sat back down in the recliner, saying nothing.

I'm sure he wanted to tell Jake Smith all my shameful secrets. Daddy is like that. He doesn't forgive or overlook. But for the first time in my life, I realized that Daddy shared the responsibility for my shame. Jake's comment about him keeping watch over the boys was eye-opening. While I was a teenager living at home, Daddy was to be my caretaker, the keeper of the gate. But he didn't. He didn't watch the boys or the gate. He sat behind that paper for years while my heart cried out for love. He let me take the fall for the abuse and the baby and the traumas. No wonder I couldn't choose a good man. I didn't know what one looked like. I never really had.

Chapter 30 CARLIE: Aunt Charlotte's Rural Detective Agency

I'm officially out of the movie business. Contract is signed, sealed, and delivered. The only caveat I scribbled above my signature was the insistence that Angelina Jolie not appear in the film. I'm not sure why that was so important to me, but it was. I figured one diva request or lack thereof wasn't too bad. I was happy to relinquish control of the movie because I really want to learn to make pork chops and I don't have time to micro-manage a movie studio.

Along with the pork chop project, I need to be working on two things: writing and matchmaking. They're not even going to start filming the movie for several months. Evidently it takes a long, long time to make a movie. And I'm not good at waiting for things. I'm not even good at watching other people wait for things. Dusty McConnell is waiting for his day in court. Clara Johnson is waiting to fall in love. Dave and Shannon are waiting for a baby. And I can't help any of them. Or can I?

On an average Tuesday morning, I woke with great inspiration. I determined to do some stealth detective work on behalf of one Dusty McConnell. I didn't decide on my own. Oh no. It's almost like I could hear the dramatic theme music wooing me in the background. I'm almost sure I heard an announcer's voice say, "Carlie Ann Davidson, Rural Detective, and her Side-kick, Aunt Charlotte, A Crime Fighting Deviled Egg Eating Duo." When you hear the call, you hear the call. I had no choice but to answer, "Yes."

When Doug left for work, I threw in a load of laundry, took a shower, and put together a crock pot meal that Ms. Ida swore was the most delicious thing she'd ever eaten, saying it reminded her of something she ate in Savannah years ago. I had my doubts. Frozen peas, cream of mushroom soup, and canned tuna seemed a bit abusive to the palette. But what did I know? Oh, and I wasn't sure Ms. Ida had really ever been to Savannah. She just read so many Paula Deen cookbooks that she thought she had.

I arrived at Aunt Charlotte's house at 10:00. She was sound asleep in the dusty rose recliner. Uncle Bart answered the door and proceeded to wake her in a very 'Uncle Bart like' way. He stood in front of the recliner and cupped both hands around his mouth, "Charlotte, Charlotte! Carlie's here! Wake up! Carlie's here!"

She startled and then rose from the recliner, "I was just resting my eyes a bit. Glad you're here, Carlie. Glad you're here."

"Aunt Charlotte, would you like to go with me to Sonic for a limeade?"

"Well, that's a mighty fine offer, and it ain't even my birthday. Sure, Honey. I'll go! Bart, can we get you anything?"

"Naw. I had a big glass of buttermilk. I'm good."

Aunt Charlotte put on her gray sweater and her tan garden shoes and got in the car.

I said in a whisper, "Look, Aunt Charlotte, I will get you that limeade, but that's not really why I came over. I need your help."

"Matchmaking?"

"Oh no. We've got bigger fish to fry. I'm talkin' detective work. Real detective work."

"Do tell, Carlie. Do tell."

I pulled out of the driveway and headed toward town. "Okay. So, Dusty McConnell says he doesn't know how that cocaine got in his truck. But I'm not so sure about that, Aunt Charlotte. I think he does know."

"You think he's lying? Carlie, Dusty don't seem like that kind."

"No. I don't think he's lying. I just think he's not telling everything he knows. He's protecting somebody, Aunt Charlotte. But who? That's the question. And guess who's going to find out? Go ahead, guess."

"Well, Baby, I reckon you and me's as qualified as anybody else 'round here."

"Precisely my point."

Aunt Charlotte and I knew where to go for information. We wouldn't be very good rural detectives if we didn't. We saw Chester coming out of the barber shop and I rolled my window down, "Hey! Chester, wanna go get a limeade with us? We're headin' over to Greenfield. We'll even throw in a burger, if you want."

Now there's something you need to know about Chester. He knows all the business in town and he never turns down free food. Phase One was in full force.

He hurried toward the car. "Reckon I could accompany you young ladies on that mission. Reckon so."

The minute Chester crawled into the backseat, I was ready to pump him for information. But that's not the way we handle things in a small town. Small talk must prevail.

"Chester, it's been a while since I've seen you! Glad we ran into you. The weather sure has been cold lately, hasn't it?"

"Whew! Colder than a frog's rear in January!"

I laughed, even though I'd heard that saying my whole life. "I saw Mrs. Ida at the craft fair last Saturday. She's lookin' good. Real good."

"Yeah, Doc Murphy told us she'd be better after that gall bladder surgery. And it was a miracle, Carlie. She ain't even scared of green pepper no more. A dad gum miracle."

Aunt Charlotte had evidently not read the etiquette section of the "Small Town Detective Handbook." She broke in with unbridled enthusiasm. "Chester, what do you know about Dusty McConnell's trouble? We figure there's a missin' piece somewhere. He ain't no drug addict, is he?"

Chester was happy to oblige. "Naw, Dusty ain't an addict. Dusty's problem is his family. Ever one of them McConnells was just 'bout worthless."

I disagreed with Chester. Human beings have worth. All of them. Even the McConnells. But I wasn't going to correct an old man when I was on a detective mission and needed valuable information. "But Dusty doesn't even see his family, does he?"

"Not usually, no. His mama, God love 'er, was a good woman but she died a few years ago when he was in prison. Most of 'em is locked up somewhere or dead. But Grover said he seen

Dusty's daddy a few weeks ago hitchhiking over toward highway 54. Yeah, hadn't seen him in years. I figure he was up to no good. Probably came lookin' for money."

Every day I thank God for His guidance and wisdom. The wisdom to pick up Aunt Charlotte. The wisdom to know that the promise of a limeade and a burger would lure Chester straight into the car like a June bug lures a prize trout. God allowed me to glean valuable detective information and it only cost $9.78.

We ordered an extra burger for Mrs. Ida and then proceeded to drop Chester off at his house right behind the Kwik Mart. I hate that Kwik Mart is spelled like that. I know there's a kid somewhere in Sharon who got five points off his spelling test because he spelled "quick" "kwik." Bless his heart. Sometimes the world just works against you.

"Aunt Charlotte, are you in a hurry to get back home?"

"No. Bart was goin' with Brother Dan today to clean out fence rows for old Mr. Simpson. He won't be home till supper."

"I say we make a quick trip to Bradford. You game?"

She smiled and did a big thumbs up. "Now, that's a fine idea, Baby. A fine idea."

We were happy to see that business seemed to be booming at Dusty's shop. The big garage door was up and he was fixing a tire for a 20-something gal who was wearing pink cowboy boots. Her jeans were so tight that a lot of extra was spilling over her rhinestone belt buckle. Her bleach blonde hair was teased in the front and she was talking a mile a minute between puffs of a cigarette. He looked up from the tire project and smiled. “What’s got you ladies out and about today?” We assured him we were in no hurry and would just wait inside. As we approached the front door, I heard the young woman say, “Dusty, you should go with me to this new cowboy bar outside Humboldt. You’d love the music.” He never looked up and said pleasantly, “I don’t really go out anymore. But thanks anyway.”

A gray-haired man was sitting on the ugly green couch waiting for Dusty to finish the tire project. A walker was positioned nearby complete with the little tennis balls at the bottom. He was reading a “Sports Afield” that was several years old. But I guess shooting stuff or fishing doesn’t change that much from year to year. If you love to read about a guy from New Jersey who went to Texas and shot a 400-pound boar hog, well, I don’t guess it matters if it was this year or five years ago.

A detective never knows what important information she might get from members of the general public so I decided to be friendly and engaging.

I waved pleasantly and said, “That Dusty McConnell sure is a good mechanic, isn’t he?”

The old man put down the magazine and said enthusiastically, “He is. I wouldn’t trust nobody else with ol’ Beulah.”

I love it when old people name their cars. I’d always wanted to name my cars. But they were never interesting enough to name. I had a black Crown Vic when I first went to college. I guess I could have called it Vic, but I didn’t. It looked like a funeral director’s car and that thwarted the joy of the nick naming process.

"Yeah, Dusty seems to be a good guy. My husband trusts him. I know that."

"And who's your husband, Missy?"

"Doug Jameson. We're from Sharon."

"Yeah, I know Doug's people. Knew his daddy real well. Fine folks. Sad that both of 'em's passed. And Doug works at the bank in Sharon, don't he?"

"Yes, sir. I'm Carlie and this is Doug's Aunt Charlotte."

He perked up and said with a smile, "Charlotte Nelson? Good gosh, I didn't even recognize ya, Charlotte. It's been a long time, hasn't it? Probably didn't recognize me either. Bob Woosley. Bart and me was big buddies back in the day."

"Bob Woosley, great to see ya! How in the world are ya?"

"I figure I'll be okay if I can get this hip healed up and my car fixed too. I felt sorry when I heard the news about Dusty though. I don't think that boy's done drugs. Not at all. He's a responsible fella. Somethin' ain't right about that whole story."

I jumped at the chance to glean information. "We don't think he did it either, Mr. Woosley. We think he's been set up. But by who? That's what we're tryin' to find out. Do you ever see any shady characters round here? Anybody that can't be trusted?"

"Naw. Not really. I think the fellas that work here are on the up-and-up."

"Well, something's not right. We know that."

About that time Dusty walked in, wiping his hands on an old grease rag. “Mr. Woosley, why don’t you just leave Beulah here and James can drive you home? I’ll call tomorrow afternoon. Oughta know somethin’ by then.”

“Thank ya, Dusty. She’s makin’ an awful rattle. Rattles at stop signs and stop lights. Rattles somethin’ awful in the mornings. Just know that I ain’t ready to shoot her yet. Not yet.”

Dusty patted the old man on the back and said with a smile, “No sir, Mr. Woosley. A good car is like a good woman. Always best to keep the one ya got and not be thinkin’ ‘bout a trade in.”

Mr. Woosley laughed and said, “True wisdom!” Dusty carefully helped him rise from the old couch and take hold of the walker. The old man smiled and patted Aunt Charlotte on the arm as he scooted by. “Try to keep that rascally husband of yours out of trouble, Charlotte.”

“Ain’t much use tryin’ to tame ‘em, Bob. I gave up on that years ago.” They both laughed. Dusty walked with Mr. Woosley to an old gray truck parked around back where a young man was waiting to drive him home.

Dusty was still smiling when he walked back into the office. “What brings you ladies in today?”

“Uh, I need an oil change, Dusty.”

“We can get you fixed up. Let me ask Al to get you started and then I’ll be back in.”

I handed him my keys and prayed that Al would keep his mouth shut about the beautiful amber oil still fresh from last week's oil change in Martin.

When Dusty walked outside, Aunt Charlotte grabbed my arm and nervously asked, "What are we gonna say, Child?"

"I'll think of somethin'. When he gets back, just let me take the lead."

Dusty walked in the door and removed his ball cap. He quickly ran his fingers through his hair, and sat down on the couch facing us. I saw what Clara saw. Humility. Kindness. Comfort. He straightened the magazines and held up a picture of an elk. "I'm guessin' a man could eat on that for a good long while. Don't you figure? Can I get you ladies a Coke or somethin'? We've got some cold ones in the back. It's on me."

"No, we're good, Dusty. We're good. How's business? Looks like you've got plenty goin' on."

"Yeah. It's decent. I mean, we're keepin' things movin'. It could be better but it could be worse too."

We talked for several minutes about the weather and the convenience store on Hwy. 22 that caught on fire. Finally, he looked down at the floor and rubbed his hands together. His face turned slightly red. I could tell he was embarrassed to ask the next question. But he must have wanted the information more than he wanted to save his dignity. "How's Clara, Carlie? Guess she's still seein' that fella from Obion County, huh?"

"She is. He went down there last weekend. So I guess they're kind of a thing now. I'm sorry. Just bad timing, huh?"

“I guess. Even if I get my trouble straightened out, it’s probably too late now. Probably wouldn’t have worked anyway.”

“I don’t know. It might have. Clara really took a shine to you, Dusty.”

Leave it to me to open my big mouth and get his hopes up. Why can’t I have a thought that doesn’t come flying out my mouth?

He looked up and his smile overtook the room. “What do you mean? Did she say somethin’ about me?”

“Well, yeah, she said she enjoyed talking to you on the phone. She was excited that you were coming to visit. That’s all I meant.”

He sighed and ran his fingers through his hair again. “But she was more excited about this other guy…evidently.”

Now I was in a quandary that even the most experienced rural detective would have a hard time negotiating. How much info should I divulge? Clara wasn’t more excited about Jake and I knew it. At least not at the beginning. She liked Dusty more. But now? Well, Jake had finally come out of hibernation and was pursuing her like a man. She seemed happy. And Dusty seemed miserable and in trouble with the law too. Just about the time he thought he found someone worth pursuing, cocaine was found in his glove box. An unfortunate set of circumstances to be sure.

“Well, I don’t really know, Dusty. She likes both of you. But if I were you, I wouldn’t worry about Clara right now. I’d get your legal trouble straightened out and proceed from there.”

His face dimmed with the harsh reality that a court date was coming. "You're right. But how does a felon explain that the drugs in his own truck weren't his? Not very believable, right?"

"I don't know. It might be easier than you think." I decided to be straightforward and unafraid. "Dusty, is there something you're not saying? Do you know who could have put those drugs there? You can tell us. You can. We know your father has been in town. Chester said he was seen out near Highway 54 a few weeks ago. Did he come to see you?"

He put on his cap and rose from the couch. "You'll have to excuse me, Ladies. I better get out there and check on Mr. Woosley's car. I appreciate you coming by though. Really. And tell Doug and Mr. Bart I said 'Hello.'"

Despite my earlier admonition, Aunt Charlotte walked right in front of Dusty and touched him gently on the arm. "Look, Dusty. Ain't no shame in havin' troubled family members. No shame at all. Your daddy is your daddy but he ain't a reflection of you as a man. Don't carry his shame as your own. I promise you'll regret it."

Dusty patted her on the shoulder and proceeded toward the door. "Thanks, Mrs. Charlotte. I'll remember that. I thank you both for comin' in. Al will be in here in a minute and get you checked out, Carlie. I need to get back to work. Come back anytime."

Dusty's unwillingness to communicate was a setback, but we weren't giving up.

Al came through the back room and smiled as he politely said, "That'll be $34.99." I knew what he was thinking. He thought I had a crush on Dusty McConnell. Why else would I come in for an oil change when clearly my oil was much more beautiful than it should have been? Well, I guess motor oil is never really beautiful but still. He and I both knew I didn't need an oil change. I didn't bother telling Al that I thought Dusty's daddy had planted drugs in his truck. I didn't tell Al that a kindergarten teacher in Georgia thought his boss was incredibly handsome even though he had an eye patch and a scar on his chin. I might lack discretion sometimes, but I was blessed with unusual silence as I pulled out my wallet. Oh, and me have a crush on Dusty McConnell? Puh-lease. I'm an inch taller than him and outweigh him by 50 pounds.

"Here's $40. Keep the change for your trouble. Thank you, Al."

When Aunt Charlotte and I got in the car, I said, "Well, it is what it is. We did what we could."

"Oh, we ain't finished yet, Baby Girl. We ain't near finished."

I respected Aunt Charlotte's heartfelt tenacity. More than she would ever know.

Chapter 31 CLARA LOUISE: Pushing Forward or Pulling Back

Driving home from school, I thought back on the events of the weekend. I remembered the odd sense of relief I felt when I was waving good-bye to Jake from Mama and Daddy's driveway. He was a good man. But I couldn't bring myself to jump in, even feet first. I was still testing the water with my big toe. He deserved my unbridled enthusiasm and I understood that. He tried to kiss me outside the gift shop at Stone Mountain but I pulled away. He apologized profusely. I gave him the whole, "It's not you. It's me." routine. He bought it too. But still, I could tell he felt rejected.

How could I explain to someone like Jake that I hadn't kissed a man since I was seventeen years old? How would he ever understand about Jason and the years of abuse I endured? Or worse, how could he believe I actually relished the abuse because I naively regarded it as love? And how would he feel about the other men? Some of them old enough to be my father. The men who crawled through the window late at night, the men who came knocking when Mom and Dad were gone. The men I repeatedly said yes to all those years ago. No. Jake would never understand. And neither would I. It was the worst kind of memory. Even though years had passed, it was like a weight hanging around my neck.

Jake's family tragedy was a happily-married sister who hadn't graduated from college. That was their primary grief and embarrassment. They would never wrap their minds around real tragedy. Abuse. Childbirth. Sadness. Loss. They would never accept their perfect little Jake marrying into such a family. And who could blame them?

As I pulled into the apartment complex, a wave of depression swept over me. Loneliness. Shame. Guilt. Meeting Jake had brought up all the things I feared most. All my childhood insecurities had re-surfaced. Now I knew why I stayed away from men. I was broken and being around men was like shining a bright light on all the unsealed cracks.

The phone rang and I knew it was him. He said he would call after school and he's faithful to his word.

"Hello."

"Hey! Clara, I miss you. How was school today?"

"Okay, I guess."

"What's wrong? Did something happen?"

"No. I'm just in a mood. Feeling a little sad, that's all."

"About what?"

"About my life. My family. Bad decisions. But don't worry about it. I'm fine. Really. How was your day, Jake? Did you sell a ton of insurance?"

"It was great. Sales are actually up right now and the boss says we're all in for a big bonus this year."

"Congratulations, Jake."

"Any plans to come to Tennessee again? I'm fine with driving to Georgia, but if you're coming to see Carlie, I'd like to know so we can make plans."

"Yeah. This weekend is the beginning of my spring break. Are you free Saturday?"

"I'll make sure I'm free. Let's go to Jackson. An afternoon movie and a nice dinner sound good? If you're stayin' a while, we can make other plans later."

"Sure. I'll find out if Doug and Carlie are gonna be home. I'll let you know. Jake, I have to go now. I have lesson plans and a bunch of stuff I need to do. I'll talk to you soon though. I will."

"Okay. Talk to ya soon. Bye."

I didn't have to go. I didn't have to do lesson plans at 4:15 in the afternoon. No one does. I just wanted to escape. And that just made me more depressed. Who would want to escape from a man like Jake Smith? Only someone who knows she's not good enough for him. Someone like me.

Chapter 32 CARLIE: Burnt Tuna and Bad Drugs

Aunt Charlotte and I parted ways mid-afternoon. When I dropped her off, she assured me that we would get to the bottom of the Dusty McConnell criminal case, no matter what it took. I knew she'd be in that broken dusty rose recliner talking on the yellow corded phone within five minutes of me dropping her off. She'd be soaking every member of our fine community for valuable information concerning Dusty McConnell and the great cocaine mystery. If anybody could get to the bottom of Dusty's legal trouble, it was Private Eye Charlotte Nelson. He might as well just fire his lawyer right now.

Evidently there wasn't enough moisture in the crock pot recipe because the canned tuna hardened like mortar all around the bottom. The house smelled like a Little Friskies factory burning to the ground. I scraped what I could into the trash and then sat the crock pot in the sink to soak. I opened all the windows and pondered supper plans. I decided to play it safe. There are a few things I know how to make with utmost precision. Chicken spaghetti is one of those things. And the way I see it, a woman whose matchmaking and detective skills are still considered questionable, well, she needs to have at least one success a day. Enter chicken spaghetti.

I heard the kitchen door open at 5:20. And in walked the most handsome man carrying a bouquet of flowers he picked in the field across from the house.

"Aww, thanks, Doug. They're beautiful."

"You're welcome. Do I smell chicken spaghetti?"

"You do."

“Fantastic.” He wrinkled his nose a bit. “And what’s that other smell? Like a cat or a dead mouse or somethin’?”

“Uh, yeah, something died, Honey. It was a tuna crock pot meal. I pronounced it dead at 3:05 but the carcass is still, well, kind of lingering in the trash. So you might want to carry it to the outside can for the final burial.”

He laughed and proceeded outside with the trash bag. He slipped his shoes off as he walked back inside. “Tell me we don’t have plans tonight, Carlie. Tell me that nobody is coming over and we’re not going anywhere and there are no conference calls or counseling sessions or pickle-making projects. Tell me it’s just you and me tonight. For the whole night.”

“Oh shoot, Honey. I do kind of have plans for tonight. Big plans.”

He sat on the bar stool with a grave look of disappointment. “Lay it on me.”

I walked up behind him, put my arms around his shoulders, and whispered into his ear. A big smile came across his tired face and he managed a few words with great enthusiasm, “I’m a blessed man. A blessed man indeed.” Chicken spaghetti was not the only success for this misguided rural detective. Married women or soon-to-be married women, take note.

When Doug left for work the next morning, I immediately picked up the phone. “Good morning, Aunt Charlotte. Any news?”

“Well, several people did see Dusty’s daddy. He had a few drinks at Blondie’s several nights in a row. Nobody knows why he was back in town and nobody in Sharon trusts him.

But even if he did put that cocaine in Dusty's truck, I can't figure out why. What would he gain from settin' him up like that?"

"Yeah, it doesn't make sense. At all. I mean, those drugs were worth money. A lot of money. No one would have wanted to take a loss like that."

"Well, I'm tempted to just put it out on Swap Shop, Carlie. Just ask if anybody has any leads."

I laughed nervously, "You're kidding, right?"

"No. I'm not kidding. Local people listen to that radio show, Carlie. They might know somethin'."

If you've never lived in a small southern town, there's something you may not know. Most small southern towns have radio shows called Swap Shop or Bargain Hunters or Swap and Trade. Local folks call in trying to sell a 20-year-old refrigerator or a size 12 prom dress or their Rhode Island Red rooster. On any given day, you could pick up a bargain on a billy goat, an old lawn tractor, a 12-gauge shotgun, or a stand-alone deep freeze. But I knew the host would get mad at Aunt Charlotte for calling in requesting information about Dusty McConnell's legal trouble. She'd have to give away a rusty wheelbarrow or an old metal bed frame to even get on the air.

"You can't do that, Aunt Charlotte. They won't let you ask for information like that on the radio. Let's think of another option."

"I say we go creepin' around Dusty's neighborhood. We don't know it was his daddy. Could be a neighbor or a friend of a neighbor."

“I’ll pick you up at 10:00.”

“You know I’ll be ready. Oh, and Carlie, do you and Doug need any more sausage? We have a fresh batch.”

“No ma’am. We’re good.”

We were good because we never really eat Uncle Bart’s sausage which we know is from a questionable meat source (think squirrel or possum) and it’s also hotter than a habanero pepper dipped in lighter fluid. Some things are just better left unsaid.

It only took fifteen minutes to get to Dusty’s house. He lives out in the country between Greenfield and Bradford. But he doesn’t have property to speak of. There’s a road which has about ten houses kind of lined up in a row. Some of them are well cared for and others aren’t. We decided to just park on the shoulder of an adjoining highway. There was a tree between our car and the street which we hoped would keep us from standing out. We popped the tops on two off-brand diet orange sodas and decided to keep watch a while. His house was a little blue clapboard house near the middle. It had a dirt driveway, old white rockers on the porch, and a beagle pup running through the yard.

“Aunt Charlotte, I think we’re supposed to keep watch at night, not at 10 in the morning. Crime show detectives never set up a neighborhood watch after breakfast, do they?”

“Well, we ain’t on a crime show. This is real life and I figure we’ll see somethin’ that’s gonna give us some clues. Keep your eyes peeled and don’t drink too much of that soda. Ain’t no porta-potties out here.”

We watched an old woman hang work clothes on the line behind a gray mobile home. A young mom and her toddler girl were swinging on a rusty swing set in the backyard next to Dusty's house. But there was no sign of mayhem or criminal activity.

"Aunt Charlotte, I think this has been a bust. I better go home and get to writing. I'm almost done with chapter 9 but I have to send 12 chapters to the publishers by next Thursday." My new book was called, "Country Girls Can Survive If they Stock Pile Peanut Butter." It was a funny look at country living and cooking and marriage.

"Patience, Child. Patience."

For some reason, I felt the need to go along with Aunt Charlotte's plans. I was driving. I could have started the car and driven off. But I didn't. I had respect for her age and tenacity. She was right. I needed patience. Aunt Charlotte was trying to help me develop patience, and help Dusty all at the same time.

"Wait. What's that truck doing, Aunt Charlotte? The white one next to Dusty's house."

"I say we sit tight and find out."

Two young men got out of the truck and stood in the driveway smoking cigarettes. A blue Trans Am pulled in behind the truck and one of the young men handed the passenger something, a package of some kind. He drove away as quickly as he had pulled in. Moments later a red SUV pulled in. Same scenario. An old aqua blue Impala pulled in next and the young men retrieved two big packages from the truck cab and handed those off.

"Aunt Charlotte, it doesn't take a rocket scientist to figure out something's fishy about this."

"Oh, absolutely. Reckon we better go pull in that driveway and ask 'em what they're sellin' over there?"

"What? No! Absolutely not!! Are you crazy? We could get killed!"

Aunt Charlotte bent over laughing and some orange soda sprayed from her mouth, "I'm messin' with ya, Baby. Just messin' with ya. Let's go talk to Raymond and see what we can do."

I pretended to hit Aunt Charlotte on the arm. But of course, I would never really hit her. I loved her deeply. We had almost nothing in common. Other than Doug, she was my closest friend.

Raymond is Uncle Bart's second cousin. He'd worked for the Sheriff's department for more than twenty years. He would know if there had been any drug complaints out on Antioch Road and if there could be a connection to Dusty's trouble.

When we entered the Sheriff's department lobby, Millie, a chubby young woman wearing a ton of bright make-up, greeted us warmly, "Mrs. Charlotte, how are ya? And what can we do for ya?"

"We're lookin' for Raymond, Millie."

"He's in his office. I'll tell him you're on your way back."

"Thank ya, Baby."

Aunt Charlotte called anyone under 50 "Baby." I didn't know why. I'd never thought to ask. I followed her down a long corridor and into a tiny office.

Raymond rose to greet us. "C'mon in, Ladies. Good to see you. How can I help you today?" His desk was covered with papers and old coffee cups and a few faded pictures of little kids who probably now had kids of their own. He was a tall skinny man who looked a lot like Uncle Bart only he didn't have a full beard, him being a law man and all.

"Raymond, I'm not gonna waste your time. Dusty McConnell's in trouble with the law but I don't think he did it. He ain't a drug addict. He's had a hard past but he's gettin' his life together and this whole cocaine thing, well, I just don't buy it. He works hard at that shop ever'day. He never seems high on nothin'. I think he's been framed. And I think I know what happened too."

Raymond twirled an ink pen between his fingers. He looked unhappy with Aunt Charlotte's declaration but he knew not to dismiss her. "And how do you think it happened?"

"Well, I think there's some young fellas dealin'drugs out there on his road. In fact, I know there is. Somethin' probably went wrong with one of their deals. I reckon they got scared or somethin' one night and they hid that cocaine in his truck thinkin' they'd get it later."

"And how would you ladies know what happens on Antioch Road at night?"

"Well, I don't know what happens there at night, but I know what was happenin' there no less than an hour ago. Right there in broad daylight. It was drug dealin', Raymond. I don't think they's passin' out Bibles, I'll tell ya that."

Aunt Charlotte proceeded with every detail of what we saw, the license plate of the white truck, the makes of the other cars, the description of the young men, the house, the driveway.

Raymond looked more serious now. “Thank you, Charlotte. I promise I’ll do some investigating.”

“Look, Raymond, I’m not tryin’ to be rude or nothin’, but you’ve got to stay on this. Dusty McConnell’s life is on the line here. It is. Now promise me you’ll see this through.”

He wrote something on a note pad and nodded his head. “I will, Charlotte. I will. But don’t worry. His life is not on the line. It’s a drug possession charge. The most he’d do is six months or so. With his record, maybe a year.”

“Well, that shows what you know about the word ‘life’, Raymond. Life is not about the length of a jail sentence. A man’s life is his dignity. It’s his character, his work. Dusty, he’s made a lot of mistakes in the past. He has. But now, well, now he’s on the straight and narrow, workin’ hard, goin’ to church, even pursuin’ a good woman. And this drug charge? If he’s found guilty, it would take the life right out of ‘em. And I can’t watch that happen. I won’t watch it happen.”

“I’ll check it out. I promise.”

“Thank ya, Raymond. We’ll be on our way. If I don’t hear from ya by tomorrow afternoon, I’ll give you a call or come by. You can count on it.”

He shook his head and with a grin, he muttered, “I expected nothing less.”

We walked back down the corridor and I could have sworn Aunt Charlotte had grown ten inches. She was just 5’3”. But after the conversation with Raymond she seemed taller than me. I knew a lot of people in Sharon thought she was odd. A raccoon in the house. A loud voice. Unusual thrift store clothing. An old house that was poorly decorated and never spotless. But they didn’t know the real Aunt Charlotte. What a shame. She was full of compassion and tenacity. A pioneer woman. As Chester would say, “When God made her, He done broke the mold and maybe that was with good reason.”

Chapter 33 CLARA LOUISE: Confession is Good for the Soul

I couldn't believe I was on another road trip to Tennessee. I was weary of the drive but I was longing to be in Sharon. Commerce held nothing for me anymore. My parents were fighting more than usual. The Kindergarteners were as ready for spring break as I was. Doug and Carlie's place provided solace from all of it. They offered everything I didn't have. A lack of conflict. A lack of loneliness. Belonging. Jake would pick me up tomorrow afternoon for another date. That made me both happy and stressed.

Doug and Carlie were waiting for me on the front porch and we all sat in the rockers for a while and drank cocoa. I envied them. Oh, how I envied them. The way they looked at each other. I envied their life together, a life full of love and sex and happiness…without baggage or fear. I asked Carlie if I could speak with her privately. Doug said he was happy to give us some time. He went to the bedroom to watch TV.

"Carlie, it's late and I'll get right to it. I don't even know how to love a man. Even if I wanted to, I don't know how. I don't. I've never had a good relationship with Daddy. I've never even kissed a man. I mean, not really. Not like the way someone would kiss someone they love. I haven't. Jake has been so nice and I like him. I do. He tried to kiss me at Stone Mountain and I couldn't do it. I still remember all the men who would kiss me and it was all just to get something else. No man has ever loved me, Carlie. Not one man. Ever. I'm 32 years old and no man has ever loved me enough to fight for me. They never even had to."

Carlie reached out her hand to grab mine. "Just start with the truth. You say, 'Jake, I have to tell you something. I haven't dated in years because my teen years were fraught with sexual abuse. But I'm working on that. I'm really trying to work through some of the things that happened to me. But I'll be honest. Those experiences were horrible. Truly horrible.' Then you tell him the whole thing. Jason and all his friends. The pregnancy. The baby. The adoption. You tell him you're fighting to believe the truth. You're fighting to see yourself the way God sees you. But you'll need help in that fight. And any man who wants to be with you, well, he'll have to be willing to go into battle with you…and for you."

"Good night, girl. You have a way with words. Can you come with me and tell Jake yourself?"

Carlie laughed. "Don't ask twice. You know I'm nosy enough to do it, but smart enough to decline. Plus, we don't want to risk one of those Cyrano de Bergerac moments, you know, where Jake THINKS he's falling in love with you but really he's falling in love with your big-butted best friend who's in a bathroom stall speaking into a little headphone mic." She laughed and added, "That would be disastrous. Look, Clara, it'll be fine. And if it's not, it's because he's not the right guy. Let's get some rest, huh? We can visit more in the morning."

I stood to give Carlie a hug. "You bring comfort to me, friend. Thank you."

"You're welcome, sister. You're welcome."

I woke up long before Doug or Carlie. I grabbed a water bottle and wrapped myself in a thick blanket and sat on the porch. Watching the sun come up over the farm was a gift. In the quietness, I prayed. "God, help me. Please help me." And in a life that had been filled with terribly ugly moments, that one moment stood out as beautiful.

Chapter 34 CARLIE: Cheering for the Home Team

Doug and I have been married less than a year so we still need a lot of privacy. We want to take care of other people but we want to take care of each other too. That's a balancing act, to be sure. We were glad Jake was coming at 1:00. We were happy for them because they would get to spend more time together. And we were happy for us too.

I love to watch the clock for punctuality. At 12:55 his clean silver Camry came gliding up the drive. Smart, Jake Smith. Very smart. You don't want to get on my bad side. He wore faded jeans and a green polo shirt nicely tucked into his belted jeans (ten points for the belt and the tuck-in). Jake's hair was dark and short and his eyes were kind of an odd but lovely Army green color. His skin was medium in tone. I'm whiter than school glue, but Jake is more the color of that flesh crayon that has now been booted from the Crayola box because we all know that flesh comes in many different colors. Anyway, Jake's skin was not white. Not brown. But a medium tannish pink.

Poor Jake. His clothing was perfect. His hair was kind of spiked, all clean and neat. But his new white tennis shoes were much too bright. But just like my willingness to forgive him for the short tie, I made a conscious choice to forgive the blinding white tennis shoes. Maybe the shoes were a gift to make up for his perfectly straight teeth.

I waved as I walked out onto the porch, "Welcome, Jake. Come in! Would you like some sweet tea or water?"

"I'm good, thanks."

"Have a seat in the living room. I'll get Clara."

I knocked gently on her door and walked in. Clara was standing in front of the full-length mirror. She looked adorable. Casual brown shoes with jeans and a bright yellow shirt cinched with a leather belt. Her hair was curled just like Charlene had curled it. Her Mary Kay was applied as if to say, "I'm applying for the job of 'girlfriend' and I'm darn serious about it too." She no longer looked like an insecure teenager. She looked like a beautiful red-headed woman. I heard Doug talking to Jake about March Madness (which has something to do with basketball or mad cow disease), so I took a few minutes for my own dating pep talk. "You look beautiful, Clara." I grabbed her hands in mine. "I'm praying for you, friend. You need to do this. You have to do this. Jake will understand. Knock 'em dead, Girl! Knock 'em dead!"

I always wanted to be a cheerleader. But for some reason, the powers that be never let me. Society has the misguided feeling that a tall, chubby, teenage girl cheering on the sidelines would make the high school boys play worse, not better. But of course, there's no real data to support that. No data at all.

I deemed matchmaking far more important than a high school basketball game anyway. And Clara was more precious to me than a pimply-faced kid hoping for two points. I had to cheer for her because no one else would. Jake and Clara drove off into the sunset in a new silver Camry. Well, it was 1:00 so the sun wasn't setting. And they weren't really at the end of a fairy tale yet either. Not yet. I prayed a simple prayer. Oh God, please don't break her heart.

Chapter 35 CLARA LOUISE: Freedom, Sweet Freedom

The movie was stupid. Too much action. Not enough dialogue. As we were walking out of the theater, Jake knew he had made a mistake. "That was intense. Was it a little too intense for your tastes, Clara?"

"Well, yeah. I'm kind of a girly girl when it comes to movies. So yeah, if more than one person dies, I'm pretty much spent emotionally."

He put his arm around me and dropped his head. "Oh, no. I'm really sorry then. I won't make that mistake again."

"Don't worry about it, Jake. No biggie."

"We've got some time before dinner. Any stores you wanna go to? I don't even know what stores women like. I don't even know if you like to shop."

"Yeah, I like shopping. But could we just go to a coffee place or something and talk? I have something I need to say and the sooner I get it said, well, the better off I'll be."

Jake looked worried or puzzled. I couldn't tell which.

"No problem. How about yogurt? There's a yogurt place next door."

"Sounds great."

I ordered a small plain chocolate yogurt. Jake ordered some huge pink swirly concoction with a lot of fruit toppings and whip cream. If Carlie were here, she could analyze the hidden meanings of our food choices. I had no idea if the big swirly yogurt meant he was in love or just that he had a preference for dumb action movies.

We sat at a quiet table in the back. Jake took the lead. “What’s up, Clara?”

Sudden tears made me mad and frustrated. I would never get this done if I couldn’t control my emotions. I stood up and walked toward the back. “I need to go to the restroom. I’ll be back.”

When I walked out of the restroom, he was checking the messages on his phone. He looked worried.

With a handful of tissue, I sat down across from him. I lowered my head and tried to speak quietly. “Jake, I’m broken. I am.”

He leaned in across the table. “I can’t hear you, Clara. What did you say?”

“I said that I’m broken. I didn’t kiss you because I don’t know how to kiss you. I want to but I don’t know how to kiss a man. I don’t and I never have.” I ate a bite of yogurt in a failed effort to provide a distraction.

A look of startling relief came across his face. “Oh, Clara, gosh, that’s not a problem. It’s not. Don’t worry about it. I appreciate that kind of innocence. Really. My last girlfriend had the opposite problem. She had done all kinds of things with all kinds of men and it was a mess. She eventually ran off with a guy she met on the internet. Looking back, it was probably the best thing that could have happened though. Look, I love the fact that you’ve never kissed anyone. It’s a relief, really.” He smiled and grabbed my hand. “That’s a good confession, Clara, not a bad one.”

Tears sprang up again and I whispered. "No, Jake. You don't understand. I'm not innocent. I'm far from innocent."

"Okay. I know I'm a guy and everything, but I don't understand. You said you've never kissed anyone and now you say you're far from innocent. What am I missing?"

"I've never kissed someone in…well, a relationship way." I quickly asked God for recall of Carlie's words. "My teen years were filled with abuse. Sexual abuse. I was 15 the first time I had sex. It was with a 25-year-old neighbor. But he wasn't the only one. There were men. Lots of men. Some of them young and some old. It was two straight years of relationship hell. Hell on earth. I had a baby. He's almost 16 now. I placed him for adoption with a couple from Louisiana." I placed my head in my hands and cried like someone had died. And someone had died. The woman I could have been died. The woman I always wanted to be died. But deep down, I wanted to believe she could be resurrected. Made new. Jake glanced out the front window then gently took hold of my hand. "I don't know what to say. What am I supposed to say? I'm sad for you. I am. Your sadness is my sadness. But I do think there's healing. If you thought I was gonna run, I'm not. I'm still here, Clara. I'm still right here and I've got no plans to go anywhere."

I managed a smile through the tears. "Are you serious?"

"Dead serious."

"And what about your perfect family? What would they think about it?"

“My family is far from perfect. And it’s not their call.” He grabbed my other hand and looked into my eyes. “I’m not seventeen, Clara. I’m a grown-up.”

And it was like a light had entered the room. Not a bright light. No. Just enough light to take the next step. I looked into his eyes and chose to believe him. On faith. “Okay then.”

“I’m starved. Let’s ditch the yogurt and get some real food! Sound good?”

“Absolutely.”

He stood and hugged me gently. I felt free. Like a weight had been lifted. I never wanted to carry it again.

We ate delicious pork barbecue and talked about work and the details of the horrible action movie. Neither of us mentioned the earlier conversation. Jake didn’t try to kiss me. In fact, he made no further physical contact with me at all. I’m sure he knew I needed some time. Healing can sometimes come in an instant. But not usually. Usually it’s a process. A painful time-consuming process. After fifteen years, I had only now even begun the process. The process of becoming a woman who could love and be loved. Jake needed to wait for me to give the cues. Thankfully, he was smart enough to figure that out.

Carlie was once again waiting up at the kitchen table, even though I know she never stays up till 11:00. Jake walked in with me and said his quick “Hello” and “Good-bye.”

When the door slammed, she said, “Sit and spill it, girlfriend.”

I laughed and pulled up a kitchen chair. She scooted a bag of Oreos in front of me. "I told him. All of it. He was very understanding too. He said he doesn't just preach redemption. He believes it."

"Well, Glory Hallelujah, Clara. See? I told you he'd understand. Am I a matchmaker or WHAT? Well, I mean, is Aunt Charlotte a matchmaker or what?"

"Yes, you did well. Both of you."

We chatted for a few minutes and then went to bed. My bedtime prayer was simple. "Thank you, God. Thank you."

Chapter 36 CARLIE: Throwing Baby Bird Out of the Nest

Jake picked Clara up early before we even woke up. The fact that I didn't feel the need to get up and supervise her every move was indicative of her personal relationship growth…or my personal relationship growth in learning to keep my nose out of her business. Doug and I ate lunch at Uncle Bart and Aunt Charlotte's after church. She had put field peas in the crock pot and then made a big pan of cornbread. Delicious. I figured she knew something because she was unusually cheery and speedy with the lunch prep. She didn't go digging in the cellar for pickled radishes or take the time to make cole slaw. No. She got busy and got it on the table and that was that. After lunch, Doug and Uncle Bart turned on the news. Uncle Bart proceeded to complain about Congress, the Senate, and the Sheriff in North Carolina who was caught stealing marijuana. Aunt Charlotte whispered, "Meet me on the back porch. We have some detective work to discuss."

She shouted over the TV, "We're in the backyard, boys!"

They both mumbled something incoherent.

We sat in old lawn chairs on the back porch. You know, those big green metal chairs that grandparents always have and type A people are always refinishing on Home and Garden TV? Aunt Charlotte never felt the need to re-finish anything. I completely agree. If it was finished once, why would we want to finish it again? That's a misuse of the word.

I spoke in a loud whisper, "What do you know, Aunt Charlotte?"

"Raymond called me early this morning. He told us to be patient because they was gettin' ready to crack a case out there near Dusty's house. Seems them fellas don't actually live there. They just use that driveway 'cause the rent house is empty right now. No one had reported them 'cept us, but he did recognize the car descriptions. Unless they actually catch the guys with the stuff, it'll be hard to prove that what they sell is what was in Dusty's truck. But Raymond told us he felt like they were onto somethin'."

"Isn't Dusty's trial in a week?"

"Yeah, but they'll find somethin' fore then. Raymond knows the clock is tickin'. He does."

"Well, in other news, seems like things are workin' out really well for Clara and Jake. They're together again today and she's going to his parents' house for the afternoon. Sunday dinner, the works. We did good, Aunt Charlotte." I reached for her hand. "Real good."

Chapter 37 CLARA LOUISE: Perfect Family Dinner

For the first time in my adult life, I felt comfortable with a man. Mr. Garrison led music so Jake could sit with me on the front row. Jake held the book and I sang, "Amazing Grace." For the first time in a long time, the words truly resonated with me. This must be what family feels like. Belonging. Not being alone.

I was terribly nervous about meeting Jake's family. But he said they were wildly excited about meeting me. He promised I would love them and they would love me back. Trusting Jake was the only option. And that option felt…well, for the first time it felt doable.

The minute we pulled into the long paved driveway of his family farm, I realized he must have been horribly embarrassed for me when he came to my parents' house. His home was two-story brick with those big white shutters on all the windows. The lawn was manicured to perfection and there were multiple flower boxes filled with color. A grove of big oak trees surrounded the house. Jake's family home reminded me of a movie set where a girl might walk out onto the porch in a big antebellum dress. Mom and Dad's house was small and the faded brown paint was peeling badly on the front of the house. The yard was an overgrown mess. A mess that had long been forgotten. My family home looked like my family. Tired and in the process of giving up.

His mom stepped out onto the huge porch which was covered with pots of bright spring flowers. She greeted us with a wave and perfect smile. You know those older women who wear a lot of make-up, but not in a gaudy way, in a really classy way? Kind of the way a judge on the Miss America pageant would look. Her clothes would be stylish and all her jewelry would match perfectly. That's the way Jake's mom looked. She was tall and a little overweight but I had never seen someone so "put together."

Jake reached out for a quick hug and then pulled back and put his arm around me. "Mom, this is Clara Johnson. Clara, this is my mom, Barbara Smith."

"Oh Clara, we're so tickled to have you! Do come in, dear. Jim is in the back with the grill. Andy's family is here and so is Emily's. Drew just called. They're ten minutes away. This is going to be such a great day, Clara." She reached out to hold my hand. "Oh, Honey, my heart is full."

I've been alive more than 30 years and I don't believe either of my parents have ever said, "My heart is full." Their hearts aren't full, not even half full.

If I thought Jake was too perfect, he came by it honestly. His dad was taller than him and ruggedly handsome. He was manning a massive grill with enthusiasm. But he managed to pull away from the project for a friendly hug. He asked if I liked steak, and my answer brought a cheerful, "Atta girl."

His orthodontist brother, Andy, was friendly but reserved. He looked a lot like Jake, only not quite as tall. His friendly blonde wife was obviously pregnant, but she wore one of those chic maternity smocks with bright swirly flowers that made her look like a woman from the Macy's window.

I liked Emily immediately because she seemed to be more like me. She was thin but wore very little make-up. Her jeans were faded and her tan sweater had a tiny stain near the right shoulder. Her oldest little girl, Mollie, had a few tangles in her beautiful curly hair and the baby, Justin, still used a pacifier even though Jake's mom kneeled down and said in a high-pitched voice, "Three-year-olds don't use pacies, Justin. Three-year-olds should act like big boys."

Drew's family arrived with big hugs and an apology for tardiness. Everyone stopped what they were doing to oooh and ahhh over their bald baby Jacqueline, only four months old. Jake and Andy looked like their dad. But Drew was the spitting image of his mother. Brown eyes and darker features than his brothers. He shook my hand briskly. "Clara, you know I must have really wanted to meet you, to come all the way up here during tax season." He laughed and patted my arm. I expressed my appreciation for his sacrifice.

The Smiths had a screened-in back porch straight from a Southern Living magazine. A massive table was set with china and plaid cloth napkins. Glasses of ice water complete with the little lemon wedges were at every place. I thought this only happened in movies. But I was wrong. There were real families who lived this way. Real patriarchs who wear expensive polo shirts and grill steaks in the backyard. Real matriarchs who do meal planning and still manage to look like they just walked out of a salon. There were real adult kids who seemed to be happy coming home to visit the folks. No adult kids living in their basement, addicted to video games. No one in prison or rehab. Everyone gathered around a pristine table to hold hands and share a pristine prayer. I thought it was a glimpse of heaven. And it was. Until it wasn't.

Jake's mom led the way. "Clara, tell us all about yourself. Jake said you teach Kindergarteners. What a wonderful and fulfilling job."

"Yes, ma'am. I do love it. I've been teaching for eight years."

"And you're still not tired of kids? That's remarkable. Emily, Julie, and Beth are around their kids all day and I know it can become a struggle for these young moms to stay cheery." She smiled and patted Julie's hand. "I guess you see that we're getting another precious grandbaby in June? We're all so excited."

"Yes, ma'am. That's wonderful. Julie, do you know if it's a boy or a girl yet?"

"We don't. And I'm not really sure if I want to know. We're going back and forth. The biggest struggle I'm having right now is with gestational diabetes. I've never had it and this time I do. I'm a little worried about my health and the health of the baby."

Jake's mom was clearly not at peace with the word "worry" being spoken at her dinner table. She patted Julie's hand again. "Julie, quit fretting now. You'll be fine, I'm sure. And the new little Smith will be fine too. The Smiths are sturdy stock. Don't you worry. Clara, I take it you like babies, yes?"

"Yes, ma'am. Babies are a blessing."

"Well, I know you're getting up in age, but not to worry. Now women are having babies in their 40's even. Lord, in my day, that would have been a fright."

Mr. Smith chimed in. "Seems like yesterday our four were under feet and now they're all off and on their own. One day you just look up and they're sittin' around the table with their own families. A blessing though. A fine blessing."

I was in awe. I quietly said, "Yes, sir."

Jake's mom patted his dad's hand. "I know this much. I will never forget the moment I held each one for the first time. It was this all-encompassing unconditional love, Clara. Four times. But all four times it was the same. This feeling that I would die for this child, gladly give my life for his, that I would do whatever it took to ensure his happiness or safety. I hope that someday you get the chance to know that feeling. It's priceless."

I don't know what came over me. Was it God or Satan? I have no idea nor will I even speculate. Maybe it was my renewed desire to live free. Honest. I looked at Jake's Mom and said with a smile, "Actually, I have known that feeling, Mrs. Smith. The feeling of holding my baby and experiencing that rush of unconditional love."

Jake looked at me like he'd just gotten called to the principal's office for something he didn't do. And he winced like he was getting ready to rat out his best friend.

Jake's mom let go of Julie's arm. "What ever do you mean, Clara? Jake told us you've never been married."

"No ma'am. I haven't been married. But I did have a baby once and I understand those feelings you're talking about. I was almost seventeen, and yes, that overwhelming love? It's exactly like you described. I would have done anything for him, still would today."

Absolute silence doesn't usually make a noise. But it did that day. No one spoke a word. But in my mind I could hear the loud rush of disappointment flooding the room. Sure, everyone was still eating their steaks or drinking their lemon water. But a bomb had hit that pristine Southern Living table. And though the Smiths are of sturdy stock, they couldn't endure the impact.

Jake's mom took a big drink of water and cleared her throat. "Where is your son now?"

"He's with his family in Louisiana. I placed him for adoption. My cousin was in college at LSU. She knew a wonderful couple from her church that had been praying for a baby for years. I got to meet them and everything. I trusted them. Still do."

Mrs. Smith pretended to be cutting her steak. Her nose wrinkled as though there were a foul smell. "And you haven't seen him? In all these years?"

"No ma'am. I gave them their privacy. I wanted him to have a regular life with a regular family."

She looked up as though a train were coming and she was glued to the tracks unable to move. "And the father was okay with that? He just signed over his rights as well? He was fine with giving away his own flesh and blood?"

"No ma'am. I declared the father unknown. And I didn't give my baby away either. I didn't just hand him to someone on the street. I made a plan, a plan that was for his good."

Jake bowed his head, rubbed his eyes slightly, and put his napkin by his plate. He glanced at me like he was trying to tell me to end the conversation. But truthfully, the whole conversation felt freeing. Like for the first time in my life, fear was being conquered and truth was winning. Besides, he had already said his family wasn't going to decide for him. He wasn't seventeen and they weren't going to take away his car for dating a formerly promiscuous woman. He was a grown-up. He made his own decisions. And all of this happened fifteen years ago anyway. I had changed. We'd all changed. No mature adult would fault a 32-year-old woman for the actions of a teenager…or a teenager's immoral neighbor.

Mrs. Smith stopped eating. "Unknown father? What does that even mean?"

"It means I didn't know who his biological father was. I still don't."

Jake spoke up while his face turned beet red. "Hey, Mom, let's change the subject, okay?" He took a long deep breath. "This whole thing happened a long time ago. Clara is our guest and we don't want her to be uncomfortable. She doesn't even know the family yet. So let's give the baby conversation a rest, huh?"

His brothers and sisters-in-law looked at me and nodded in supportive agreement.

"Honey, nobody's trying to make Clara feel uncomfortable. Least of all me. Clearly, she's very open about her…well, her situation." She looked directly at Jake as though she were now scolding him without making it sound like a scolding. "And we all know why she's here today. I mean, you wanted us to meet her so you must like her. And you want us to like her too, right? We can't like someone we don't even know. We're just trying to get to know her."

His dad rose from the table and said pleasantly, "I'm stuffed! Who has room for another steak or potato? We've got plenty. And it's homemade ice cream for dessert out on the deck. Who wants to help with the setup?"

The kids jumped up and ran outside. Julie and Emily joined them. Jake's dad grabbed a few plates and patted his mom on the shoulder. “A great meal, Barbara. I love the way you did that asparagus. Delicious.”

Okay. What was happening here? And how was it happening in a perfect family? Was this some kind of alternate universe? Surely any minute now the furniture would start spinning and I would realize it was all just a dream.

I had just shared a dark and painful secret. I was hoping for compassion and support. I expected them to respond the way Jake had responded. But Jake’s mom was openly expressing her displeasure with my past and what she probably believed was my present. But that wasn’t even the oddest part. At least she was communicating.

The oddest part was the rest of the family’s reaction. They were doing regular stuff. His dad was talking about asparagus. The young women were walking outside to watch the kids. Drew stood up to go turn on a ballgame in the living room. It was like we were talking about the weather or something. I knew my family avoided emotions at all cost. But this family? I thought they would have rallied around me. I expected a litany of “That must have been such a tough decision, Clara.” “Bless your heart. I’m sure he was beautiful.” But, no. A lack of perfection had somehow crept into the Smith’s family dinner party. And it would quietly be escorted out.

Jake stood and walked over to plant a kiss on his mama’s cheek. “That was good, Mama.” He turned toward me and said, “Hey, Clara, let’s go out on the deck and help Dad with the ice cream. Mama, I hope you’ve got chocolate syrup.”

“Sure do. And some of that caramel too. I’ll get the bowls.”

My steak was less than half eaten. I never even touched the potato. I noticed the sisters-in-law hadn't eaten either. I couldn't help but wonder if the stress was unbearable for them. Did they just sit and go through the motions every time? Did they keep their real lives bottled up so they'd never be on the receiving end of her scorn or disappointment? I had a feeling I'd never know. That I didn't even want to know.

We stayed at their home for two more hours. A few games of cards. Yard darts. Boy scout stories and bad school pictures. Justin cried when he burned his hand on the grill. Jake's mom wrapped it in ointment all the while telling him that good little boys do what they're told and don't touch things they're not supposed to touch.

That was it. Little Justin and I had the same problem. I hadn't been good. At all. And she would have none of it. They all pretended the table scene had never happened. Jake's new girlfriend surely didn't blurt something out about her shameful past or the fifteen-year-old son who lives in Louisiana. But I knew. I knew it was all still there, just bubbling beneath the surface.

At 3:30, we stood in the front yard and waved our good-byes. I had no idea what was going to transpire in the car. At first, there was silence. And then more silence. I'm not a good communicator usually. If someone depends on me for leadership in verbal communication, well, they must be pretty bad off.

"Jake, I'm sorry. I don't know what came over me. I think I've just been so broken and so hidden all these years. I thought I was on this new plan of sharing the truth. And I crossed the line. Clearly, I crossed the line. And I'm sorry. I didn't know your mom would react like that, but I'm sure I just surprised her and it's my fault. I'm just glad you said they're not making decisions for you…cause I'm sure your mama's gonna tell you to run." I laughed nervously while I scanned his face for information. "She'll probably tell you to run and never look back. But you won't, right? You said that you weren't going anywhere."

Jake didn't look happy or sad. He just kept looking straight ahead. "Don't worry about it, Clara. They'll get over it."

But they wouldn't. I knew it and Jake knew it. That's when I knew his family was a lot like mine. Bruised and broken. The difference? They were all "perfect" enough to cover it up. You could look at my parents' faces and see their sadness. You could look at their house and see the hopelessness. But not at the Smiths' house. No. Everyone was clean and beautiful. But it was never enough. Emily had embarrassed them terribly with her lack of a college education. Little Justin disappointed them because he wasn't mature enough to give up his pacifier. Julie wasn't strong enough to face her fears about the pregnancy. All of these were tragedies…until now. Now their precious baby, Jake, had brought home a woman who had given birth to a baby. And she didn't even know who the daddy was. Emily, you can thank me later. With one fatal swoop, I made you and your lack of education look a whole lot better.

Chapter 38 CARLIE: Love On the Run

Monday morning

Doug has to wear a suit and tie today because lots of bank people are gatherin' in Martin for some kind of regional highfalutin bank meeting. Doug looks good in a suit. More than good. Ridiculously good. In fact, I'm not sure he should be walking around Sharon and Martin in a suit because women are going to physically chase him or pull up to him in their cars and roll down the windows and say silly things like, "You're SO cute. Are you married?" And then he's gonna say, "Heck yeah, I'm married. And she's the greatest too, so back off." And then they're gonna feel all sad and downtrodden and discouraged. And I'm not the kind of woman who wants to inflict that kind of pain on single women. Seriously. (I know. Doug doesn't really talk like that, but still.)

Usually Doug and I have at least 30 minutes of coffee time in the morning. But not today. We overslept and he has to be in Martin by 7:30. So I made a "to go" cup and threw a granola bar and a banana in a big Ziploc bag and sent him on his merry way, praying he wouldn't unknowingly inflict emotional pain on the women of Sharon or the surrounding area.

At 9:00, I realized something was wrong with Clara. She never sleeps this late. She came home before supper last night and didn't want to spill the beans either. She suggested we watch a movie so she could rest her mind. Rest her mind? I don't think so. She's avoiding something. I also haven't heard from Aunt Charlotte this morning about Dusty's situation. Get with it, people. I need to stay informed.

I decided to make a lot of kitchen noise so as to wake Clara gently. I dropped a non-stick frying pan on the stove top. I hit a metal bowl with a big whisk. Right before I was gonna drop the muffin pans on the floor, she came walking out of the guest room wearing gray sweats and a red Georgia t-shirt. I knew she was glad to see me so I rang out with my cheeriest of greetings. “Good morning, Sunshine.”

“Are you building a skyscraper in here? Why so much noise?”

“Uh, no. Just the regular stuff. Thought I’d make us some whomp biscuits. Have a seat and I’ll get your coffee.”

“Carlie, look, I’m not staying until Wednesday. I’m leaving this morning. You and Doug need your privacy and I need to get back home anyway.”

“What? What are you talking about? We have plenty of privacy. You’ve spent most of the time with Jake. You haven’t been in our way. And speaking of Jake, what’s goin’ on? There’s somethin’ you’re not sayin’.”

She rubbed her tired-looking eyes and took a big gulp of coffee. “I don’t think it’s gonna work, Carlie. I’m sorry. I tried. He tried. It’s just not a match. We come from two different worlds and it’s not fair to either of us. And it doesn’t help that I messed it up pretty badly with his family yesterday.”

“How did you mess it up? You don’t tend to mess stuff up, Clara.”

“Oh, I did this time. You won’t believe it. I told them about the baby, the men, the adoption. Big massive mistake. They’re like this perfect everybody-do-right family and I embarrassed myself and Jake. I don't think he'll get over it. And I'm not sure he even should. I have not gotten one text, call, or e-mail since he dropped me off at 4:30 yesterday afternoon. When we left his parents' house, it was early. I figured we'd go do something fun. He said he needed to drop me off early and get back to his apartment. He needed to rest up for the big work week."

I didn't like where this was going. "Rest up? He's an insurance salesman, not a bear wrestler. That's ridiculous. What was that big declaration Saturday night about staying with you and not walking out? That's it. I'm gonna call him right now and get this straightened out."

"Don't you dare! Look, I appreciate your help but I've decided. I'm not ready for a relationship. All of this stuff with Jake just proves that. Let's go back to the way things were. You be happily married. And I'll be lonely and content. Deal?"

"No. Not a deal. Not a deal at all."

Clara put her coffee cup gently in the sink. She didn't even drink half of it. She reached for my hand and looked out the kitchen window above the sink. "Look, the buttercups are starting to bloom." Her eyes were filled with sadness as she turned to face me. "You won't change my mind, Carlie. I've already got my stuff packed. I'm going to take a shower and be on my way. I love you. I do. If you love me, let me have some time to get this worked out. Give Jake some time, okay?"

I hate it when people ask for time to get something "worked out." Let's say a busy mom gets asked to be the president of the Parent Teacher Association. What's the first thing she says? Give me some time to get it worked out. I don't buy it.

"Give me some time." is code language for, "Not on your life. I'd rather be covered in molasses and thrown on an ant bed."

But Clara is a big girl, even though she has a tiny rear end, and I have to respect her boundaries. Or at least look like I am. The minute I heard the shower running, I called Aunt Charlotte.

"Aunt Charlotte, it's all gone to pot over here. Something's not right with Jake and Clara. She's going home this morning. I know. I agree. Well, yeah, come over as soon as you can. I don't know how much longer we've got."

In less than 30 minutes, Clara strolled out of the bedroom rolling her little black suitcase which was probably perfectly organized with all the socks rolled up in one section and the clothes meticulously folded. She had on very little make-up and her hair was still damp and in a pony tail. Old jeans and a purple t-shirt that said "Commerce Elementary ROCKS!" In the background of the t-shirt was a graphic of a young kid with an electric guitar and two huge speakers. I don't know. Sometimes I think we'd be better off going back to one-room school days when schools didn't have t-shirts or fancy computers or mandatory guidance classes about hygiene. I mean, people fell in love and got married long before mandatory hygiene classes were invented. And those folks stayed married too. Maybe that's the problem with relationships now. Everyone is too darn clean.

It was the first time since Charlene's make-over that it almost seemed she was regressing to the old Clara. Or maybe she was just in travel mode. She wouldn't see anyone she knew and I guess the "not pulled together" look was excusable.

"Clara, you can't leave right now. You have to wait for Aunt Charlotte. She has a gift for you. She's on her way."

"A gift?"

"Yeah. I'm not sure what it is, but one thing I can promise. It'll be interesting. And it probably won't be new. So just smile and act happy. That's what we always do."

Aunt Charlotte burst through the creaking kitchen door carrying a gray plastic Sears bag so loaded down that part of its contents poked through the bottom of the bag. She was grasping the bottom and talkin' a mile a minute. "Mornin', Girls! Mornin'. What's this I hear about you leaving, Clara Louise Johnson?"

"Yes, ma'am. I'm heading back to Commerce."

"Well, I sure hate that. I was hopin' I could show you how to make them pickles Carlie and I are becomin' so famous for makin'. Ever body who's eaten one says it's the best pickle they ever ate. Chester even wants to financially invest in our company. But he only had a five-dollar bill so I told 'em not to bother."

"Oh, I appreciate it, Mrs. Charlotte. But no, I better be on my way. Thanks a lot. Maybe next time."

"Well, that's a shame seein' as how I brought the cucumbers and the jars and ever'thing."

Aunt Charlotte looked nervous. She should be nervous. Pickle makin'? That was her brilliant idea to lure Clara into staying long enough for us to knock some sense into Jake Smith? She felt like pickle makin' was gonna seal that deal? Oh, Aunt Charlotte. This one's got Kaboom written all over it.

Clara spoke with quiet confidence, but I could see the pain written in her eyes. "It's been a pleasure, Ladies. Come to Georgia and see me."

Aunt Charlotte and I looked at each other with despair. We had failed at our mission to keep Clara in Tennessee. We hugged her and told her to come back soon. She drove away while we stood on the porch waving.

Then Aunt Charlotte raced into the house like the porch was on fire. She quickly called Debbie to get Jake Smith's phone number. I thought we should let sleeping dogs lie. But Aunt Charlotte felt like the hound needed to be poked with a big stick.

In a matter of minutes, I heard Aunt Charlotte's loud pseudo-professional voice. "Hi, Jake, this is Charlotte Nelson. How are you today, Hon? Yes. Yes, I agree. Life insurance is a good investment. But baby, I'm calling today about a personal matter. Carlie and I don't know what happened 'tween you and that lil' Clara Johnson. But she's high-tailing it back to Georgia right now and we figure, well, we figure you might not want that to happen. Yes. Yes, I'll get off the phone and let you take care of that. I will. Come see us in Sharon sometime, Honey. Bye." A look of satisfaction rested comfortably on Aunt Charlotte's chubby face. "Carlie! He's gonna call 'er right now. Yes, sirree. We done good. Real good."

Chapter 39 CLARA LOUISE: Don't Wimp Out at Wimpy's

Everybody says the road to I-40 is one big speed trap and I don't need a ticket especially considering what I've been spending on gas lately. But no more. No more trips. No more wandering aimlessly. I'm staying home for a while.

The phone reminded me that Carlie wouldn't let me go so easily. I expected as much. But when I scanned the screen, I saw Jake's number. He must be planning his farewell speech.

"Hello."

"Clara, what are you doing? Are you really on the road back home?"

"I am."

"Well, don't be. Listen, I've had some time to think about the way yesterday went. And I'm sorry. I'm sorry about what Mom said but I'm even more sorry about what I didn't say. I want you to give me another chance, Clara. Don't just blow out of town. Where are you?"

"I'm almost to Greenfield."

"If you're willing to stop, stop and I'll come to you. How 'bout that?"

"I guess that'd be okay. There's a hamburger place on the left. Is it too early for lunch for you? How about just meeting me there? It's called Wimpy's."

"Yeah, I know Wimpy's. That's fine. I'll explain to my boss and be there as soon as I can. Should make it by 11:30."

"I'll be waiting. Bye."

Doug and Carlie had told me about Wimpy's. It was best known for a giant burger. But I wasn't hungry at all. I felt like I'd never be hungry again. The wait staff was so friendly and an older woman told me to sit wherever I liked. I chose a booth that was kind of hidden. A young woman with blonde braids brought me a glass of water and I told her I would wait for my friend before ordering.

I sat in the booth for more than 45 minutes, long enough for the staff to feel sorry for me. Finally, they stopped asking if I wanted more water or an appetizer. They wanted to save me the embarrassment. At 12:00, I wanted to get up and leave but I didn't. I knew I owed Jake an explanation. He wasn't ignoring me. Something had just delayed him. I observed the townspeople as I waited. Friendly talk of weather and crop planting. An old bald man in a wheelchair was flirting with a friendly old woman in the other booth and I found it pleasantly amusing. The door opened and I prayed it would be Jake. But it wasn't Jake. Shock and an odd sense of happiness.

Dusty McConnell stepped through the door, took off his cap, and ran his fingers through his hair. He spoke pleasantly to the older woman at the counter, "Mornin' Ms. Jessie. Is my order ready?"

"Not yet, Dusty. Give me a few minutes. Here's your drinks."

"No rush. Those fellas need to keep workin' anyway." He laughed and sat on a stool with his back toward me. He sipped on a big drink and asked the petite older woman next to him if she ordered the giant burger. She patted his arm and said, "Not today, Hon. Not today." He wore faded blue jeans and a green t-shirt that said, "Farmers feed the world." No disagreement from me.

One might think I had a decision to make. Would I go over and speak to Dusty? Or would I sit quietly hoping he wouldn't notice me? But I didn't even have to think about it. I would remain deathly quiet. Dusty McConnell was going to appear before a judge on drug charges. Dusty McConnell couldn't even leave the state of Tennessee. Besides I was waiting for my insurance agent who already knew all my ugly secrets but liked me anyway. No, I wouldn't approach Dusty. I would sit still and pretend we'd never even met. I wanted to look away but I couldn't. From the first time I met him, he fascinated me. He was good-looking and his voice was pleasant. It's like he could be an emcee or something. But there was something more. A kindness in the way he spoke to people.

I watched him bend the bill of his cap back and forth while he watched the news on TV. Ms. Jessie shook her head, "Dusty, the world's going to hell in a hand basket." He laughed, "Well, not the whole world. I'd say our corner of it's still pretty good, Ms. Jessie. And I, for one, don't plan on spending any time in hell. Somebody paid my way."

"You're right, Honey. You're right." She smiled and handed him a big bag. "I put extra napkins in there. And a cookie for each of ya. On the house."

"Thanks, and tell Jerry thanks for cookin' it too. Have a good day!" I felt a wave of incredible sadness as Dusty McConnell rose from the creaky stool and headed toward the front door. He wasn't a hardened criminal. At all. He was the opposite. He was scarred, but unlike me, he had recovered. He wasn't hiding from people. He was kind and considerate and full of life. Humble and hard working.

Jake walked in and waved at me from the door. For some reason, a reason I'll never understand, Dusty McConnell's head turned slightly and then he jerked. Jake walked quickly to the table and Dusty just stood there staring at me. He nodded his head slightly. He didn't touch the door or sit back down. He just stood there holding a food bag and a drink carrier. It was like the day he stood next to my car. Waiting. Observing. Jake sat across from me and immediately apologized for the tardiness but my eyes were still looking at the front door.

Jake fumbled with his keys. He was clearly frustrated. Was he frustrated with me or with his work? He spoke as though he were in a terrible hurry. "Mr. Jones wanted us to stay for a conference call with corporate. I couldn't tell him no or my name would be mud."

I reassured him, "It's fine. Really."

I saw Dusty moving toward the table and I felt sadness and joy. I couldn't explain it. Jake looked ridiculously handsome in a white shirt, silver tie, and dark blue pants. Dusty looked like a mechanic who had removed his coveralls because it was a pleasantly warm day and he was coming to pick up lunch at Wimpy's. How was any of this to be explained? Only one absolute truth lingered in the air. Farmers feed the world. On that much we all could agree.

Jake was talking endlessly about work and his many obligations when he noticed Dusty standing at the booth. He paused and said, "Can we help you?"

He put out his hand, "I'm Dusty McConnell. I'm friends with Clara here." He looked straight at me. For the first time, I noticed the color of his eye. It was a beautiful bright blue like those pictures I'd always seen of Caribbean waters. It didn't match his dark skin and hair at all. He set the drink carrier on our table and held the paper bag in his right hand. He put his left hand in his pocket nervously. "Clara, it's good to see you again. How's the car runnin'? Any problems?"

"No, it's doing well. Real well. This is my friend, Jake Smith." Jake looked at me and cringed. I wondered if it was that word "friend." "He sells insurance in Union City. Dusty fixed my car when I broke down one time on the way home from Carlie's. He's a mechanic in Bradford."

"Nice to meet ya, Jake."

"You too, Dusty."

Dusty picked up the drink carrier and looked straight at me. "How are you, Clara? Are you doin' okay?"

"Pretty well. Yeah. No complaints really."

His voice got quieter and he looked at the floor and shuffled his feet a bit. "Well, that's good. That's real good."

I noticed his tan work boots were severely worn. The laces were matted and covered in dirt and oil. There was something about how the jeans and the boots came together to produce a wave of attraction. Jake worked hard every day. He labored and I respected his labor. I glanced across the table. Jake was scanning the menu and ignoring both of us.

I didn't want Dusty to walk away. He started to turn from the table but I spoke in a desperate effort to stop him. "And what about you, Dusty? Are you doing okay?"

He quickly placed the bag and the drink carrier on the table and put both hands in his pockets while he glanced out the window and then straight at me. He shook his head and spoke matter-of-factly, "Truthfully, not so good, Clara. Not so good. I mean, business is fine. Yeah, lots of business right now." He paused and looked at Jake for a good long time and then at me. "It's my personal life that's been a disappointment lately."

I couldn't help but smile uncomfortably. "Is that right?"

"It is. Sadly, it is." He smiled and stared right at my face. There was a gentleness there. The kind of gentleness that only comes to one who's lived hard but then been pardoned. I don't know. Refreshing.

Jake chimed in, "I hate to interrupt but I'm kind of on a time crunch right now. Dusty, it was good to meet you."

Dusty smiled like he knew something was happening between us. "Oh, well, yeah, I'll let you guys get back to what you were doin'. Clara, it was good to see ya again. Be safe. Jake, keep sellin' that insurance."

He walked out the door and never looked back.

Jake continued talking, never missing a beat. "Okay, about yesterday, I'm sorry about Mom. But I'm even more sorry that I didn't do anything about it. I am." I must have been looking into space. "Clara? Clara, did you hear me?"

"Uh, yeah. Your mom. You were talking about your mom. Don't worry about it, Jake. What could you do? It was my fault. I shouldn't have spilled the beans. Not on the first meeting. I don't know what got into me. Really."

"Yeah, that's okay." He reached out for my hand. "Look, Clara, it's been a long time since all that bad stuff happened to you. You're not a teenager anymore. Why don't you try to put that all behind you and make a new life now?"

Under normal circumstances, I wouldn't say that was bad advice. I might even say it was good advice. Kind of. But I got a gnawing feeling that Jake was just trying to smooth over his personal trouble. He needed to fix me. His mother would never tolerate someone who was broken and he needed to super glue me together. And quickly.

"I'm all for the new life part. I am. I'm trying to make a new life. But I'll never forget what happened and I'm not even sure I should." I saw the young blonde waitress heading for the table so I quickly spoke. "Maybe there's a way my story could help others. I mean, maybe if I weren't so timid about it, I could help other women who've been through the same thing, or help girls who are going through it right now."

Jake's countenance fell as the young woman asked, "What can I get you two?"

"Clara, what do you want?"

"I'll just take a Coke. I'm not really hungry."

"I'll take a Coke and a burger and fries to go."

To go? Jake drove to Greenfield to settle the deal, make it all okay. But he didn't have time to see what I needed to settle.

"Jake, do you have to get right back?"

"Yeah. Mondays have been busy lately and daylight is a'wastin'. I thought you were staying 'till Wednesday. Thought I might convince you to go back to Carlie's."

"Well, thanks, but really, I need to get back home. I've been on the road too much lately and I'm tired." I looked down at the table because I couldn't face him. "I'm going to ask you something, Jake, and I don't want you to be afraid to tell the truth. I've lived the last fifteen years of my life under a rock. I have. I wore no make-up, didn't care about my clothes, all in an effort to keep men away. And it worked too. It worked until I saw my roommate fall in love." I folded the cheap paper napkin over and over again. "Something about watching that process changed my perspective. It changed me. I started having hope. Carlie taught me to not be afraid of being a woman. She even convinced me not to fear attention from men. I know you don't understand it, but that's what I was doing. I lived in constant fear." I looked up and tried to smile. "But no more, Jake. I'm serious. I've decided to live honestly. And I want to know that my honesty isn't going to be a problem. For you or for your family. If it is, well, we need to part ways."

"No problem, Clara. So, will you stay? Till Wednesday at least?"

"I guess." I'm not sure why I decided to stay. Part of me dreaded spending a week alone in my dreary apartment. Another part of me wondered if I needed to give Jake more time, more time to accept me, more time to get to know me. All the while wondering if he could someday even love me. All of me.

I drove into Doug and Carlie's drive and laughed out loud when I saw Carlie and Ms. Charlotte on the front porch. They were jumping up and down and dancing and flinging their arms in the air in celebration of my arrival. I felt loved. And that was the gift I needed.

I opened the door and Ms. Charlotte yelled out, "Welcome back, Baby! Welcome back!"

I think it was the first time I'd ever been given a "Welcome Back, Baby" party. We all knew there was only one way to handle it. Make pickles.

Chapter 40 CARLIE Three Days Later: Here Comes the Judge

Clara went home yesterday. She said the time with Jake had been fine, but I didn't buy it. She didn't seem like a woman in love. He didn't seem like a man smitten anymore either. Something had happened. Something she wasn't willing to talk about. But something I knew I would drag out of her eventually.

I sent my publishers a completed transcript. "Country Girls Can Survive if They Stock Pile Peanut Butter" should be on the shelves by mid-fall. The fall would bring a few book signing trips and maybe even another trip to Hollywood.

Dave called to tell me that Doug's cousin, Shannon, had slipped into a dark place emotionally. A few times he got quiet on the phone. He loved Shannon deeply and none of his love could erase this terrible pain. The more they tried to have a baby, the more bad news they received. They were now researching adoption but the thought of starting a whole new journey seemed overwhelming. I thought about the boy Clara gave birth to many years ago. What was he like? What were his parents like? Did she ever hope to meet him? Had she ever thought of making contact? I prayed a simple prayer: "Lord, please find a baby for Dave and Shannon. And please heal Clara's heart."

Aunt Charlotte was still working feverishly on the Dusty McConnell "We don't believe he did it" cocaine mystery, but time was running out as he was scheduled to appear before Judge Richards in the morning at nine. Raymond said the boys in the white truck turned up clean, at least for now. Something about that didn't sound right though.

Not that I would know. I admit I'm not the most experienced person when it comes to felonious drug activity. I still remember the day Tim Perkins walked into Geometry class bragging about the "special brownies" at his Friday night party. I asked a simple question. "What made them so special?" He replied, "You know? Weed." I told him I'd never heard of putting weeds in brownies but I thought walnuts or marshmallows were always a nice touch. The whole class laughed. It took Janice Carpenter twenty minutes to explain it to me at lunch. Tim and his friends called me "Naïve Nellie" the rest of our junior year. Mama said I should wear it as a badge of honor.

Next morning 8:45 am Court House

Doug had several appointments at the bank and couldn't get away. Aunt Charlotte and Uncle Bart gladly accompanied me. Aunt Charlotte wore her best dress which was a bright green double-knit number with big fake pearl buttons down the front and a wide black plastic belt which could barely perform its job duties despite control top pantyhose which she swore were cutting her in half. Uncle Bart wore black dress pants that were a tad too short and a white shirt with every button fastened. Was I embarrassed? No. I'm not an 8th grade girl trying to get the "cool kids" to like me. I'm a grown-up.

Dusty McConnell's face looked unusually pale but he smiled when he saw us walking down the corridor in front of the court room. He was wearing khaki pants and a light blue oxford shirt with a navy blazer and some fancy brown cowboy boots. As the barber shop men would say, "He cleans up good." For just an instant, I wished he were Clara's boyfriend. I don't know why exactly. Maybe I was remembering him sitting on our couch talking about how Clara couldn't put an alternator in a car, and how she respected the fact that he could. As a matchmaker, how could I not be moved by his desire to be respected, and loved?

Aunt Charlotte hugged him and wiped a tear from her eye. "How you doin', Dusty? You okay this mornin'?"

"I've been better, Mrs. Charlotte. My lawyer wants me to plead guilty. Says I'll get less time that way, that maybe I'd be out in less than a year."

Aunt Charlotte grabbed him by the arms. "Absolutely not! Dusty, were those drugs yours?"

"No ma'am."

"Then why in tarnation would you stand right there before a judge and tell him you were guilty? Good night, Baby. That's straight-out lying. I didn't graduate high school and even I know that much."

Dusty smiled and spoke nervously. "I wish it worked that way, Mrs. Charlotte. I do. I don't know how the drugs got in my truck, but no one else seems to know either. And that's a problem. A big problem."

A tall, thin, older lady with stacked gray hair and a carved wooden cane approached me and said, "Excuse me. Can you tell me how much time you figure I'd get for an arson charge, if it's my own house and I just need the insurance money?"

"Uh, I'm sorry, Ma'am. I'm not a lawyer."

Her nose wrinkled and she said with disdain, "Well, then why the heck would you come to the court house dressed up like a lawyer?"

I placed my hand on her back gently. "I'm sorry, Ma'am. Didn't mean to cause any confusion." She unhappily turned and limped away. That's when I knew my choice of black dress pants, and a red power blazer had been the right one. The black and white polka dot scarf must have just sealed the deal.

I hugged Dusty. There was that odd but pleasant pine tree scent again. I wondered if it was some kind of mechanic hand soap or something. I told him Doug regretted not being there. "We're for you, Dusty. We are."

His lawyer approached us and said, "It's time to go in, Dusty."

He turned to follow his lawyer. Looking back he tried to force a smile, "I know, Carlie. And thank you. Thank you all."

I'm deathly afraid of court rooms for the same reason I was afraid of the principal's office growing up. I don't like to be in trouble and I don't like to see anyone else in trouble either. I'm also keenly aware of the fact that judges, like principals, can make mistakes. Oh, not on purpose. No. They can make mistakes because they're human. Like the time Tommy Carithers had to stay after school for a whole week for starting a food fight in the middle school cafeteria. Only Tommy didn't start the food fight. Bill Meyers threw the first ketchup-covered hamburger bun. It hit shy Katie Johnson on her left cheek and she got ketchup in her eye lashes too. I know. I was there. But when Tommy, in an act of naive chivalry, pelted Bill with tater tots, one of the tots hit him in the eye and he cried out in agony like a Shakespearean actor. His dramatic ability convinced Mrs. Morrison that he had severe cornea damage. In middle school, ketchup on your eyelashes will never compete with a term like "cornea damage." Tommy served his detention time like a true martyr. Five years later he married Katie Johnson and they have three kids who raise sheep for the 4-H.

Uncle Bart led us to the front of the court room. I saw several law enforcement officers and lots of community people in the room. I wanted to believe people were there to support the ones being charged or the ones who had been victimized. But I knew some of them were there for sport. Like gladiator days, without the blood.

"All rise. The honorable Archibald Richards presiding."

I sighed with sweet relief. The judge was short and round and I felt confident a bald man named Archibald would be a man of mercy, after the playground bullying he must have survived. Thank you, Lord, for small favors.

The judge and the lawyers said a bunch of legal stuff I didn't understand about a young woman who was charged with drug possession. It only took fifteen minutes for the judge to sentence her to probation and community service because she didn't have a rap sheet. They didn't use the term "rap sheet." I got that from TV.

When the bailiff called Dusty's name, my stomach started churning. Dusty did have a rap sheet and everyone in the court room knew it.

The judge addressed him directly, "Mr. McConnell, you understand that a drug possession conviction is a violation of your probation, not just a violation of probation, but a serious crime."

"Yes, sir."

"What do you plead?"

“Not guilty.”

His lawyer looked like a major league pitcher who’d been hit with a line drive. He straightened his tie and looked through some papers. “Your honor, may we have a minute? Just one minute?”

“Mr. Ray, are you saying you and your client haven’t consulted before now? This is not the time for a consult.”

“No, sir. We’ve consulted. Evidently my client has changed his mind and we need to confer for one moment. Just a moment, sir. I know your time is valuable.”

“You have two minutes.”

Dusty and his lawyer were trying to whisper but we were close enough to hear the heated exchange. I prayed right then and there that Aunt Charlotte would not be responsible for Dusty McConnell’s extended sentence. Aunt Charlotte knew nothing about the law. Maybe his lawyer was right. Maybe it would be better to play it safe and do a little time rather than risking a longer sentence. But something didn’t seem right about that. At all.

Dusty rose and looked at the judge with confidence. Where he got that confidence, I had no idea. He looked just like Tommy when he decided to serve his term as a martyr for the cause. Resolved.

“Judge Richards, I’ll be representing myself today. I’m sorry for the delay.”

The attorney gathered his things and huffed out the back door of the courtroom.

“Mr. McConnell, in your particular situation, it would be highly advisable for you to have an attorney present. This is not your first criminal charge.”

“I’m aware of that, your Honor.”

“Well, then, let me get straight to the point. On January 31st, at 8:45 pm, Officer Timothy Cline stopped you for a minor traffic violation. Is that right?”

“Yes, sir. My tail light was out.”

“And?”

“Because I was on probation, the officer asked if he could search my vehicle. I told him it would be fine. I wasn’t worried. I knew he wouldn’t find anything.”

“But he did find something. Is that right?”

“Yes, sir. He found cocaine in the glove box.”

“Well, Mr. McConnell, that seems like an open-and-shut case then, yes?”

“It would be. Except it wasn’t mine. I don’t know whose cocaine it was or why they put it there. I have no idea. But I do know it wasn’t mine. I’ve done some bad things in my life, criminal things. I don’t have to tell you that, Judge Richards.” He bowed his head. “You remember.” He looked up again. “But I don’t do drugs. I own a business. I’m trying to get my life in order and I promise I had never seen that cocaine before that night, before Officer Cline removed it from the glove box. Truthfully, I planned to come into this courtroom today and lie. I’m embarrassed by that fact. That’s what my attorney wanted me to do. That's what I agreed to do. But I can't. I'm sworn to tell the truth. I wish I knew who planted that in my truck. I wish I knew why. But I don't."

The judge held up his hand while a young woman handed him some papers. He wrinkled his brow and even his bald head wrinkled slightly. Kind of like those wrinkly dogs on Hallmark cards. She said a few things. He said a few things. Even though Aunt Charlotte stood and leaned forward, she still couldn't hear what they said. I prayed the judge wouldn't hold her in contempt of court. I don't even know what contempt of court is really, but if anyone had the possibility of doing some jail time for court behavior, well, I think we all knew it was Aunt Charlotte.

"Mr. McConnell, it seems there's been an unusual turn in your case. There's someone here in the court room willing to testify on your behalf. The court calls Lucas McConnell to the stand."

The crowd made that loud sighing sound that would normally get them in a lot of trouble with the judge, but evidently the judge was distracted by the idea of a new witness. Aunt Charlotte patted me on the leg and whispered to Uncle Bart, "The Lord has done a miracle, Bart."

I looked at Dusty and saw him lower his head. He should have looked relieved. But he didn't. He looked tormented. A tired old man came dragging down the aisle. Dirty torn pants and an old army jacket. A weathered face covered by a red and gray beard. He wore a Cardinals ball cap that looked 50 years old.

"Mr. McConnell, you'll need to remove your cap."

I heard him mutter, “Yes, sir” as he removed the dirty cap and smoothed his hair, just like Dusty always did. Except Dusty’s daddy didn’t have on a blue blazer and brown cowboy boots. And I doubted he smelled like pine trees. If death took human form, it would look like Lucas McConnell. He sat in the provided chair near the front. They didn’t put him behind that little chamber gate like they do on big TV criminal cases. He just sat in a wooden chair between Dusty and the judge.

“Mr. McConnell, I’ve been informed that you’re here to provide a statement. Is that right?”

He spoke slowly and in low guttural sounds, “It is.”

“Do you know the origin of the cocaine that was found in Dusty McConnell’s truck on January 31st?”

“I do.”

“And what is that origin?”

“I stole it and put it there.”

“You’ll need to explain a little better than that, Mr. McConnell.”

“I stayed with Dusty for a few days in January.” He pointed to Dusty who was looking down at his paper and refusing to make eye contact with his father. “I hadn’t seen him in years.” His voice cracked and his hand swept quickly across his face. “I needed to tell ‘em somethin’, him being my son and all. Doc says I’m in bad health. Anyway, some boys was comin’ round next door a lot while he was at work. I knew they was dealin’. One day they left a package in a big hole behind the porch steps of the empty house. Covered the hole with a garbage can. I’m sure they thought nobody was around to see ‘em. But I saw ‘em. I needed money. I been livin’ in Louisville and I knew I could get a lot of money for whatever it was they was sellin’ and protectin’.”

“That doesn’t explain why the cocaine was in Dusty’s truck. If you planned to keep it and sell it, why did you put it in his truck?”

“Late that night, I got in the hole and got out that package. But there’d been a lot of police patrolin’ around and the only open door was on the front of Dusty’s house. I got scared. Dusty’s truck was parked behind the house. Figured I’d just get up early and get it out before Wally came to get me at sunup.”

“Wally?”

“Wally’s a guy I met at a pool hall in Jackson. I called him and told him I’d make it worth his while if he could get me back to Louisville. But Dusty must have gotten a wrecker call early that mornin’ ‘cause when Wally showed up, the truck was already gone. I didn’t know what to do. I wanted him to take me to Dusty’s shop so I could get the stuff. But a few miles down the road, Wally found out I didn’t have money, so he dumped me out on 54. I hitchhiked to my cousin’s house near Paris Landing. They got an old trailer out back behind their house. Been there ever since. Dryin’ out. Or damn near tryin’. A few weeks later, my cousin’s wife said she heard on the radio where Dusty had gotten in trouble with the law again. I knew what it was. But figured his lawyer would find a way for them boys to take the hit somehow.” He bowed his head and bent the bill of his cap back and forth. “Reckon not. When I heard the case was coming to trial, well…” Lucas McConnell’s voice cracked. He no longer represented death to me. He wasn’t alive and well, but he was alive. “Well, truth is, I ain’t done nothin’ right by this boy. Not one thang. But today I do. I'm tellin' the truth, Judge. You gotta believe me. Dusty ain't into drugs. He's a hard worker. A hard worker with a worthless daddy." He bowed his head further and said quietly, "And you can't fault a man for that."

The judge called for a recess and asked to confer with some law enforcement officers and the district attorney's representative in his chambers. We were to meet back in fifteen minutes.

Dusty walked over to where we were sitting. He didn't look at his father one time. Not once. His father remained in the wooden chair as though he planned to wait it out. I didn't know if it was relief or appreciation on Dusty's face. He spoke calmly to the three of us. "Maybe this'll finally be over, huh?"

Aunt Charlotte leapt to her feet and hugged him tightly. And when Aunt Charlotte hugs, it can nearly cut off your air supply. "Dusty, the Lord, the Lord done smiled on you, child. You told the truth and the Lord blessed it."

"Yes, Ma'am."

The judge walked back into the court room and we all remained deathly silent. Well, all of us except Uncle Bart who asked Aunt Charlotte if she still had Juicy Fruit in her purse and could she get him out two sticks. She loudly whispered, "Gosh darn it, Bart, you are a mess."

The judge looked resolved. The prosecuting attorney spoke loudly, "In light of this testimony, I make a motion that charges be dropped and that Dusty McConnell be released." The judge agreed and asked law enforcement to take Lucas McConnell into custody for further questioning.

Aunt Charlotte started clapping. The judge wrinkled his face and head again, "Order. Order in the court. We'll take a ten-minute break and then start with the next case."

I saw the relief wash across Dusty's face. Aunt Charlotte was right. This wasn't like the Tommy Carithers tater tot case at all. Truth had prevailed. But it wasn't over quite yet. Dusty's daddy was getting ready to be handcuffed by the bailiff when Dusty walked up and put his hand on Lucas McConnell's tired shoulder. "Thank you for coming today."

"You're a good boy, Dusty. A decent man. I'm sorry. I am." His voice cracked. The bailiff handcuffed him and led him away.

It was a banner day on the courthouse square in Dresden, Tennessee. Dusty McConnell was a free man. But that's not all. Uncle Bart sprang for pizza for all four of us at Pizza USA. It was a day of miracles.

Chapter 41 CLARA LOUISE: A Family Gone Bad

Every time I drove down Mom and Dad's street, I felt a twinge of nausea and depression. Things had gotten significantly worse. Dad was drinking more. Mom was spending more and more time at the neighbor's house. I told them I would bring dinner tonight in hopes of helping, helping them and helping me. I used to come only once a week. But I wanted to do better. Plus, I had this odd hope that we still had time to become a real family. Not the kind that uses plaid cloth napkins, but at least the kind who talk to each other.

I knocked and opened the back door. "Mom, Dad, I come bearing barbecue!" I knew Dad would be half asleep in the recliner. Mom was probably in the bedroom reading a romance novel. A familiar trail of broken green linoleum led me from the kitchen to the living room. Then life stopped. In one abrupt moment. At 6:34 pm on March 29th all my dreams of family ended. Dad's body was hunched over in the brown recliner, blood all over the newspaper. Mom's remains were lying almost peacefully on the green rug by the front door. A small amount of blood pooled by her head. I'm sure I jumped. I don't remember. I quickly ran to the neighbor's house screaming that we needed help. Mrs. Irene called 911 and she and I met the police and the ambulance in the driveway. But I knew the truth. No ambulance was needed. They were dead. Irene and I stood in the yard while neighbors we didn't know gathered on the street to gawk.

The police taped off the front door and two body bags were eventually removed through the back door of the tired little brown house on Mill Street. A policewoman sat with me on the front porch. She put her arm around me and with incredible kindness, she asked some questions. I answered them as best I could. Irene's nephew drove me to the morgue for identification and paper work. By that time, my tears were gone.

Doug and Carlie arrived at 5:00 am, knocking loudly on Mrs. Irene's door. I fell asleep on her couch but Mrs. Irene had kept watch all night, saying she couldn't sleep. I remember having an incredible headache. When Carlie grabbed me, my whole body melted into her arms. Doug patted my back and told me he understood. He was probably the only one who did. Both parents dead. The horror of being alone. But Doug had Aunt Charlotte and Uncle Bart and other family members who rallied. No one in my family was good at rallying. I didn't even know where most of my relatives lived.

Doug and Carlie put me in the backseat of their car and drove straight to my apartment. She insisted I drink a bottle of water and eat a cheese sandwich. She and Doug held my hands and prayed out loud for me while I wailed. Snot kept coming out my nose until finally my nose started bleeding. I laid back on the bed holding a wash cloth over my nose but the room was spinning. Carlie put on classical music, packed my bags, called my pastor, and did a load of laundry. Doug made coffee and called Jake. I could hear the kind diplomacy in his voice. "Jake, there's been a terrible tragedy and you might want to make plans to come to Georgia." He then called Commerce Elementary, explaining to Mr. Hobbs that I would need a few weeks off. We stayed at Carlie's parents' house for the next three nights. I checked out of life completely. Barely surviving. But Carlie agreed to live life for me, for a while. She made me eat and drink. She planned the funeral. She and Doug talked to police. Doug filled out reports and called distant relatives. But mostly, mostly they fended off the press. We didn't watch TV at all or even turn on the radio. Carlie's mom cooked for us and played Boston Pops CDs. I took sleeping pills every night, prescribed by Dr. Jacobs.

Finally, the day of the funeral arrived. It was a relief. Carlie laid out my clothes. Black pants and a tan jacket. She told me I must wear make-up as it would help me feel better. It was easier to just do what she said. The funeral home wasn't crowded at all. I knew it wouldn't be. Police had surrounded the place so that press wouldn't disturb us. I searched the room, curious that anyone had come at all. A few people Daddy worked with at the plant. A few neighbors. Carlie's parents. Mom's bowling team. My pastor and his family. The women from my Tuesday night Bible study. A few relatives from Birmingham. Mr. Hobbs and a group of teachers from my school.

Jake and his mom drove down in time for afternoon visitation the day before the funeral, but he had to get back for an important afternoon meeting so they left this morning at 5:00. I was horrified when he said his mother was coming. But she hugged me at visitation and swore up and down that she was there to support me during my "time of need." I think she was there to show Jake how very broken I am. It was the perfect opportunity. The perfect illustration of a family gone bad.

I sat next to the aisle on the front row. Carlie sat on the left of me. Doug sat to her left. Mom's sister and her husband came from Birmingham but said she didn't want to sit on the family row. I think she was embarrassed. Who can blame her? People would surely talk. Everyone in Commerce knew the truth by now.

My pastor did the best he could as he didn't even know my parents. He read scripture and talked about the blessing of my presence in his congregation. He finished with more scriptures of peace and comfort and a prayer for the healing of my heart. During the funeral, Carlie never let go of my hand. Doug had his arm around Carlie the whole time and would often squeeze her shoulder with love and affirmation. It was a passing down of the blessing. Doug loved and supported Carlie unconditionally. She turned around and loved and supported me during my time of need. The pastor's prayers for comfort had already been answered.

At the end of the funeral, our row stood and the funeral director asked the funeral goers to come up row by row to show their respect. The coffins were closed but each person paused at the front and then hugged me or shook my hand. Dad's boss handed me a hundred dollar bill folded up. Mrs. Irene wept so hard that Doug escorted her to the back and got a bottle of water for her from the kitchen. But me? My tears had been spent. I was now just going through the motions, waiting for the end. When the pastor called the last row, I was hardly looking up anymore. I leaned into Carlie and I heard her whisper, "Oh my gosh."

I had never seen him in anything other than jeans or the work coveralls. He had on khaki pants, a white shirt, a tan striped tie, and a navy jacket. It was the first time I had seen him without a cap or at least one in his hands. He kindly told Mom's bowling team they could go up first.

I couldn't concentrate. I took a drink from the water bottle. Mom's bowling comrades hugged me one by one and then Mrs. Eula handed me some cards from the kids at church, saying that everyone was praying for me. I could see Dusty waiting patiently behind Mrs. Eula. His face was red and he rubbed his lips together nervously. When it was his turn, I put my hand out and said, "Wow, you came a long way, Dusty. Thank you."

"No problem. I wanted to just tell you how sorry I am. I know about tragedies and about suffering." He lowered his head and spoke quietly, "It's like a nightmare and you think you'll never wake up." He raised his head and stared right into my eyes. “But you will wake up, Clara. Hard to believe now, but you will.”

I wiped a tear that came out of nowhere. “Well, thank you for that. I hope you’re right.” I didn’t know what else to say or how to say it. I had an overwhelming desire to hug him, to lay my head on his shoulder, and let him take care of me. But I couldn’t. I wouldn’t.

Carlie stepped up to the plate, unafraid as usual. “Dusty, you sure came a long way. Are you going to the cemetery?”

“I am.”

Carlie touched him on the arm. “We’ll see you there then. And we’ll make some plans for afterwards.”

He spoke briefly to Doug and then looked back at me and nodded. We walked to the parking lot and I saw his truck pulled into the funeral processional behind Mrs. Irene’s old Grand Marquis driven by her nephew.

Doug and Carlie and I rode in the hearse. Cars pulled over and stopped on the side of the road to show their respect. That’s what all southern small town people do, if they’ve had any kind of parenting whatsoever. When someone comes flying by a funeral procession, you know that’s it’s an out-of-towner or someone who just didn’t have much in the way of parenting.

Only about 25 people drove to the cemetery. Brother Jim said a prayer and then led us all in “Amazing Grace.” The funeral employees lowered my mom’s body into the ground and then my dad’s. Brother Jim’s wife, Carol, hugged me for a long time. “We love you. We’re here for you. This may not be the right time to talk about it, but you're going to need grief counseling, Clara. Sooner the better."

"Yes, ma'am. Could you set that up for me?"

"Glad to do it."

I dreaded the afternoon. Doug and Carlie were leaving for home after lunch. They begged me to come with them. But I wasn't sure. I felt like crawling under the covers and sleeping for days. Maybe I would rest up and then go to Tennessee in a few days. Mr. Hobbs said I should take as much time as I needed to recover. God only knew how long that would take or if it were even possible. I chose to believe it was.

Mrs. Eula called a few days ago, saying the women from church wanted to provide a funeral lunch. But I declined. I wanted to keep things simple. And truthfully, I knew none of the family members would want to stay. And they didn't. I don't come from that kind of family. My cousins didn't even come to the burial. They said their good-byes at the funeral home. Mom's sister hugged me at the cemetery and I knew I would never see her again.

Doug and Carlie planned to pick up a pizza and meet me at the apartment. I asked Mrs. Irene if she wanted to join us. She declined saying she needed to lie down for a while and her nephew had a job interview that afternoon at Subway. While I was talking to her, I noticed Dusty and Doug sitting on the tail gate of Dusty's truck. It looked like the truck had been meticulously washed. The funeral was at 11:00. He must have left the house at 3:00 am. It was crazy for him to have come all this way. This was my mess, not his. And besides, I have a boyfriend. At least I think I do.

Everyone went home except the four of us. Carlie approached me and asked quietly, “What do you want me to do about Dusty?”

“What do you mean?”

“Well, he came all this way. We can’t let him just turn around and go home. We should at least feed him, don’t ya think?”

“I guess. But not at my apartment. We should go out somewhere.”

“That’s fine.”

Doug and Dusty walked up to the oak tree where we were standing. Doug said, “Well, ladies, let’s go eat and put our feet up, yes?”

Carlie suggested we go to a pizza place near her parents’ house. She rode with me in the hearse back to the funeral home where we would pick up their car. Doug rode with Dusty in the old red truck. What I would have given to be a fly on the wall of that truck.

Chapter 42 CARLIE: Funeral Pizza

Is it wrong to matchmake at a funeral? I hope not. I wouldn't even attempt it if Jake were here declaring his undying love. But he's not. He's in Tennessee trying to swing some kind of insurance deal. And in my book there is absolutely no excuse for his absence. None. The only excuse for his absence would be if he were having to attend the funeral of his own parents. And according to current reports, all his family members are alive and well. So here's the bottom line. If I were a man and I liked a woman enough to try to kiss her outside the gift shop at Stone Mountain (which hey, I'll be the first one to admit the Celtic music they pipe into that shop is pretty romantic) I believe I would find a way to be at the tragic double funeral of her parents. End of story.

So now I had two jobs. Help Clara with the grieving and help Clara get her man priorities straight. And I only had two hours to do it. Challenge accepted.

"Clara, we're almost to the funeral home. Is there anything else you need to get from inside?"

"No. I asked the ladies of the church to do what they wanted with the flowers. I don't want any at my apartment. I told Mrs. Irene to take the green plants. She likes those. I'm supposed to come in next week to settle up with the funeral home. So, no. We can just leave. It's over."

I held her hand and said nothing. When we pulled up, Dusty's truck was already parked next to our car. I wasn't sure how we should work the travel arrangements. The matchmaker in me wanted Clara to ride with Dusty. But I also wanted to be sensitive to her grief and to Jake Smith, despite his glaring absence. When we got out of the hearse, she thanked the driver and then waved at the men, saying, "We'll meet you there." That was actually a pretty decent plan. It would give Doug even more time to get valuable information from Dusty. Information he could pass along to the matchmaker on the long drive home. I prayed a simple prayer as I drove to the pizza shop. "Lord, please tell me Doug and Dusty aren't discussing the weather or their high hopes for duck season."

Clara put on lipstick and straightened her hair some. I didn't think it was remotely disrespectful to do so. Her parents were gone but she needed routine and order…and of course, love.

Lunch wasn't as uncomfortable as I thought it would be. Doug and Dusty had both removed their jackets and left them in the truck. Doug rolled up the sleeves of his dress shirt. Dusty loosened his tie and said he was glad he didn't have to wear one every day. I was happy we were seated at a square table so there wouldn't be that uncomfortable "sitting next to each other in a booth" moment. Clara didn't need that.

Clara seemed more relaxed than I had seen her in days. Maybe the funeral had given her a new beginning, a comfort, the courage to press on. We determined to keep her on light-hearted subjects and it worked. I scoffed at her disdain for mushrooms. She laughed at the fact that a girls' 6th birthday party was being held in the next room, saying, "Yeah, I knew Carlie would pick a place like this. She's a woman of class and taste. But where's my Barbie coloring book, Carlie? You didn't even buy me a coloring book."

Dusty ate a lot of pizza and laughed at all our corny jokes. Each time Clara spoke, he looked straight at her. I could tell he was completely mesmerized. He must have known we knew. I mean, an eight-hour drive? C'mon, Dusty. We weren't born yesterday. But then the oddest thing happened. He pushed his chair back from the table and said quietly, "I have to get back home today so I best be leavin'. Clara, I'm real sorry about your parents. I know what it's like to lose someone close like that. I do. And it's terrible. Just know that I'm real sorry about everything. I came out the other side of somethin' terrible and so will you. You will." He stood and extended his hand to her and with his other hand, he patted her on the shoulder. "I'm sure they were proud of you, Clara. Real proud."

She shook his hand but the disappointment was written all over her face. "Thank you, Dusty. Thank you for coming to the funeral. Really. It was a total surprise." I stood and hugged Dusty. Doug stood and put out his hand. "Dusty, I'll get with ya next week, man. See you soon."

And then he was gone. No attempt to woo her. No hanging around with hopes she'd fall in love or at least in like. No. Dusty wasn't planning on wearing out his welcome. He figured 16 hours of driving should speak straight to her heart. And it did.

Chapter 43   CLARA LOUISE: The Road to Recovery

I know people thought it was odd. I went back to my kindergarten class two days after the funeral. I didn't need to sit around the house in sweat pants watching Lifetime movies. I needed to work and be around people. I had planned to drive to Tennessee after a few days but decided against it. The week went remarkably well. I had two counseling sessions which were helpful. A few of the children had seen the news or heard their parents talking which meant they had questions. I answered every question the same way, "There are some things Ms. Johnson doesn't want to talk about." Carlie called every afternoon with the same two questions: What have you eaten today? Did you sleep well? She must have read a book about grief that convinced her that those were primary issues. And they were, I guess. I made myself eat and I still took the sleeping pills at night.

I hadn't been back to the house. I knew there were things I needed to do. Clean the food out of the refrigerator. Cancel their driver's licenses. Get some personal items and pictures. Make a financial plan. Close bank accounts. But instead I pretended the house didn't exist. My counselor said that was fine for now.

Jake called the night of the funeral and a few nights later. But there was an odd distance between us. I wanted to blame it on his mom. But she wasn't to blame. I told him about the counseling. He asked how many months it would take. I thought that was an odd question. I told him it might last the rest of my life. Silence. And for the first time, I understood our problem. Jake Smith's not a bad guy. He's kind and good and loving. That night at the yogurt shop, he told the truth. He did plan to stick by me. He knew I was wounded and broken. But he had a plan. He was going to fix me. You know, like when a man buys a broken down old '57 Chevy with a plan to restore it. Knock the dents out. Make it shiny again. Make it new. But now Jake realized that no matter how much God healed me, restored me, there would always be a little glitch. A glitch he couldn't live with.

I talked to the counselor about it and she helped me make a plan. I was going to Doug and Carlie's next weekend. Jake and I would go out on Saturday and I would explain that I would probably be broken for a very long time. It would hurt but I would let him off the hook.

But the plan never got off the ground. Jake Smith called me five nights after my parents' funeral and told me our relationship wasn't going to work. His voice cracked. He said he knew the timing was bad but he thought it was worse to drag it out. He was right. If I were twenty, I would have cried and begged and tried to super glue myself together so that I could win his affections. But I no longer had the energy. Plus, I was learning in counseling about real love. This wasn't it. It was a freedom of sorts.

Carlie begged me to still come for the weekend. On Wednesday I asked Mr. Hobbs for Monday off so I could have a long weekend and he graciously consented. I knew he would. I no longer dreaded the drive. The thought of leaving Commerce brought relief.

Chapter 44 CARLIE: The Cocoa Bean Has Healing Properties

Clara was on her way and I didn't feel like straightening the house so I did what every messy woman in America does. I put every out-of-place item in a large 30 gallon garbage bag. I tied the bag up and happily put it in the hall closet for safe keeping. If Doug starts looking for flip flops or the electric bill or yard darts, I'll have to remember to look in the bag of shame.

Clara arrived at 10:00 pm and even though I was sleepy, I drank cocoa with her on the porch. It was becoming tradition. "So, how are you feeling? About Jake? Your parents? Life?"

"I hate to say it but I feel relief about Jake. Like the pressure is off. I don't have to be better than I can be. Does that make sense?"

"I guess. And what about your parents?"

"I miss Mama. I want to miss Daddy but I can't really. I mean, I hardly knew him. Then that becomes its own grief. The whole daddy daughter thing." She pulled the blanket around her shoulders. "The idea of wanting him to love me and protect me, knowing that he didn't or he couldn't. The counselor is helping me walk through those things though. She is. And of course, having to forgive them, both of them."

We talked for more than an hour before we called it quits for the night. I got a late night e-mail from Shannon requesting prayer for an appointment with an adoption agency. Ashley Harrison left a phone message, saying she had lost 15 pounds and they were to start shooting scenes next week. The book was to be released in late September. Things were moving along at a rapid pace. I only had two things to do now: learn to make pork chops and find a man for Clara Louise Johnson. Not a bad "to do" list.

After breakfast, I explained to Clara that I had to speak at a luncheon at the University of Tennessee in Martin and Doug would be going with me. But not to worry. Aunt Charlotte wanted to take her to lunch and would arrive promptly at 12:00. I may never learn to make pork chops, but one project is getting crossed off the "to do" list. Today, if possible.

Chapter 45 CLARA LOUISE: Tater Tots and Tears

Doug's Aunt Charlotte had grown on me. I didn't know what to think at first. But now I found myself looking forward to being with her. She blew in the door at 12:10, her face red and sweaty.

"Sorry I'm late, Darlin'. Had some dog and coon trouble this mornin'. The dog chased the coon and the coon got down in the cellar, broke some jars of pickles and tomato relish and an old jar of moonshine from Doc Lawson," she leaned in and spoke in a whisper, "for medicinal purposes only, of course." She poured a glass of water and wiped her face with a paper towel. "Law, the smell down in that cellar. Smelled like Jack Daniels done took up with a hot dog vendor. Bart was cussin' that coon and we was both cleanin' up the mess best we could. I think we got it all done, but if I smell like a bar maid, well, you'll have to forgive me."

I laughed and said, "No problem, Aunt Charlotte." I said it before I even realized what I said. "Oh, I'm sorry. I didn't mean to say 'aunt'."

"Well, I mean for you to say it. I'd be mighty proud to be your aunt. You don't have to be born in my family, Clara. Carlie ain't born in this family. But she's my family as sure as Doug or anybody else."

"Thank you, Aunt Charlotte. Thank you."

I told her I would drive my car and just take her home after lunch. Uncle Bart had dropped her off because she doesn't drive. I didn't know why and felt no need to ask. "Where do you want to eat, Aunt Charlotte?"

"Let's go to Wimpy's in Greenfield."

I smiled, remembering the kindness of the people there. It made me remember Jake too and the loss of the only real boyfriend I'd ever had. But I also thought of Dusty and the way he looked at me that day, and the day of the funeral. Carlie hadn't mentioned him, which surprised me. I wanted so much to contact him and tell him I was in town. But it seemed forward and silly. Plus, he knew I was seeing Jake and he'd think I was one of those silly girls that went from boyfriend to boyfriend. But I wasn't that girl at all. I'd never even had a boyfriend or kissed a man. Not really.

Wimpy's was more crowded than last time. Probably because it was Saturday. The same pleasant older woman was there. She found Aunt Charlotte and me a booth near the front. Aunt Charlotte saw a friend from church and excused herself to go make small talk. I looked at the menu and decided to order all the good stuff, burger, tater tots, and a Dr. Pepper. I was ready to order but my lunch companion seemed to be camping out at the other table, talking about the Community Center Quilting Bee and Ida's upcoming 80th birthday party to be held in the basement of Westside Baptist. Finally, she yelled out, "Clara Baby, why don't you just order me what you're gettin'?"

I nodded and the older woman promptly took my order. The sun was shining through the window as I meticulously wiped the dried ketchup from the menu. It was a good day, a day of hope and blessing. That's when the little bell on the front door rang out and Dusty McConnell walked in. He didn't take off his cap and smooth his hair. He wasn't wearing a cap. He wore brand new blue jeans, and a starched plaid cowboy shirt and the brown cowboy boots he wore to the funeral. He didn't hesitate or talk to Mrs. Jessie or act like he was there to pick up an order. He walked straight to my table and I could hardly breathe.

Aunt Charlotte came running over and hugged Dusty real big. While fanning herself with a napkin, she looked straight at me and said, "Oh Baby, I'm so sorry I can't stay for lunch. Margaret said the Sunday School material got delivered up at the church and we've got to get it organized 'fore in the mornin'." She leaned in and whispered, "Margaret will be in fits if it's not done right." She shrugged her shoulders, as if to say there was nothing she could do about Margaret's obsession about Sunday School material.

I smiled real big and said, "Really? So you brought me to Wimpy's and now you're standing me up for lunch because of a Sunday School emergency? Is that the story you're sticking with, Aunt Charlotte?"

She broke out in raucous laughter, grabbing her stomach, saying she shouldn't have worn tight pantyhose 'cause her life will surely be cut short. She winked at me, "Don't you question an old lady, Clara Louise Johnson." She reached down to hug me and bid us both farewell. Dusty slid into the seat across from me.

Clean-shaven and smiling. His wavy brown hair was combed perfectly in place except for a few little wisps that refused to be controlled. His hands were clean but covered in scars. I hardly even noticed the eye patch anymore. The chin scar was still there but it was made less significant by his kind smile and gentle voice. "Clara, I guess you're stuck with me. I mean, if it's okay."

I smiled and nodded. "So, who's really behind this little plan?"

His perfect teeth were showing through a crooked grin. "Who do you think?"

"It's got Carlie and Aunt Charlotte written all over it."

"Carlie called me yesterday afternoon to tell me you were coming to town. And I'm glad she did. She told me you weren't with the guy in Union City anymore. Said Mrs. Charlotte wanted to work out this little bait and switch plan. Carlie and I thought it was silly. But it made Mrs. Charlotte happy so we did it."

"You're kind to go along with it, Dusty."

His voice got quiet and he looked out the window and then down at the table. "Oh, it's not kindness on my part." Looking right at me, he said, "I wanted to see you. And I don't mind sayin' that I was happy to find out you're not with the insurance guy too. I don't know what happened, but I'm glad it did."

"We just weren't right for each other. The truth is…" I started crying a little and he unfolded the white napkin and handed it to me. "Well, I'm kind of bruised and broken, y'know? Oh, I'm healing and I'm hopeful. Real hopeful. But Jake? Jake needed someone who is new and shiny. Or at least someone who looks new and shiny."

"Don't be fooled, Clara. No one's new and shiny. Not really. Was the break up about your parents?"

"Yeah. And other stuff too. My life has just been, well, it hasn't been much of a fairy tale. You don't want the whole story. Probably bore you to death." I wiped another tear.

"I've got all day, Clara. If you want to tell me, you can." He took a drink of water.

I talked for two hours. I told the whole story of Jason, the men, the baby, the adoption. He asked pertinent questions, but never in judgment. He seemed overflowing with hope, a belief in new beginnings, and a commitment to the truth. At one point, he stood up and got Kleenex from Mrs. Jessie. He re-filled my water glass when the women were taking a break. I didn't leave out one detail, from my distant dad to the neighbors who talked about me to the move to Commerce.

"It was so bad. So emotionally gruesome that when we moved to Commerce, I decided I would never touch a man again. I wouldn't care about my appearance. I'd avoid men at all cost. And I did. Until now."

He tapped lightly on the table with his thumb. "What made the change?"

"Doug and Carlie. When I saw the way Doug treated Carlie, well, I had never seen anything like it. He took care of her. And she respected him. It was amazing to watch. She'd tell me these stories, and I remember praying, believing that it was possible for me too, that all men weren't like my dad or Jason. So Carlie took it upon herself to find 'my Doug' as she would say." I laughed. "And you know Carlie. She doesn't give up easily. She tried her best. Things were going pretty good with Jake and then my parents…well, it was just so bad, so dark. I knew Jake wasn't the kind of guy who could swim in those waters. And that's okay. Really. I understand it now. The way he looked at me was like, he was in a hurry for me to get better. And I am getting better. I'm not one of those 'all about me' people. I'm planning to live a full life. But it will be a process. And I may always be limping. At least a little bit."

He spoke with authority. "A limp's not always a bad thing. Sometimes it's a reminder of being spared something worse. Have you forgiven your parents?"

"I have or at least I'm trying to. I'm working with an unbelievable counselor. She's helping me walk through some tough steps right now. I knew they were both miserable. They'd been miserable for a long time. I wanted them to get help. There are a lot of people at my church who have been through depression, suicide attempts, bad marriages, addiction. I told them they could get help there, that they didn't have to be embarrassed or alone. I thought maybe they were coming around and then, well, there they were….dead."

I continued, "At first, everyone assumed it was a murder suicide. I knew it wasn't. When investigators found the bank account had been drained, they started checking my parents' computer and other accounts. Evidently Mom had inherited some money when Aunt Martha died and she'd been hoarding it in a separate account, probably because she was planning to leave my dad. I didn't know Aunt Martha even had money and I don't think my dad knew either. The guy who killed them was Aunt Martha's neighbor back in Birmingham. He'd met my mom several times and I guess he knew she was set to inherit the money. So when my aunt died, he found Mom online, shared condolences at first and then, well, it's a long embarrassing story. He was a smooth operator. She was terribly lonely. She gave him a bunch of money and evidently it became a full-blown cyber-affair. At least it was to her. It's a mess. They think my dad found out about the money and the affair and had threatened to kill the guy. I guess that's why he did what he did. There's still a lot I don't know and I've decided I don't want to know. The police found him outside Atlanta a few days after they were killed. I'm sure I'll have to testify when he comes to trial."

“I’m so sorry, Clara. I am.”

“The whole thing still seems unreal, y’know? Like something from TV. Let’s just change the subject. Besides, I’ve been wondering something. Why did you come to the funeral? I mean, you drove all that way, knowing I had a boyfriend. Then you drove all the way home that same day. That doesn’t even make sense.”

“Mr. Bart and Mrs. Charlotte came to the shop the day after your parents died. They told me they’d been killed. I asked her to find out about the funeral plans and let me know. If I could work it out, I knew I would go to the funeral. Sometimes it helps to be around somebody else who’s seen tragedy…and lived through it. It’s kinda like seein’ a big sign that says, ‘Keep going.’.” Dusty looked down at the now empty hamburger plate and smiled, “And I also knew that if it didn’t work out with the insurance guy, I wanted you to know, uh, that I’m not just words, but actions. All the way home that day I prayed. I wasn’t trying to nudge him out, but if he was already on the way out…” He looked straight at me and smiled, “Well, I wanted you to know the kind of man I am, Clara. The kind of man I want to be. That I’m not afraid of making sacrifices.”

In 32 years I had never pursued physical contact with a man. Ever. I never ran into the house to jump in Daddy’s lap. I wasn’t the one who started things with Jason or the other men. I just let people do what they wanted to me. I was numb. A non-person. Unfeeling. Eventually I decided that physical touch was for people who could still feel, not for people like me. But for the first time in my life, at a hamburger place in Greenfield, Tennessee, I reached my hand across the table and lightly touched the top of Dusty’s hand. He jumped a little and his face turned red. But then he slowly reached out and took my other hand. He wrapped his big scarred hands around both of mine. Like he was covering me, protecting me. His hands were rough but his gentle touch brought a sense of calm. I was alive again. A tear came to my eye. Not sadness, but joy.

I looked down and smiled a bit. "Gosh, I've gone on and on about my family, Dusty. I never even told you how happy I was to hear about your legal victories. Carlie told me the whole story in detail. Amazing. And speaking of forgiveness, it sounds like you've had to do a lot of forgiving yourself. She told me about your dad."

"Yeah, never was much of a dad. Drank too much, hit my mom a lot. People who don't know me well probably think I got this scar and eye patch in prison. But prison wasn't near as bad as home." He pointed to the patch. "Metal pipe when I was twelve." He pointed to his chin, "A screwdriver when I was fourteen. He didn't like me standing up for Mom. I understand that now. He was weak. It must have been a terrible feeling to be so weak that hitting a woman made him feel strong."

I didn't bring up his wife, Melissa, and the baby. That would be for another day. We talked another two hours about work, West Tennessee, and his long journey toward a decent standard of literacy. We shared about church and family, the families we were born into, and the families we had chosen, the families who had beautifully made up for the ones we were born into.

At 4:30, Mrs. Jessie patted Dusty on the back and asked with a smile, "Can I get ya'll some supper?"

Dusty rubbed his lips together and apologized. But she said, "Oh Honey, I'm just messin' with you. You've done nothin' but bring me joy today. Just watchin' you two. It's a blessing. Take your time. We're here all evening." She wiped off some tables and switched channels on the TV.

I didn't want to leave. I didn't want him to leave either.

"Clara, I'm not much of one to go to fancy places. Is there somewhere you'd like to go?"

"I don't care. I'm fine with driving around or sitting at a park somewhere."

"I'll show you the local sites. How about that?"

"Sounds good!"

He paid the bill and left Mrs. Jessie $10. His truck was old but immaculately clean. He opened my door and I slid onto the worn vinyl seat cover.

He drove by the school he attended in Sharon. I asked about his favorite teacher and his worst memories. Mrs. Carson was his favorite. She believed he was smart and let him talk to the whole 8th grade class about small engines. Mrs. Jensen made him spell in front of all the 5th graders and he still remembers the agony and embarrassment when he spelled patience p-a-s-h-e-n-s.

We drove down the street where Uncle Bart and Aunt Charlotte live. He showed me the little green house where he spent his childhood, the fenced-in dirt yard that housed hound dogs and a few chickens. I thought about what he'd said earlier, how prison had been less abusive than his home. He drove by Carl and Betty Jenkins' house, the couple who had taken him in after the tornado tragedy. He swallowed hard and said, "They walked with me through some dark places, until I could see the light again."

The tour ended at his shop in Bradford. He pulled in right by the front door. He turned off the truck but country music was still playing softly on the radio. For the first time I smelled what Carlie smelled. But it wasn't like pine trees. I couldn't place it, but it smelled clean, like the way I thought a waterfall would smell.

He spoke with enthusiasm. "I know you've been here before but thought you might like a real tour. I mean, look around, Clara. This IS my kingdom." He opened his truck door and pointed to the building. "I'm thinking of having a moat dug 'round the front here."

I played along. "Oh, you definitely need a moat. Seriously, it looks like business is booming, if the parking lot is any indication."

He looked out the back window. "Not too bad. I'm thankful." He walked around the front of the truck and opened my door. He put out his hand and I happily took it. "I'll be glad to show you around, if it doesn't sound boring."

"Boring? Are you kidding? Anyone who can make it in business nowadays is a rocket scientist."

"I'm pretty driven. Daddy never held down a job. His brothers were all a lot like him. Carl and Betty Jenkins helped me go to trade school right out of prison. I worked here for Mr. Hopkins for a year and a half. He'd owned this shop for forever. Then he sold it to me three years ago when he was diagnosed with lung cancer. He had no children, sold it for a lot less than it was worth. He knew I was a felon and would have a hard time getting the loan. Said he couldn't take it with him. I'll never forget it. The shop takes a lot of sweat, but

I'm not afraid of getting dirty." The enthusiasm in his voice grew. "I love working on cars. I do. It's a challenge when you listen to an engine and can hear that something's not right, and then you figure out what can make it right." He unlocked the front door, but paused a minute and turned toward me. "And for the record, I'm not afraid of things that aren't new and shiny either, Clara. Sometimes the best vehicles have a little wear on 'em. And the shiny ones that look brand new? Sometimes they're not worth a dime."

He turned on the light and then opened the door that led to the garage. I could smell motor oil, cleaning fluid, dust, and work. "I'm putting a new engine in Mr. Janson's hot rod over there. It's gonna be incredible when it's all done." He pointed to the far corner, "Replacing the transmission on Mrs. Perkin's van on Monday."

I knew what was happening. Dusty needed me to acknowledge that what he produced had value. "They must trust you. A lot."

"I hope so. Hope I can manage to keep my name out of the paper too, at least for a while." He smiled and moved a gas can out of my path, then turned out the garage light and headed for the door. I had never wanted to kiss a man. Not that I could remember. Until then. In the darkness of that shop, I wanted to place my hands on his face, scars and all. I wanted to touch his hair and lay my head on his chest, believing he would protect me. But I didn't. I walked into the office and out the front door like the thought had never even crossed my mind.

We drove to Sonic for cheese tots and limeades. He talked about the best and worst of country music and his grandfather's collection of George Jones records. I told him my favorite book was "War and Peace" and then laughed when he thought I was serious. He recalled the first time he saw "Star Wars." I grieved the fact that he hadn't seen "Pride and Prejudice." He held my hand and we talked about the power of forgiveness.

At 11:00 he pulled into Doug and Carlie's driveway. I had already texted them that I would be late. We walked onto the porch and I said with a chuckle, "Thanks for lunch. And supper."

He put both hands in his pockets and looked around nervously. "No. Thank you, Clara. I hope I can see you tomorrow. Can I pick you up for church? My church isn't big or fancy, but I'd like you to come with me, if you're willing."

"I'd love to."

"Great. I'll come by at 10:00 then. See you in the morning." He looked at me, hesitated a bit, then walked right off the porch. I was disappointed. And the disappointment made me happy. Hearing him whistle on the way to the truck made me even happier.

Doug and Carlie were both waiting at the kitchen table. She must have convinced Doug that the news this time would be so exciting that it would be worth staying up for. He was eating Oreos and she was pouring milk.

I happily called out, "Grab another glass, Carlie."

She came running over with a hug that had such intensity I thought my ribs would break. "Forget milk and cookies, sister. As your official matchmaker, I need all the details."

I sat down and grabbed a cookie. "It went well. Real well. I like him. A lot."

Carlie was standing behind Doug's chair. She enthusiastically kissed him on the cheek, and put her hands on his shoulders. "Oh Honey, our little girl's in love!"

I laughed, "Did I say the word love? No. I said I like him a lot. That's what I said."

Doug seemed unusually invested in the conversation. "We're happy for you, Clara. I know for a fact that he's happy."

I had been dying to ask Doug some questions and this was the perfect time. "Doug, I'm glad you're up. I've been wondering, well, what you and Dusty talked about in Commerce, at the cemetery, in the car."

He raised his right hand. "I'm sworn to secrecy, Clara. A man's word is his word." He grinned as he reached for the bag of Oreos. "But I can tell you this. Dusty McConnell is the real deal. He's been through the wringer, but he came out the other side…clean."

I couldn't sleep that night. I daydreamed about pine trees and waterfalls. About Dusty's hands and his less-than-perfect face, that looked perfect to me. Striking and handsome. About his stories of prison, some bad, but mostly the stories of hope he'd found there. I thought about his words, "My prison sentence was like a big U-turn sign. A chance to go a different way." I thought about Doug and Carlie's enthusiasm. How Doug had said he was trustworthy. I didn't know Dusty McConnell well, but I wondered, I couldn't help but wonder the one thing I'd wondered my whole life. Could he love me?

Chapter 46 CARLIE: Roman Holiday in Sharon, Tennessee

Aunt Charlotte and Uncle Bart came over early for Sunday breakfast even though they never come over for Sunday breakfast. They were fully dressed in their church clothes even though it was 7:30. At least they called before they came, five minutes before. Uncle Bart sat in the living room with Doug while Aunt Charlotte drank coffee at the table patiently waiting for Clara to come walking out of the guest room. At 8:05 her wish was granted. Clara came out wearing blue jeans and a faded brown t-shirt. No make-up, hair not fixed, but smiling from ear to ear. Beautiful. It was like her face was glowing. You know how they always say pregnant women glow, yeah, it was like that. 'Cept I knew for sure she wasn't pregnant. I suspected it might be love.

Aunt Charlotte jumped from her chair and announced loudly, "Clara Louise Johnson, get your skinny little self over here and give me some love." Clara happily reached down to give Aunt Charlotte a hug. "Have a seat, Baby, and I'll pour your coffee. Carlie and Doug tells me you was out cattin' 'round with that Dusty McConnell till late in the evenin'." Even though Doug was reading the paper in the living room, I could hear him laughing out loud at Aunt Charlotte's bold declaration. She smiled and continued, "Sorry I had to run out on ya at lunch. But hey, the Lord called me to a sacred task and who am I to question his timing?"

Clara happily recounted the day's events for Aunt Charlotte's enjoyment. After every story or detail Aunt Charlotte would wipe her eyes with a paper napkin and say, "Praise the Lord" or "You don't say!" When all was said and done, she yelled loudly, "Bart, I'm all for goin' to church this mornin', but I done had some kind of church service in here at the kitchen table. My heart is full, Honey. Full to the brim. The Lord done smiled on us real good."

Dusty knocked on the door at 9:50. Ten minutes early. Ten points for you, Dusty McConnell. Fifteen minutes early would have caused you to lose five points because fifteen minutes early borderlines on a lack of consideration. I know. It's a delicate issue. But the sweet spot of punctuality is five to ten minutes early and there's really no discussion about it.

I had never seen him looking so happy. Khaki pants and a dark green shirt. Polished boots. Big smile. He sat at the table with Doug and me while we finished our coffee. At 10:00 Clara opened the guest room door and it was like a light came pouring into the kitchen. Dusty stood and his mouth dropped open. She looked more beautiful than I had ever seen her look. More beautiful than the times she went out with Jake. More beautiful than the day I got married. I understood why now. Clara felt this overwhelming sense of acceptance from Dusty, a sense of protection and safety. And it had changed her. All of her. She might be limping but she was no longer walking in fear.

Her hair was perfectly curled around her face. Make-up just right and she smelled like the Macy's counter, only with none of that sassy attitude. She had on a solid blue dress that tied at the waist. The skirt was long and flared. She looked kind of like Audrey Hepburn in all those old movies. You know the tiny little waist and the flowing skirt. And Dusty looked like Gregory Peck in "Roman Holiday" when Gregory looked at Audrey like he'd never seen a more beautiful woman. He fell for Audrey Hepburn and the whole audience is just rooting for them to get together even though we all know she's some kind of European princess and he's an American journalist. But Gregory Peck wore a suit a lot in that movie and Dusty McConnell is more of a cowboy boot kind of guy. Plus,

Gregory Peck didn't have an eye patch or a scar on his chin. And Clara is a kindergarten teacher rather than a princess, but still. The look of love is the look of love.

Dusty couldn't even speak. So, of course, I was glad to speak for him. "Girl, you are lookin' GOOD this mornin'! Dusty, you should see how she normally looks in the mornin'. Seriously. Not like this. At all. Completely different. Trust me." Clara laughed and Dusty smiled. He held out his hand and said, "You look beautiful, Clara. Unbelievable in fact." She reached for his hand but tripped on the rug in her high heels. He reached out and caught her by the arm. It was exactly like one of those moments in a romantic movie. Except I was in my bright orange housecoat and if I were going to play a matchmaker in a real movie, I would be sure to wear regular clothes, not a housecoat, and definitely not an orange one, as it makes me look like a tangerine.

Clara spent all day with Dusty. She had to leave on Monday and he had to work, so she met him at Wimpy's for lunch on her way home. She texted me three words from a gas station in Chattanooga. The words every true matchmaker longs to hear: I love him.

Chapter 47 CLARA LOUISE Five Weeks Later: Learning to Love

Yesterday was the last day of school. Hugs. Coffee mugs filled with cocoa packets. Flowers and apples and best wishes. I greeted parents and spoke words of assurance to the children about the joys that awaited them in first grade. But all I could think about was pulling into Doug and Carlie's driveway today. It always felt like home. Dusty had been to Commerce three times in the last month. He stayed with Bro. Jim and Mrs. Carol every time. When I asked what they thought about him, they both used the same word, "humble." Brother Jim said, "There's not much you can do with a proud and haughty man, Clara. He wants his own way and he'll find a way to get it. But a humble man? Well, there's no end to what He can accomplish." I memorized their words and trusted their wisdom.

Before I even pulled into the driveway, I saw the familiar red truck. Carlie said she was going to invite him for supper. As I got closer, I saw all three of them on the porch. Doug and Carlie were sitting on the porch swing and Dusty was in a white rocker whittling. I had seen my grandfather whittle many times and I assumed it was an old man's pastime. But evidently not. Dusty looked up and smiled. He wiped the pocketknife on his jeans and folded it up and put it in his pocket. He walked quickly to open my car door. I got out and hugged him like I hadn't seen him in months. But it had only been five days. Five long days. He whispered, "I missed you so much. How was your trip?"

I whispered back and touched his face, "It was good because I knew you would be here." We held hands and walked toward the porch. Carlie announced loudly that she made chicken spaghetti because she didn't feel it was right to torment Dusty with him being a first-time dinner guest and all. The food was delicious. Doug made homemade ice cream on the porch after supper. For a split second, it reminded me of being at Jake Smith's house that day. I felt no disdain for Jake or his family though. Just a flood of relief. We played Pictionary and Carlie showed us the garden she'd planted out back. She'd forgotten to mark which seeds she planted where so she said summer would bring the joy of surprise. Surprise. I no longer feared that word.

At 7:30, Dusty said he wanted to take me for a drive. He was unusually quiet but occasionally he'd reach over and touch my hand. Silence no longer sent fear into my heart. Silence with Dusty was comfortable. Restful. Some things no longer had to be spoken. I didn't ask where we were going but I figured we were going to the shop because we passed the Bradford city limits sign. I asked if he would take me to the Doodle Soup Festival this year. He laughed and promised he would. Country love ballads played softly in the background and I felt an incredible sense of peace. Happiness. It startled me when he pulled the truck over on the shoulder and turned off the ignition.

"Does this spot look familiar?"

I grimaced, "It does. If I remember correctly, I was stranded here once, and after a pretty failed matchmaking attempt too. SO I'd been rejected by a man and then my car was stuck on the side of the road. Plus, and this was probably the worst part… I had very little hope of ever really attending the Doodle Soup Festival. It was a depressing day all the way around." I laughed and looked right at him. "But thankfully, well, this good-lookin' man came riding up on a white horse to save me."

He put his hands on the steering wheel, lowered his head, and grinned. “You have a terrible memory, Clara. Do you want me to straighten out the story?”

“I’m all ears.”

He reached out to hold my hand but was still looking out the front windshield. His voice was serious. “It was a Sunday afternoon. Real cold. There was this man. Decent-lookin’, I guess.” He paused and smiled. “He’d only loved one woman really and she was gone. Only had one child and she was gone too.” He lowered his head and swallowed hard. “The memories haunted him, especially at night. Unbearable sometimes. So he prayed. Right there that Sunday morning in the middle of the choir singing ‘Rock of Ages.’ He prayed God would do a miracle. Give him another chance. That maybe this time he’d do it differently. Y’know? Be more appreciative. More understanding.”

I scooted closer.

He continued. “I ate lunch with Carl and Betty that day. Then got a call from Greenfield. Not for the wrecker. Just an old friend needing an estimate on fixin’ an ol’ truck in his grandparents’ yard. We talked a while and then I headed to the shop to check on some inventory. That’s when I saw your car. Parked right in this spot. I even laughed and said, ‘God, is that my woman up there?’ But it was a joke. I figured it would be an older woman. I mean, you do drive an old lady car, Clara. But when I looked through the window, I remember thinkin’ you looked pretty good for an old woman.” We both laughed quietly. “You were right to not trust me though. You didn’t know me. I understood that. But the more you talked, the more I wanted to get to know you. I didn’t want Doug to show up because I wanted you to need me, Clara.”

I spoke for the first time. "I do need you, Dusty."

He turned his head toward me. "Then marry me, Clara." He grabbed both my hands and covered them with his. "I love you. And I won't leave you. Ever. You can count on me to protect you. I promise. Will you marry me?"

I didn't think about it. I didn't need to. I spoke one simple word with confidence, "Yes."

He sighed with a sense of relief. He gently placed both of his rough hands on my face and leaned in to kiss me. "Thank you, Clara. Thank you."

He wiped the tears from my face and for the first time I ran my hand over the scar on his chin. "Does it hurt?"

He smiled. "No. Not anymore."

I've heard of men jumping out of airplanes with a proposal written on the parachute. I've seen stories of men who planned fancy dinners and hired string quartets. Then there's the common story of having the proposal written on the big Jumbo Tron at a professional ballgame. But Dusty McConnell had the best proposal of all. He understood my greatest fear and spoke straight to my heart. Every man I'd ever known had used me, left me battered and exposed. But not Dusty. His scarred hands would protect me. He promised.

Chapter 48 CARLIE: Praise the Lord and Pass the Pickles

9:30 pm

"Doug, did Dusty say when he planned to come back?"

"No, Honey. I'm not his dad. And you're not Clara's mother either."

"Well, I know but I'm worried. They could have had a wreck or car trouble or they could have gotten snatched up in a horrible tornado. The sky was looking kind of green earlier today. And we don't always hear the sirens out here, y'know?"

He laughed. "Carlie, they both have cell phones. Besides, I feel certain that we'd get the news if a tornado had swept up a 20-year-old Chevy truck and thrown it into another county. Aunt Charlotte would have known five minutes before it happened, don't ya think?"

I scooted next to him on the couch. "Great point, Honey. Great point."

At 10:00 pm, the Paducah news anchorman announced that Elton John would be appearing in Memphis in the summer and that a petition had been started by a local radio station to get George Strait to be the opening act. Now there's a concert I'd pay $100 to see. About that time, we heard a light tapping at the kitchen door and Dusty and Clara came strolling in.

I jumped up from the couch and said, "Hey, guys! There's leftover ice cream in the freezer, if you want some. I think I even have some of those pink sprinkles you like, Clara."

Clara said nonchalantly, “No. I need to get busy making some plans.”

“Plans? You can make plans when you’re back home in Commerce. I bet Dusty will take some ice cream. How ‘bout it, Dusty?”

“No. I need to help Clara with the plans.”

“What’s gotten into you two? Why are you being so industrious and what are you planning to do anyway?”

Doug walked into the kitchen and put his arm around me. Clara started smiling and Dusty shuffled his feet and put his hands in his pockets.

And that’s when it hit me. Nobody ever accused me of being a rocket scientist. “Oh my gosh! Are you guys? I mean, are you?” I was tongue-tied and flustered and I started crying at even the thought.

Clara ran to me, grabbed my arms, and said, “Yes, Carlie! Yes! We’re getting married.”

Doug shook Dusty’s hand and patted him on the back. “Congratulations, man! We’re happy for both of you!”

I just kept hugging Clara and then I just kept hugging Dusty. About that time Aunt Charlotte blew in the door. Uncle Bart followed behind with less enthusiasm. No light knock. No pre-visit phone call.

Aunt Charlotte asked, “Is something going on here? Is there somethin’ I need to know? Willie Carlisle called and said you was parked down there on the side of the road in Bradford for a long time.”

Clara hugged Aunt Charlotte and said, “I’m getting married! To Dusty. I’m getting married and moving here, Aunt Charlotte!”

“Well, praise the Lord and pass the pickles! It’s time for a celebration! Carlie, you got any champagne or apple cider?”

“Let me look.” I scoured the refrigerator. “We’ve got grape juice and Diet Sprite.”

“Well, mix ‘em together and let’s have a toast.”

On May 19th at 10:25 pm the six of us raised our red Solo cups into the air to toast the upcoming nuptials (be careful how you say that word) with a mixed drink of grape juice and Diet Sprite. Aunt Charlotte cried profusely. Uncle Bart handed her a Kleenex and asked Doug if the drought had hurt the farmers yet. The newly engaged couple walked into the living room with me to look at the calendar and set a date.

Dusty put his arm around Clara and spoke softly. “I know women sometimes like to spend months planning a wedding and caring about the cake and the dresses and all that but, for me, I want to cast my vote for sooner rather than later.”

Clara grabbed his hand and said, “Well, you’re in luck, Dusty. I’m not one of those silly girls who is worried about the wedding or the cake. I want to be married. To you. So I’m fine with the sooner.”

I spoke up with a voice of authority, “Well, as your official wedding planner, and I assume I can just assign myself that job, I’ll ask the first question. Where would you like to get married?”

Clara answered quickly. "Maybe it's bad that I've thought about this before tonight, but I already know. If it's okay with you guys, well, I'd like it to be small and simple and I'd like to get married here. In the backyard. Are you okay with that, Carlie?"

My voice cracked but I tried to remain ever-professional (seeing as how I was the wedding planner and all). I grabbed her hand and said, "That will be just fine."

Dusty looked at the calendar and said, "What about June 25th? That's five weeks from now. Is that enough time?"

Clara touched him on the knee and said, "Perfect."

I have an opinion about weddings. Actually, I also have an opinion about guacamole and profanity in Broadway plays and little girls wearing make-up and well, about a lot of other things. But we're talking weddings right now. Weddings can be beautiful and meaningful without spending months planning them. I mean, look at funerals. Most funerals are planned in two days but they usually have tons of flowers and special music and meaningful words from a minister, not to mention a delicious potluck meal in the church basement afterwards. This is not rocket science, people. Get with the program.

At 11:30 I politely escorted everyone out the door, saying the bride needed her beauty sleep and the newlyweds needed something else. Uncle Bart laughed and patted Doug on the back. Aunt Charlotte shook her head as she walked out the door and said, "That Carlie!" Dusty gently kissed his bride-to-be and told her he'd pick her up for church at 10:00. He brushed her hair off her forehead with his hand and said, "Sleep well."

I happily sent Clara to bed and told her we'd plan the whole wedding tomorrow afternoon. I looked at Doug and said with a smile, "We're not engaged. We're married."

He replied with one word, "Hallelujah."

By 5:00 Sunday, the plans were made. Diane Perkins would sing. Doug and I would hire the catering with a local woman we loved. We called Clara's pastor and he agreed to come from Commerce to do the message and the pronouncing of the man and wife part. Clara chose two bridesmaids and Dusty chose two groomsmen. Dusty wanted Carl Jenkins to be his best man and Doug to be a groomsman. Clara asked me to be matron of honor and I couldn't believe what she said next. She wanted Aunt Charlotte, 63-year-old Aunt Charlotte, to stand up with us. It was perfect. Not in fashion sense, but in life.

Clara went back to Commerce on Wednesday morning with a detailed list of assignments from her life coach. Oh, did I forget to mention that I'm a life coach now? Yeah. I didn't do too well with the matchmaking, but life coaches mostly tell people what to do and I think I have a real gift for that.

Clara would turn in notice on her apartment, contact Mr. Hobbs with her resignation, and see the counselor about getting re-assigned to someone in our area. There was one more thing she needed to do. But it was pure dread. She had to face the house. She hired someone Mrs. Irene knew to throw everything in the refrigerator away and clean the house. She made arrangements to give all the furniture and household goods to a local shelter. A realtor was prepared to list it. But before any of that could happen, she needed to go through and gather personal items. Pictures, family memorabilia, anything she didn't want destroyed. Dusty promised to be there to help her. In a few weeks he would say the words, “for better or for worse.” Good thing he understood what they meant.

Chapter 49 CLARA LOUISE: Dark Corners and Cobwebs

It was a happy and sad day. Dusty was coming. My love. The one who looks out for me. But I'd also be walking into my childhood home for the first time since my parents were killed there. And for the last time too.

I knocked on Mrs. Irene's door so she could meet Dusty. She came out into my parents' yard because she's a bit of a hoarder and was embarrassed by the state of her living room.

The three of us stood there and she filled us in. "The realtor came by, said painting the outside might improve the value. But I told him you'd already decided to just sell as is. Opal got it all cleaned up and lookin' real good though, Clara. Real good. Your mama was a good housekeeper so there ain't much to worry with. Neither of 'em collected junk." She held my hand as I wiped a tear. "I'm sorry, Clara. Real sorry."

"I know. Thank you, Mrs. Irene. I don't know what I would have done without you. I don't. When we get finished, I'll bring the keys to you and then the realtor can pick them up from you tomorrow. Is that okay?"

"Sure. Do you want me to go in with you, Darlin'?"

"No ma'am. Dusty's here." Dusty reached out for my hand.

"Well, you're blessed to have a good man. Blessed."

Dusty thought we should pray before going in and I agreed. Dusty prayed different from anyone I'd ever heard. He never used "thee" or "thou" or big words. He just said it. Said what he needed or what he was worried about. He wrapped his arms around me and prayed a prayer I would never forget.

"God, this is sad for Clara which makes it sad for me too. A bad thing happened here. Lots of bad things. Help Clara walk through this house and do what she needs to do. Remind her of some happy times. Make it a time of healing please. In Jesus' Name, Amen."

Dusty removed the key from my hand and led me to the back door. The door was jammed but he used his shoulder to pry it loose. The house smelled like a combination of Lysol and stale bread. Dusty walked on the broken green linoleum and said, "Is there anything in the kitchen you'd like to keep, Clara?" I dug through the cabinet for a yellow bowl my grandma had used for making biscuits. "This is it."

We walked into the living room and he held my hand. I spoke calmly, "Daddy was in that chair. It's where he always sat. Mom was laying by the front door. There used to be a rug there. I'm sure they took it to the police station. There are four or five old photo albums in that bookshelf that I should take." He gathered them up and put them on the coffee table and then took the yellow bowl and placed it carefully on top.

I started walking down the dark hallway. The paneling was an ugly dark brown and pulled away from the wall in several places. The avocado green carpet had been matted and dirty since my childhood. I pointed to the bathroom. "There's only one bathroom and there's nothing in there I want." As we approached my childhood bedroom, I doubled over in what seemed like physical pain. Dusty bent over to pick me up. He whispered, "This is the past, Clara. It's over and done. I promise."

We walked into my old bedroom. I stood by the bed and wept like there had been a death there. I reached for him and he pulled me to his chest which had become a place of safety.

"My innocence was lost right here. Lost forever. And what did Daddy do? He did nothing. Not one thing."

Dusty held me as tight as he could. I could hear him praying but I don't remember what he said. I just remember peace coming over me. It wasn't like the bad things had never happened. No. I could still remember them, every one of them. It was more like the scars stopped bleeding. Now I knew what Dusty meant about his chin scar. It would always be there. His own father had abused him with a screwdriver but as time passed, it didn't hurt as much.

I wanted nothing from that old room. No books or yearbooks or sheets or teddy bears. I walked away. I went to my mom's closet and found a red coat I had given her for Christmas when I was sixteen and had my first part-time job at Walgreen's. Dusty held it over his arm. I picked up a music box my great-grandmother had brought over from Poland and he took it. We already had the bank statements and insurance papers. I spoke calmly, "I'm ready to go, Dusty."

"Are you sure?"

"Yes."

"Clara, I'm saying this because I love you. Is there anything you could get that would be a good memory of your dad?"

I had to stop and think. I walked into the hallway and immediately took an old picture off the wall. I turned it around to show him. "We went to Six Flags when I was ten. I'd never been anywhere. My uncle took this picture of me and my parents. Mom had it blown up and she framed it because all three of us were smiling, and 'cause, well, it made us seem normal I guess. Happy."

He looked at the picture and smiled. "You were a beautiful girl, Clara. Still are."

He gathered the things from the coffee table and we walked toward the back door. I turned one last time and forced a smile. "Mama could make some killer brownies. She sure could."

Dusty locked the door and pulled it closed. For the last time in my life.

Chapter 50 CARLIE Two weeks later: Movies and Moms

It's hard to believe we'll be hosting a wedding in two weeks. I'm flying to California in the morning at the invitation of Ms. Watson. She's proud of how the movie is going and wants me to be a part of it, for a few days anyway. I know she wouldn't want me to stay for a month. But that's fine because I wouldn't want to stay for a month. I'll only be gone three nights. Doug can't come with me this time. He has some meetings at the bank and I understand. I asked Shannon to come with me. Dave was overjoyed as he said she desperately needed the time away.

California was still very California-ish. But I agreed with Ms. Watson. The movie seemed to be coming together better than I could have ever expected. Ashley was knocking it out of the park and her co-star, Crystal Van Gogh, was phenomenal. No, she's not kin to Vincent Van Gogh and she doesn't like for people to ask either. She's most famous for her starring role in a Disney Channel TV show and her short-term relationship with Justin Timberlake. If I haven't said it lately, I love living in Sharon, Tennessee.

Chance Baldwin wasn't our host at the studios this time. Emily, the beautiful curly-headed blonde woman who had been my greatest supporter in meetings, had been assigned to take care of us. When she met us in the lobby, I gave her a big hug. But her thin frame was clearly at least six months pregnant.

I pretended to pat her tummy. "Emily, I had no idea! Congratulations!"

She cowered. "Thanks."

"What's wrong?"

“I’m what’s wrong.” Her voice softened. “This whole situation was a mistake. The father and I have been together for more than two years. The baby wasn’t planned but I thought we were both pretty okay about it, even talked about getting married. Well, I guess I was the one talking about it. But he left for New Mexico two months ago. Said he can’t be ‘tied down to a family’ right now. Evidently, even the thought of it affects his…” She held up her hands pretending to make quote marks in the air, “his creative process.”

I replied, “I thought parents could still be creative. I mean, I’m sure there are artists and song writers and actors who have kids, right?”

“Ha ha. Yeah, but not according to him. Who knew that a D list lounge singer was so committed to his career, huh? My parents are back in Boston and not able to help right now. I have to work full-time. I want my baby to have a dad too, not one who ditches his responsibilities, but a real dad. I love this baby, Carlie. I do.”

“But?”

“But I’m thinking about making a different plan.”

We sat at the studio coffee shop with Emily for more than two hours while she poured out her heart. At one point, I put my arm around Shannon and silently prayed for a miracle.

Chapter 51 CARLIE The Finale

It was hotter than it should have been on the day of Dusty and Clara's wedding. Well, I guess it's not for me to determine what the weather "should" be on any given day. Thankfully, the forecast had predicted the heat wave accurately and Doug had rented these big cooling machines you can use for outdoor events in the summer. You can hide them by renting these pretty white terrace-looking things too. I reminded Aunt Charlotte not to stand in front of the cooling machines with her dress hiked up. A story for another day.

Speaking of dresses, it was a challenge for Clara to choose bridesmaid dresses that would look good on a really tall, chubby 33-year-old and a really short, chubby 63-year-old. I mean, how many brides face that kind of challenge? But she did it. We did it. I think we got the dresses from the "grandmother of the bride" collection instead of the bridesmaid collection but we didn't tell Aunt Charlotte. Besides, we looked good in our long flowing lavender dresses. The dresses were sleeveless and made of chiffon but they came with these beautiful beaded long-sleeved jackets…because grandmothers don't usually want to show off their arm fat. And truthfully, neither did I.

Doug and I bought matching gray suits for Doug, Dusty, and Mr. Jenkins as part of our wedding present. We knew Dusty wouldn't want to wear a fancy tux and he shouldn't have to. A fancy tux just didn't go with his persona. And yes, every person has a persona, even if they're not famous.

Folks started gathering at 6:30 for the 7:00 wedding. I told Uncle Bart he could skip wearing a tie, if he helped park cars. He was happy to oblige. Several people came from Commerce. Teachers and church friends. Dusty's uncle and aunt came from Paris. Tennessee, not France. I doubt that had to be clarified, but better safe than sorry. Mrs. Jessie came along with some of the other folks at Wimpy's. Several people from Dusty's church in Bradford came, including the pastor and his young family. The two boys who work at Dusty's shop cleaned up real nice, wearing khaki pants and ironed shirts. Al was flirting with the young blonde piano player who plays every week at First Baptist. Truthfully, I'm thinking the young blonde piano player might turn out to be the best outreach campaign that church has ever had.

Uncle Bart parked the last car and then asked everyone to take a seat as the ceremony was about to start. Brother Jim walked up front with Dusty, Mr. Jenkins, and Doug following faithfully. I peeked out of one of the rental terrace things to get a good look at Dusty. He rubbed his lips together a bit and then ran his fingers through his hair. I think that's just Dusty's nervous tic. You know how some people grind their teeth or click their fingernails together. Dusty does the hair thing. He smiled broadly as the music started playing. I helped Aunt Charlotte position her white rose bouquet and handed her a wad of Kleenex to hold discreetly under the blooms. She walked down the aisle slowly and proudly like a blue ribbon hog at the fair. (That's a good thing. No, really. It is.) I did everything I could to hold back tears as I turned to Clara and said, "I'm leavin' now, but I'll be right down front if you need me, okay?" She laughed. "Clara, are you ready for this?

She reached out and patted my hand. "I am."

I walked down the aisle, pretending I was marrying that hot-to-trot Doug Jameson again. Even though I was wearing the grandmother dress, he was giving me the eye and I was giving him that powerful "come hither" look too. Just as things were starting to sizzle between us, we remembered we were here to celebrate Dusty and Clara's wedding and I stood faithfully next to Aunt Charlotte and glanced toward the back for Clara's march down the aisle.

The music changed and the crowd stood. Audrey Hepburn, disguised as Clara Louise Johnson, walked confidently down the aisle and there wasn't a dry eye in the house. She wore a simple sleeveless white dress with lots of pearls and beading and a beautiful wide satin sash around her tiny waist. A simple thin veil draped behind her stunning red hair. I looked over at Dusty and he was star struck. In love. I couldn't help but think about the years I'd lived with Clara. All that time she'd been in hiding. Fearful. But now? Now she was all out in the open. Willing to love. And be loved. I nudged Aunt Charlotte and asked for a Kleenex. She handed me a wad of rose petals by mistake.

Brother Jim spoke of the sacred institution of marriage. Commitment. Unconditional love. Sacrifice. Respect. But he also talked about the need for fun, companionship, physical intimacy. Doug winked at me and I winked back. Only I can't wink very well and it may have looked like a reaction to pollen in the air. Eventually, he asked Dusty and Clara to face each other and share their vows.

Dusty spoke first, "I promise to love you, Clara. To take care of you, to protect you. In good times and in bad. I will never leave you. Ever. If someone wants to hurt you, he'll have to get through me first, Clara. I'm serious." He grabbed her hands and enveloped them in his own as she cried and as he spoke with more intensity. "Clara, from this day forward, by God's grace, I am watching the gate. I am. God is keeping watch over me. And I am committed to keeping watch over you. So you can rest peacefully. I'm giving you my name as a seal of that promise."

I handed Clara a rose petal to wipe her eyes. Less than effective. Then she began, “I’ve never trusted a man, Dusty. But God has worked in my heart and I’m changing. Today I vow to trust you, to walk with you. I vow to respect you and be kind to you. I make a promise in front of all these people to walk toward healing, even if I limp sometimes. I vow to walk in forgiveness and repentance, asking God to help me love you with every fiber of my being.” She spoke with clarity. “I’m free, Dusty. I want to walk with you in that freedom.”

Well, everyone in the back yard was crying. I mean, who wouldn’t be? Even Uncle Bart acted like he had the sniffles. It didn’t even bother me that I wasn’t the matchmaker for these two. Evidently a broken down Ford Focus is a better matchmaker than a tall chubby writer. I’m not going to spend a lot of time analyzing that. Besides, we all knew who the matchmaker was. Dusty and Clara exchanged rings. They kissed passionately. And that, my friends, is the end, no, the beginning of a great love story.

The next morning, Doug and I sipped coffee and reminisced about our own love story. Each marriage has chapters, some pleasant, some difficult, but all with a glorious purpose.

I sat a gift bag in front of him on the table. “Honey, I have a little present for you.”

“A present? And it’s not even my birthday.”

“I know. But what can I say? I’m generous.”

He pulled back the tissue paper and held up a little white stick. “Carlie, is this, uh, is this…” He stood and smiled as I reached out to hug him.

"Doug, you work at a bank. Surely you recognize a plus sign."

THE END

Book #3 "Doug and Carlie: Matchmakers on a Mission" December 2013

Acknowledgements

I'd like to thank my husband, Philip, and our two sons, Stephen and Jonathan, for their willingness to load the dishwasher and their endless support of this project. Special thanks to Philip for being a hard-working, dependable college professor who provides for our family. His hard work gives me freedom to do mine. His love gives me inspiration. I'm forever grateful.

I'd like to thank my dad and mom, Jack and Regina Golden, who raised me to see the potential in wounded souls. Their God-inspired service to those in need has changed my life.

I'd like to thank my in-laws, Les and Sylvia Smith. Your love for each other and the world speaks volumes.

Special thanks to my mom, Regina Golden. She spent hours and hours proofing this book and all preceding books. Her endless knowledge of comma placement, hyphens, and grammar has blessed me beyond measure. I'm especially thankful for her words of encouragement along the way. There are times I would have given up had she not convinced me to keep going.

I'd like to thank my dear friend and fellow writer, Merry Brown. This book would have never happened had she not pulled me out of a dark place with the words, "Why don't you meet me three times a week and we'll write?" She has been an endless source of encouragement, support, and friendship. Her savvy tech ability has produced my book covers and my back covers. She even wrote the funny lines on the back of this book. She keeps me from flinging my computer through a window almost daily.

God is the source of all healing and restoration. To Him be the Glory forever and ever.

17214775R10161

Made in the USA
San Bernardino, CA
04 December 2014

"I loved Lisa Smartt's *Doug & Carlie's Love Conspiracy*! All I can say is give me more, more, more!"

Merry Brown, Martin, TN

"You've got to be kidding me! How has a major publishing house not snatched Mrs. Smartt up and given her a contract and a house at the beach? Life truly is a mystery!"

Concerned Citizen, These United States

"This story warmed my heart. I mean it. *Doug & Carlie's Love Conspiracy* literally warmed the cockles of my heart."

Every Woman, Planet Earth

Lisa Smartt lives on 16 wooded acres on the outskirts of Dresden, Tennessee, with her more-than-wonderful husband of 25 years and two way-above-average teenage sons. She travels nationally as a motivational humorist and writes a weekly newspaper column called, "The Smartt View." Her future aspirations include organizing her purse, eating more green leafy vegetables, and cleaning out the hall closet.

ISBN 9780615793672
90000
9 780615 793672